Slightly Off Balance

KAYLIE HUNTER

This book is a work of fiction.
All names, characters, places, businesses, incidents, etc., are the imagination of the author. Any resemblance to actual persons or otherwise is coincidental.

Copyright 2017 by Kaylie Hunter

Books By Kaylie Publishing

All rights reserved.

No part of this book may be reproduced without the written permission of the author apart from brief quotes used in reviews and articles.

Cover design by Melody Simmons

BOOKS BY KAYLIE

DAVINA RAVINE SERIES
ONE GONE MORE BEFORE LONG
TWO LIES SOMEONE MUST DIE
THREE FREE DON'T LOOK FOR ME
FOUR FEARS BEHIND THE MIRROR
FIVE MORE LOCK YOUR DOOR
SIX WAYS A DEADLY MAZE

KELSEY'S BURDEN SERIES
LAYERED LIES
PAST HAUNTS
FRIENDS AND FOES
BLOOD AND TEARS
LOVE AND RAGE
DAY AND NIGHT
HEARTS AND ACES
HUNT AND PREY
HEROES AND HELLFIRE

STANDALONE NOVELS
SLIGHTLY OFF-BALANCE
DIAMOND'S EDGE

To stay up to date on new releases, visit our website:
BOOKSBYKAYLIE.COM

Chapter One

They say when you're having a near-death experience, your entire life flashes through your mind. Well, the twenty-six years I've spent on this planet must not have been that exciting, because the only thing I was thinking about was—*Why the hell did I wear my pastel, polka-dot, cotton granny-panties today?*

"You outdid yourself this time, Sullivan," I muttered to myself as I released one of my hands from the death-grip-hold on the outer rail to attempt tucking my skirt back between my legs.

"Quit moving," a male voice ordered from below.

The voice, a lot closer than the last time I was ordered to stay still, startled me enough to cause me to re-grip the metal bar.

I tipped my head back, looking down at Rod as he climbed the Ferris wheel in his volunteer fireman getup.

"I said, *quit moving*." He grinned, looking up at me.

Of all the people they could send to save me—did it have to be Rod Thurman?

From his sun-kissed hair to the tips of his toes, the man was smokin'. His only rival for female attention was his twin brother, Reel. Of course, in a town the size of a penny, Rod and Reel pretty much cornered the bachelor market.

I know—Rod and Reel? It was their father's fault. Their birth certificates read *Rodney* and *Ryan*, but in Pine Valley, once you were graced with a nickname it stuck like dried cement.

Their father, Everett, had told his first wife he was going on a fishing trip with the guys. The result of that so-called fishing trip was Loretta Hines getting knocked up—thus the town joke became the birth of their twin boys: Rod and Reel. With Everett being the town drunk, I suspected an abundance of alcohol was involved in concocting the nicknames.

From below me, Rod flashed his pearly whites my way. His bulging muscles flexed as he pulled himself up another few feet.

Ugh, I mentally sighed. Why did I have to come to the carnival tonight? Why did I get on this stupid Ferris wheel? "Lord, hear my prayers. Just end it now," I whispered.

"What was that?" Rod asked.

"Nothing," I mumbled.

I looked past him at all the spectators on the ground. Everyone above the age of eight held a cell phone, recording my humiliation and waiting for my shoelace to tear so they could replay my fifty-foot plunge. This was more embarrassing than the time I fell face first into the wishing fountain in the courtyard.

"You know, most people would look scared as hell if they were hanging upside down from a Ferris wheel with only a shoelace keeping them from falling." Rod laughed, now only a few feet away. "But you look just plain frustrated."

"Double knotting my shoelaces was to ensure that I never embarrassed myself again like when I fell down the stadium bleachers at the home basketball game. I'm wishing this time I'd have just fallen and gotten it over with."

"Falling isn't an option. I'd get my ass kicked if anything happened to you," he said, climbing another section. "Besides, the town will find someone else to laugh at in a few days."

"Oh really? You going to convince all those people down there to delete their videos of my big ass in polka-dot granny panties?"

He chuckled. "I hope they post the videos. I could look at that ass all day long, polka dots or not."

Rod moved under the crossbar beneath me, and now his face was inches away from mine. His smile was so bright, I would've looked away if it weren't for the humor dancing in his bright blue eyes. Rod was known as one of those happy-go-lucky guys, always finding the humor in any situation and spreading his positive energy like a virus to everyone in his vicinity.

He moved his harness clip to the side rail I was holding and then stepped up another foot so his chest was inches from my nose. I felt him strapping a harness belt around my waist and cinching it tight. As he moved over to clip the harness to the side bar, I leaned with him, inhaling his cologne.

"Are you smelling me?" he asked, chuckling.

I shrugged. "There's nothing else to do up here."

"Quit moving—" he started to say.

Hearing the shoelace rip, I squeezed the sidebar with all my might. I knew it was hopeless though. I had been stacking those extra holiday pounds on since I hit puberty and refused to go on a diet. If the harness strap wasn't secure, I wouldn't be able to hold my own weight. I closed my eyes as my body weight fell... three inches.

Frozen, I had to mentally argue with myself to open my eyes because I knew the situation had gone from the most embarrassing moment of my life to—I'll have to move to another country.

I opened my eyes.

Rod had wrapped his arms around my waist and was holding my weight as I remained suspended upside down. Only now, his face was nose deep in the front side of my polka-dot granny-panties, and he was laughing which was causing all kinds of confusion to my girly parts as his chuckles vibrated along my more sensitive areas.

"Shit! You have to drop me!"

"I'm-na-gonn-doppp-yuuu," he mumbled into my panties.

"Quit talking! Quit laughing!"

I looked at his harness and saw that only one of his clips was secured. I reached over and secured his second clip to the crossbar.

Reaching up, I moved my hands between our bodies, searching for the second clip on my own harness. In the process, my hand grazed his own sensitive area, discovering he was excited, in a manly kind of way.

"Really?" I said, forcing my hand up higher, digging around between us to find the other strap.

He tried to say something, but it just came out mumbled, and the vibrations almost made me forget what I was doing.

"Stop talking! Until your face is out of you-know-where, just shut up!"

He stopped talking but laughed even harder.

My hand found the strap between his shoulder and the top of my hip. With a hard yank, the strap freed, and I secured it to the crossbar. I tried not to think about the hundreds of witnesses filming us.

"Okay. I have the harness straps secure. You can let go now."

He mumbled something incoherent into my panties without releasing me. I suspected there were rules against him allowing me to decide for myself that I was safe. Taking the matter out of his hands, I apologized, "Sorry about this," before whacking him in the you-know-where.

Reacting as any man would, he pushed back, loosening his hold on me. I pushed with my arms as hard as I could to break his hold. My heavy thighs and ass flipped past my head, and I was instantly right side up, dropping about two feet until the tension on the harness straps stopped me.

Several spectators screamed during my short plummet, but I was more focused on my current situation. Grabbing the crossbar above me, I pulled myself to the outside rail, dragging the harness strap with me.

"Son-of-a-bitch. That was mean, Tweedle," Rod grumbled from above me.

I was somewhat relieved when he used my nickname. I looked up and grinned. Rod and I had known each other since early childhood. The only time I'd ever made him truly angry, he spoke my full name, drawing out each word like a ticked-off parent: *Deanna. Marie. Sullivan.*

I moved the harness clip from the crossbar above me to the outside rail. Wrapping my legs around the bar, I slid down, stopping at the next crossbar.

"And where in the hell do you think you're going?"

"I've had enough. It's time for me to go home and eat Klondike bars and watch Big Bang Theory reruns."

"Figures." He laughed. "You get me all wound up and now you're just going to leave me hanging?"

"I'm sure you can find a girl easy enough to take care of your, *uhm*, boy troubles."

"As in the girl has to be easy? Or... It'll be easy to find a girl?"

"Both. Either. I don't care." I moved my butt off the rail, opening a gap between my lap and the bar. While balancing my weight on my thighs along the crossbar, I moved the safety clips down to the next section.

"Hey, you really shouldn't be doing that. It's not safe. You haven't been trained," Rod said, sounding serious.

"Try to stop me," I said as I swung my thigh off the crossbar and slid down another five feet.

"I mean it. Wait for me to take you down."

"And humiliate me even more? No thanks," I said, repeating the same steps and sliding again.

Rod was trying to catch up, but I was already two sections ahead of him and had a good groove going. I was also highly motivated.

For every section he moved, following regulation rules, I moved two sections. When I reached the bottom, another firefighter helped me unbuckle the harness, and I did what any semi-intelligent woman would do—I ducked behind the control booth, climbed over the three-foot railing, and ran away.

I ran away from the spectators, the firefighters, and the police. I ran as fast as my jelly legs could carry me, sneaking out the back gate of the carnival.

Almost wiping out as I skidded around the corner of a cinderblock building, I looked up, and a peaceful happiness spread throughout my body. Parked curbside, leaning against her rusty Subaru, was the best friend a girl could ever ask for.

Tansey grinned as she opened the passenger door and stepped back. "Figured you'd head this way. Nice panties by the way."

"Don't start with me. I'm in desperate need of chocolate and ice cream."

She leaned inside, pulling out a box of Klondike bars from a grocery bag sitting on the floor.

I laughed, tearing open the box as I climbed into the passenger seat. "I really wish you were gay."

"But then you'd still be straight," Tansey said, getting in the driver's side.

"I'd convert for you."

"That's the most romantic thing anyone has ever said to me."

"I hear you there, sister. Your predicting my escape route, ready with a getaway car *and ice cream bars*, is the most romantic thing anyone has ever done for me."

We both laughed as she started the Subaru and pulled away from the curb.

"How did you end up hanging upside down on the Ferris wheel, anyway?"

"It all happened so fast, I'm not really sure. I leaned forward to look down, and the gate swung away from the seat, with me dangling over it. As my ass rose up, I slid further down. Then I fell. I thought I was a goner, but my shoelace miraculously caught on the latch."

"You scared the crap out of me."

"How'd you know, anyway?"

She looked over at me and sighed.

"Just tell me. Get it over with while I have another five Klondike bars handy."

"They were live streaming it on Facebook. I was watching the video on my phone on the way over. I was halfway to the fairgrounds when Rod reached you. I figured you were relatively safe at that point, so I stopped at the corner store for Klondike bars."

"Streaming live on Facebook?" I looked inside the Klondike box on my lap. "I'm going to need more."

"There's another box in the bag. I figured this qualified as an emergency."

"What would you've done if Rod had dropped me and I'd died?"

"I would've eaten both boxes in your honor, of course," she said, smiling. "Then I would've hunted Rod Thurman down and murdered him."

I unwrapped another Klondike, passing it to her, before unwrapping a second one for myself. "To best friends," I toasted.

Chapter Two

Tansey bypassed Main Street and cut through residential neighborhoods to get to my house. Being my best friend since kindergarten, she went to the spare room where she kept an assortment of clothes, including flannel pajamas. I went to my own bedroom and changed into pink pajamas with bunny rabbits plastered all over them and baby blue fuzzy slippers.

In the kitchen, I put two Klondike bars each into oversized cereal bowls and put the rest of the ice cream in the freezer. By the time I joined Tansey in the living room, the TV was already playing one of my favorite episodes of *Big Bang Theory*. Life was quiet and happy for all of about two minutes when someone knocked loudly on the back door.

"Don't answer it," I said, looking at Tansey.

She just grinned. We both knew who it was, and he had a key. If we got lucky, he wouldn't use it.

We didn't get lucky.

"You can run. You can hide. But I'll always find you, Tweedle-Dee," Uncle Mike called as he entered through the back door and into the kitchen.

Since grade school, Uncle Mike had called me Tweedle-Dee. The nickname had stuck and now almost everyone called me either Tweedle-Dee or just Tweedle. My mother and Reel Thurman, Rod's brother, were the only ones who called me Deanna.

Tansey and I ducked to hide, but Uncle Mike just chuckled as he walked into the living room. He was still wearing his cop uniform, but his utility belt was gone, and his uniform shirt was unbuttoned, advertising the worn-out Tesla T-shirt underneath, indicators that he was off the clock.

"I brought you a couple things. Your car is in the driveway, your purse is on the table, and here—" He tossed me a package. "—your mother stopped me and told me to give you these. She also said she has to reschedule your breakfast date tomorrow."

I looked inside the bag and pulled out three packages of underwear—bikini-cut in dark colors, satin fabric, and four sizes too small for my butt to squeeze into. I tossed the packages to Tansey who was always appreciative of my mother's wishful thinking regarding the clothes sizes.

"Sweet. A year's supply of underwear." She giggled.

"I'm just glad I don't have to meet her for breakfast."

"Like you would've shown up," Uncle Mike said, rolling his eyes.

Uncle Mike pushed me over to the center of the couch, taking the end seat and stacking his stocking feet onto the coffee table. He smiled as he snatched my bowl of ice cream.

"What are we watching?" he asked.

"*The Big Bang Theory*. It's the episode where—"

"Enough said," Uncle Mike said, interrupting. "By the way, your mother thinks you need to go to therapy. She said having oral sex on a Ferris wheel is a sign of some kind of psychological-social-bullshit disorder."

"Is that what she called it? Psychological-social-bullshit?"

"That's what I heard. I have no idea what she really said."

"You didn't tell me you were having oral sex on the Ferris wheel," Tansey said with wide eyes.

"Don't get too excited. I wasn't doing the oral sex thing until I was already hanging upside down."

Tansey scrunched her nose up in confusion. "What?"

"You didn't keep watching the live video, did you?"

"When I left the store with your Klondikes, you were already halfway down the Ferris wheel. What did I miss?"

Uncle Mike passed his phone to her, and she watched the screen.

"Holy shit!" Tansey giggled. "I missed the best part! His nose is right in there!"

"His nose was up close and personal. His mouth was—"

"Stop!" Uncle Mike ordered. "I love you two dearly, but you are not having this conversation while I'm in the house."

We turned to look toward the kitchen as we heard the back door open. High heels clacked across the wood-plank floor, and my sister turned the corner, glaring at us.

"You just had to embarrass me in front of the whole town, didn't you!" Darlene hissed as she stormed into the living room.

"You forgot to lock the door, Uncle Mike," Tansey said.

"You know you aren't allowed to wear shoes in my house," I said. "In fact, you're not allowed in my house. I distinctly remember telling you I didn't want to see you again."

Darlene cocked her arm, hand on hip. "What were you hoping to accomplish with that little stunt at the carnival tonight? Huh? If you thought you could steal my boyfriend with that juvenile move, you were wrong!"

"You have a boyfriend?" the three of us asked in unison.

"The fireman! Rod Thurman! We're dating! And you shoved your hoo-hah in his face! And filmed it!"

Uncle Mike chuckled. "First of all, I think he shoved his face in her hoo-hah."

"And she wasn't the one filming it," Tansey added.

"Rod is dating *you*!?" I asked again, still trying to get past the boyfriend comment.

"You'll pay for this," Darlene said, pointing a finger at me before she stormed back toward the kitchen. "I'll teach you a lesson you'll never forget!"

When the door slammed shut, Uncle Mike jumped off the couch and ran to lock it.

"Why do I always hear the Wicked Witch theme song in my head when she's around?" Tansey laughed.

"She has a boyfriend?" I asked Tansey.

Uncle Mike returned, picking up the remote and backing the video up so he could replay the part that he'd missed during my sister's tirade. "Word in the precinct is that Rod lost a bet and had to ask her out. That was about two months back. I heard it was the shortest date of his life and he wished he would've worn a chastity belt because she kept trying to shove her hand down his pants."

We heard the back door open again, and I turned to glare at Uncle Mike.

Uncle Mike lifted his hands, palms facing me. "I locked it; I swear!"

"It's just me," Aunt Carol called out. "I brought dinner, so put the ice cream away."

I grabbed half a Klondike out of my former bowl as Uncle Mike hurriedly ate the other bar. Tansey was barreling through her own bowl at a pace that was guaranteed to freeze brain cells.

"Okay, fine," Aunt Carol said from the entrance to the living room. "Eat your dessert first, but when you're ready, I have pot roast and potatoes in the kitchen."

Aunt Carol walked into the living room and leaned over the back of the couch, kissing me on the cheek. "I'm glad you lived, Tweedle-Dee. And your mother wants me to have a conversation with you about public sexual acts. I told her that if Rod Thurman wanted to give me oral sex, I'd do it in the middle of town square."

I smiled at Aunt Carol.

"Your husband is sitting right here!" Uncle Mike complained.

"My husband is diabetic, overweight, and eating ice cream before dinner. Maybe he needs a few mental images of what my life will look like when he dies." She patted Uncle Mike's shoulder before walking back to the kitchen.

Uncle Mike sighed. "God, I love that woman."

I giggled. "It takes a special kind of woman to tolerate you."

"Tweedle," Aunt Carol called out. "Where are all your dishes?"

"At the nursing home."

"Why on earth would all your plates and bowls be at the nursing home?"

"I couldn't sleep last night so I made blueberry cobbler. Then I made apple cobbler. Then I made peach cobbler."

"And what does the cobbler have to do with your dishes?" Aunt Carol asked from the kitchen doorway.

I dragged myself off the couch and went to search for plates. "Well, I didn't want to end up eating all that damn cobbler, so I divided it between all my dishes before taking it to the nursing home. Except the nurse said it was too late for dessert, so we had to put it in the refrigerator. I was supposed to swing by after work to pick up the dishes, but I forgot."

"I'll run by tonight and pick them up," Aunt Carol said, rolling her eyes.

Opening the pantry cupboard, I pulled out the four-person picnic basket set that my mother had given me last year for Christmas. I'd never picnicked in my life, but inside the basket were four perfectly clean plates and real silverware.

I held up the basket, showing her my find.

Aunt Carol shook her head, smirking.

Tansey entered the kitchen, pulling the picnic blanket from inside the basket before carrying it back to the living room. I followed her with the plates and silverware, and Uncle Mike helped Aunt Carol carry the food.

We had the perfect picnic, free of bugs and slobbering dogs, while watching *The Big Bang Theory*.

Chapter Three

THE NEXT MORNING, I CONTEMPLATED calling in sick, but Uncle Mike made an early morning visit to my house and ordered me to get out of bed.

"You might as well get it over with!" he hollered from the kitchen. "Your aunt said if she sees your car in the driveway still by midmorning, she'll drag you over to your mother's house."

"I'm up. I'm up!" I grumbled, forcing myself out of bed and into my bathroom.

I quickly showered and tried on three outfits before I settled for a comfortable cotton shirt and long skirt. Even after the debacle with the Ferris wheel, I preferred a skirt over having denim swishing between my rounded thighs.

In the kitchen, I found a to-go coffee with a small note stuck to the top. The note was from Uncle Mike and read: *Tweedle, show them what you're made of. Love, Uncle Mike.*

I folded the note and stuffed it in my bra—just in case I needed that extra kick in the ass later in the day.

Grabbing my keys and coffee, I headed toward the door. "You can do this, Sullivan!" I cheered to myself.

Halfway to work, my car started speeding up on its own.

At first, I thought I was having a blonde moment, but after taking my foot off the gas pedal, my car continued to increase speed.

I threw both feet on the brake pedal, but nothing happened.

Panicking, I turned the keys to the off position before yanking them out of the ignition. The car's engine died, coasting to a stop.

I sat there trying to decide what to do. The sun was just beginning to crack the sky, and the streets were empty. No one was around this early in the morning and Uncle Mike would already be at work.

I could leave the car and walk the rest of the way. Or... I could start and stop the car all the way to work. *Why not?* I thought, looking around. The streets were empty, so I wouldn't be endangering anyone.

Decision made, I started the car and traveled a few blocks closer to town until the speed climbed to double the city speed limit. I turned the ignition off and coasted another block.

I was now two blocks away from the bakery. I typically parked behind the bakery in the back lot, but I wasn't sure whether I could pull around the dumpster and maneuver into the small parking spaces. The on-street parking offered angle slots which would be easier as long as I slowed enough that my car didn't jump the curb.

I took a deep breath, restarting the car and aiming for Main Street.

Cutting the engine with three-quarters of a block to go, I took advantage of the empty street and swung my car wide before cranking the wheel in a semi U-turn to get the car to face the right way.

The bakery was directly in front of me, but I was going too fast. I wasn't going to stop in time.

Opening the driver's door, I dragged the heels of my shoes on the asphalt as I reefed on the emergency brake with all my might. Half hanging out the door, I couldn't see how far away I was from the sidewalk, but I felt the car ricochet off the curb. The impact stopped the car but tossed me the rest of the way out onto the asphalt.

Sighing, I rolled over and inspected myself for injuries, not finding any, but my clothes were covered in black asphalt smudges.

After brushing off the dirt, I grabbed my purse and closed the door before surveying the area. Surprisingly, the car was parked perfectly between the white lines and six inches from the curb.

"That-a-girl!" I thumped the roof.

Starting for the bakery front door, I stopped when I realized my shoes felt funny. Looking down, I saw that half the tread was gone. Luckily, I kept a locker at work which was well stocked with spare clothes and shoes. I took out my keys, unlocking the door.

I started working at the bakery when I was only sixteen and ten years later, forty pounds heavier, and despite having to get up at the crack of dawn, I still loved working here.

The best part was that everyone was in a happy mood as they indulged in their cake, brownies, donuts, or muffins.

But today, as the bakery got busier and busier with each hour that passed, the customers' sugar highs were only fueling their jokes at my expense. Only twenty minutes after opening, I'd decided to spend as much time as possible in the kitchen.

And hours later, that's where I was still hiding when I heard my mother's screechy voice yell at Samantha. "*I know she's here.* Her car is parked out front. How dare she show her face in town after what she did yesterday."

Choosing to show mercy on Samantha, I stepped out of the kitchen to face the firing squad myself. "Good morning, Mother." I smiled a fake smile, sidestepping behind the display counter. "I made cream puffs this morning. Would you like one?"

"What do you think you're doing?" my mother hissed. "As if you haven't done enough damage to our family's reputation, you come here like nothing happened?"

Samantha looked at me, looked at my mother, and then—like any sane person stuck in the middle of a family feud—bailed for the safety of the kitchen.

"Is that a no to the puffs? How about a chocolate éclair?" I smiled brightly.

"And that underwear! What were you thinking?"

"I was thinking that it was on sale, in my size, and in comfy cotton to make my butt feel all cozy. Though, if I could have predicted flashing my ass to the whole town, I'd have worn the ones with the pastel confetti design. Or maybe the colorful rainbow ones, but those may have made my butt look crooked from the angle of the videos. Wouldn't want the neighbors thinking my ample backside was crooked, so probably the confetti design."

"You're going to hell."

"I wasn't planning on it, but you never know. I'm still young. I might just murder someone yet." The thought of pushing my mother and sister down a flight of stairs popped into my head, but I shook the thought away. I'd never kill them. Maybe maim them a bit, but never kill them.

"You ungrateful, spiteful girl," Mother snapped before pivoting on the ball of one foot and stomping out of the bakery.

The handful of regulars sitting at the nearby tables clapped and cheered. I stepped out from behind the counter and took a bow, which led to louder claps and cheers.

Samantha giggled, peeking her head out from the kitchen. "I swear, I hear the Wicked Witch theme song every time I see your mother."

"Seems to be a family theme song. Tansey hears it when my sister's around."

"Well, lucky for us, you're Dorothy in that movie."

I grinned. "Oh damn. I'm all out of ruby red slippers. How will I ever get home?"

"I would give you a ride," a male voice answered from behind me.

Dog-gone-it, I knew that voice. I turned, and there he was. Rod Thurman.

Looking out the storefront window, I saw the town firetruck parked in front of the bakery. The other firefighters were loudly encouraging Rod.

"I've had my fill of firemen lately. Either leave or place an order."

His grin widened as he leaned forward on the counter.

"I'll take a dozen donuts."

I turned into the kitchen, pushing Samantha back as I entered. I pulled out a bakery box and smashed up twelve day-old raspberry-filled donuts into a mushy mess before closing the lid.

Storming back to the counter, I tossed the box in front of Rod.

"On the house. Thank you for saving me yesterday."

Mimicking my mother's move, I turned on the ball of my foot and stomped back into the kitchen.

Samantha snickered, following me into the kitchen. "I can't believe you just did that."

Samantha, a good fifteen years older than me, owned the bakery. Most business owners would've had a meltdown after watching me smash up the donuts and give them to a customer, but Samantha appreciated my humor and knew my baking skills were worth a few ruffled feathers.

Seeing the trash bag was full, I pulled the bag. "He deserved it. He stuck his nose into my *business* without permission."

"He can stick whatever he wants in my business, any day he wants," Samantha said before returning to the service counter.

I shook my head and carried the bag of trash out to the alley. The lid of the dumpster slamming shut startled me, and I watched a teenage boy hurry away.

His clothes were worn and his untrimmed hair was oily and uncombed. He glanced back and quickened his pace when he saw me watching him.

"Hey, kid." I smiled, stepping toward the dumpster. "You hungry?"

He turned to look at me but continued to backstep away. His eyes danced in every direction, only occasionally looking at me directly.

"I won't call anyone. Just wait here. I'll bring you out something to eat."

I wasn't sure whether he'd still be around when I came back out, but depositing the trash bag inside the dumpster, I entered the kitchen and pulled my lunch from the refrigerator, adding an apple and a handful of oatmeal raisin cookies. Stepping back outside, I didn't see him anywhere but walked to the end of the alley and set the food on the sidewalk, hoping he would see it.

I didn't know who the kid was, which was odd being Pine Valley was such a small town, but homelessness didn't just happen in the big cities.

Besides, skipping lunch might make up for the three cream puffs I'd eaten for breakfast.

Chapter Four

By eleven Samantha took pity on me and let me leave early. Our prankster regulars kept bringing me underwear. Some had funny designs. Some were fancy satin little numbers. Some looked downright uncomfortable to wear. And all of them were embarrassing to receive as gifts in a bakery shop.

Carrying an oversized bakery bag filled with undies, I strolled at a whimsical pace down the sidewalk, peeking into several store windows. I didn't dare enter any of them on a day when everyone was seeking to offer me a good-hearted ribbing.

Rounding the corner, I slammed into someone with enough force to knock me backward. Strong arms wrapped around me, pulling me forward to stop my fall. I tried to move a leg off to the side to balance myself, but it was tangled with the other person's leg. In a blink, we were crashing down on the concrete sidewalk.

It took me a minute to realize I wasn't hurt. Whoever was underneath me had broken my fall with their own body. I looked up—and froze.

Brilliant, blue, intense eyes focused on my own. "Are you hurt?" Reel whispered, cupping the side of my face.

Only inches away, I could feel the heat of his breath on my cheek. I hadn't seen Reel, Rod's brother, in years, but somehow it was like time skipped backward.

"Deanna," Reel whispered, lifting his head closer to mine. "*Are. You. Hurt?*"

I found myself leaning toward him, eager to close the space between us to kiss him, but his words broke through my foggy brain, startling me out of my stupor. I jerked back, turning my face away as my cheeks heated. "I just flattened you to the sidewalk, and you're worried about me?"

"Answer the question," Reel ordered.

"No," I said with a sigh, rolling off him. "I'm fine."

Reel sat up and pulled me into a sitting position beside him. Grabbing each appendage, one at a time, he inspected me for damage. I rolled my eyes and ignored him.

"You skinned your knee," he said.

"I did that yesterday."

"At the carnival?"

I shook my head as I rolled over onto all fours before climbing up into a standing position. "Mr. Nicholson's dog got loose again, and I was trying to help catch him. Little shit tripped me."

"Mr. Nicholson or his dog?"

"Did you just make a joke, Reel Thurman?"

He shrugged. "It happens on occasion."

I looked at Reel and the surrounding sidewalk. The bakery bag had torn during our fall, and both Reel and the sidewalk were covered in colorful panties of all sizes and colors.

"Explain this," Reel said, holding one of the pairs out in front of him.

"I was on my way to the church store to donate them," I said, grabbing the pair he held and several more that draped over him. "The good townsfolk of Pine Valley were generous enough to supply me with new underwear options."

Reel grabbed another lacy pair that wouldn't have fit me at the age of ten.

"Because of the Ferris wheel yesterday?"

"Of course. Why else would they be buying me underwear?" I said, rolling my eyes. "And I'm sure you can imagine that the jokes about how your brother saved me won't be dying anytime soon either."

"How is Rod saving you funny?" Reel asked, getting up from the sidewalk and helping me gather the underwear, stuffing them into the ripped bag.

"You didn't watch the video?"

"No," he said, seeming angered by the question. "I was told I shouldn't watch it."

"Who told you not to watch it?"

"Rod called to tell me you had an accident on the Ferris wheel but that you were fine, but not to watch the video."

Odd, I thought but shrugged off the comment. I picked up the last pair of underwear, but they didn't look like underwear to me. With the handles of the bag looped through my arm, I held them up and was turning them to figure out what body parts went where.

Reel took the undies, turned them around and showed me which way they went.

"No way." I blushed, looking at the crotchless panties in a big-girl's size.

"Never seen crotchless panties?" Reel asked.

"It's not that," I said, shaking my head. "Mrs. Crookburn gave me this pair."

Mrs. Crookburn was a retired teacher, very retired. She was pushing the hundred-year mark and still drove, despite Uncle Mike pulling her license over two decades ago.

Reel looked at the panties he was holding and laughed. *Laughed.* I hadn't heard him laugh since we were kids. Back then, Reel laughed all the time.

"Go, Mrs. Crookburn," he said, tossing the panties into the bag.

After checking one last time to make sure I'd picked everything up, I started walking again. "Sorry about trampling you. I have to be off now."

"You're heading to the church resale store?" Reel asked, jogging to catch up.

"They close early on Fridays," I said, nodding and turning left to cross the street.

"I'll go with you. I just bought a house and need some things."

"You bought a house in Pine Valley? Why? You're always out of town for work."

"I've been thinking of cutting back on the security jobs and staying home more."

After a tour with the Army, Reel had taken a job with a security firm that hired him to protect celebrities and other rich people. It required him to travel a lot, so he'd never moved out of his father's house, even though he was two years older than me.

Rod had never moved out either, but with their father being the town drunk, I figured Rod stayed to keep his father out of trouble. I also thought that

Rod and Reel were the ones paying the bills, so really, Everett lived with his sons.

"I'm sure your family will love having you home more," I said, without looking over at Reel who was now walking beside me.

Reaching the store, Reel held the door open for me to walk through. I went straight to the register, dumping the ripped bag on the counter.

"I was hoping to see you today, Tweedle," Gail said, smiling warmly. "I heard everyone in town was buying you bloomers. We have several women that could make good use of them."

"I'm not sure all of them would be appropriate to dole out. Some of them are a bit X-rated."

"Yes," Gail gasped, holding up the pair of crotchless panties. "I'll definitely sort them first."

"Deanna," Reel called out. "Help me pick out curtains."

I meandered around a rack and stopped beside Reel looking at a large selection of curtains. "What room are you shopping for?"

"The kitchen and living room. The kitchen is big and square, almost identical to your aunt Carol's. The living room is combined with the dining room and has six oversized windows like your mother's house."

"What colors are in your kitchen?"

Reel looked at me, confused.

"The counters, the flooring, the walls? What colors?"

"The floor is wood planked, and the counters are tan."

"And the walls?"

"White."

"Go with either the light blue or the bright yellow."

"Which do you like better?"

"The blue," I said. "And look, they have matching dish towels too."

Reel started loading up all the blue kitchen curtains and towels, and Gail brought over one of the two mini shopping carts for him to dump everything into.

"Gail, do you still have the cream and navy satin curtains my mother donated a few months back?"

"They're in the back," Gail said, grimacing.

"Why are they in the back? Are they on hold for someone?"

"Sort of. I was saving them for you. I know how much you love those curtains, and if you ever move out of your rental and buy a house, I knew you'd want them."

"That's sweet, but I like my rental and don't plan on moving anytime soon. Go ahead and dig them out to show Reel."

Gail returned a few minutes later with an oversized box.

"It's all here. Including the white sheers and the curtain rods."

Reel took the box and set it on the floor. I opened the top and pulled out a corner of the fabric to show Reel. "What do you think?"

"I have no idea. I'd be fine nailing sheets over the windows, so you tell me. Are they nice?"

"These curtains are a lot more expensive than sheets. My mother redecorates every year, and these were by far my favorite, which explains why she only kept them for six months. But if you want to go cheaper, we can get some fabric, and I can sew some curtains for you."

"I don't care about the money."

"Will they look okay with the carpet in your living room?"

"Wood flooring throughout the house."

"Well, if money isn't an issue, then I think you've got your curtains," I said, standing back up. "Anything else you need?"

"Everything. Pots, pans, dishes, furniture, pictures." Reel rubbed a hand roughly across his forehead.

Gail and I laughed.

"Where's your truck?" I asked.

"By the post office."

"Go get it. Gail and I will keep shopping for you. Make sure you come back with your wallet. This is going to dent your bank account."

"No, it won't." Reel smirked, escaping the store.

I released a long breath that I hadn't noticed I'd been holding. I had purposefully avoided spending time with Reel over the past few years during his rare visits. Too many embarrassing memories.

Realizing I was still staring at the door that Reel had left through, I shook off the memories and looked back at the shelves.

"People in this town are scared to death to talk to Reel Thurman, and yet you trot him around like a puppy," Gail said.

"Why would anyone be afraid of Reel? He's harmless."

"*Please.*" Gail rolled her eyes, grinning. "Since his teenage years, grown men have turned and gone out of their way to avoid him. One glare from Reel has been known to cure addictions, stop affairs, and stop the birds from singing their morning songs."

"He's not that scary." I laughed, though I could understand why others would think him scary. Reel wasn't a mean person, but he was over-the-top protective. For as far back as I could remember, Reel wasn't afraid to give someone a good thrashing if they'd wronged someone he cared about.

"It's weird, Rod and Reel are such opposites," Gail said, turning her attention to a shelf of cookware and adding a large frying pan to the cart. "Rod is an outgoing happy person and the center of every good party."

"I don't know. I was close to both of them growing up. Maybe it colors my opinion of them. Hey, have you seen a homeless teenage boy around town?"

"No, and I haven't heard of a kid coming into the shelter. You sure he was homeless? My son looks like a derelict after spending a week at his father's. I have no idea how he can stand the smell of himself."

"Maybe," I said, though I knew otherwise. When I'd left the bakery, I'd noticed the bag of food I'd set out was gone. At least I knew he had eaten something today. Until he asked for help, I supposed that was all I could do.

Shaking off the thought, I focused on shopping. It wouldn't take Reel long to walk to his truck, so I started loading another cart with dishes.

Chapter Five

By the time Reel returned, I had finished going through the store, and Gail had recorded everything on the sales slip. We were piling everything outside on the sidewalk when Reel pulled up and stepped out of the truck.

Anger was radiating off him in waves, and Gail stepped closer to the store.

I laughed. "What's got you all bent out of shape?"

"I had a chat with Rod. Buck Peaton was kind enough to show me the video of the carnival yesterday."

"So?" I asked, confused.

"Never mind," Reel said, shaking his head. "Sorry I took so long."

"It's fine. We just finished. You'll need more stuff, but it's a good start. I'll load the truck while you go pay."

"I'll load the truck," he said, passing me his wallet.

I followed Gail into the store to pay for the order. It felt a bit weird paying with cash out of Reel's wallet. And I really wanted to snoop, but I scolded myself for the thought.

I was putting the change back when I spotted an old photo staring back at me. Rod and Reel were about ten, both straddling their mountain bikes. Tansey and I stood next to Reel. He had his arm crooked around my neck and was looking at me. My eight-year-old self was laughing, with my arms wrapped innocently around his waist.

I didn't remember the picture, but it didn't surprise me either. The four of us grew up within a three-block radius, and Aunt Carol was always close by, taking pictures.

"Well, isn't that cute," Gail said, leaning over the counter to look at the photo. "What else is in there?"

"I don't know." I grinned, closing the wallet. "And we aren't looking."

I turned to leave and noticed Reel standing at the door, grinning at me.

"I didn't snoop." I felt my cheeks heat as I held up his wallet. "The picture was right there."

"You can snoop," he said, shrugging while holding the door open for me.

The sun was melting the air around us as I walked with Reel toward the truck.

"Do you have time to go to the furniture store?"

I checked my watch. It was almost 1:00.

"Can we stop by The Bar for a burger first? Tansey's working, so I'll get us a discount."

"Deal. A cold beer sounds good."

Casey Pritchard had owned the local bar for half a century, naming it The Bar. The joke was that if you wanted to go out drinking, it was the only game in town, thus everyone would go to The Bar.

Tansey had started working there when she turned eighteen, followed by moving into the upstairs apartment six months later. The apartment was spacious, with an open layout and industrial oversized windows that offered plenty of natural sunlight for Tansey to paint.

"Why aren't you at work?" Tansey asked as she walked by with a tray of beers.

"Left early. There's only so much ribbing a girl can take," I answered as I slid into one of the large booths.

Reel surprised me by sliding in next to me, moving me to the inside seat.

Tansey delivered the beers to the nearby table and returned wearing a grin. "The usual?" she asked me.

"Yup."

"The usual?" she asked Reel.

"Yes," he said without looking at Tansey. He was searching the room, his intense eyes making contact with anyone who dared look his way.

Tansey snorted before walking off toward the kitchen.

"Are you looking for someone?" I asked him.

"Habit," he answered, looking down at me. "Downside of working security for a living."

"Any interesting cases lately?"

"Interesting? No," Reel said, shaking his head. "Dangerous, yes. But it's finally over."

"What's over?"

"A friend of a friend had a kill contract out on her, but it's been handled. She and her family are finally safe."

"*A kill contract? As in a hitman?* Is that why you were gone so long this time?"

Reel nodded but didn't say anything.

"Did you kill the bad guy?" I whispered so no one else would hear.

"No." He chuckled, leaning back in the booth and throwing his arm along the top rail behind me. "She wouldn't let us."

I exhaled my relief. "Good. I mean, I get it. You are out there dealing with some real nut jobs, but it's not very Christian to kill people."

Reel shrugged. "Sometimes it has to happen."

"But this was one less time."

Reel smirked. "I'll let Kelsey know you approve of her decision."

For some reason, hearing Reel talk about another woman rankled me. I fidgeted in my seat. It wasn't like Reel and I had ever dated. Nor had we spent any significant amount of time together after he left for the Army. But hearing him talk about his life, another woman, just reminded me that I didn't really know Reel anymore.

"I expect my friend Grady will marry Kelsey before the year is over," Reel said, pointedly staring sideways at me with a raised eyebrow and his lips curved upward.

"That's nice," I said, distracting myself by unrolling my silverware from the napkin.

Reel laughed and several people startled, jumping in their seats.

Tansey rolled her eyes as she delivered a beer to Reel and a root beer float with whipped cream to me. "Kitchen's backed up, so the burgers will be a few minutes." She slid into the seat across from us. "What are you two up to?"

"Shopping," I said before sucking the sugary syrup through my straw.

"For what?" Tansey asked, looking back and forth between Reel and me.

"I bought a house," Reel answered. "Deanna's helping me with the girly crap that I need."

"Do you need furniture?" Tansey asked.

"I have bedroom furniture being delivered, but I need everything else."

"The furniture store in Cooper City is going out of business. Everything is on sale."

"They're closing?" I said, surprised. "Dang it. I don't have the money for that sectional couch yet."

"I know," Tansey said, pouting. "I called to find out how much they'd lowered the price, but even if we pooled our money, we wouldn't have enough. Unless, of course, you dip into the Master Plan account."

"I'm not breaking the rules for a couch," I said, shaking my head.

"The Master Plan account?" Reel asked, turning those intense blue eyes on me.

"Don't make fun of us," I scolded, pointing my index finger at him. "We've been setting money aside in those accounts since we were twelve. We are quite proud of them."

"And yet, I still can't get my account balance higher than Tweedle's," Tansey said, frowning. "I swear, every time I get close, she pulls a rabbit out of her hat and caters some big job on the side and blows me away."

"How much could either of you have possibly saved, working minimum-wage jobs?" Reel asked, chuckling.

I grinned. "$36,220.52."

"$32,400.11," Tansey said, smirking.

Reel looked from me to Tansey and back again. "You're serious?"

"Every penny we can spare goes toward the Master Plan," I said.

"I'm almost scared to ask, but what's the Master Plan?"

"I want to own my own paint studio and gallery," Tansey said, her eyes lighting up at the thought.

"And I want to own my own bakery," I said.

Reel nodded, drinking his beer as he listened to us detail our dream business ventures. Our conversation ended when the kitchen bell rang, indicating an order was ready. Tansey delivered our food a few minutes later and handed me a to-go container before checking on her other tables.

I cut my burger in half and placed it, along with half of my fries, into the container. I then shoved the container to the other side of the table, far away from me.

"What are you doing?" Reel asked.

"Saving the other half for dinner."

"Why?"

"Because my thighs thump when I walk. I sound like a baby elephant."

Reel reached over and dumped the food back onto my plate. "Eat, damn it. You don't need to lose weight."

"Tell that to my mother," I muttered before taking a bite of my burger.

"There are a lot of things I'd like to tell your mother, but I fear you'd never speak to me again if I did," Reel grumbled, eating his own lunch.

I didn't ask what he would say to my mother. I didn't know a single person in town—including her own brother—who liked her. She took snippety to a whole new level.

My uncle had told me that the only time she was ever happy was when she had first married my dad. But, as the years went by, she returned to being bitchy. By the time I hit kindergarten, my dad had moved away in the middle of the night. He never came back. He never wrote a letter, sent a birthday card, or called. On many levels, I didn't blame him. By the time he left, my sister Darlene, being a year older than me, was already starting to follow my mother's uppity habits and criticizing everyone for everything. They'd both targeted Dad on a regular basis.

But it still hurt. He didn't love me enough to stay in touch. To my knowledge, he had never contacted Grandpa Sullivan, either. He walked away from all of us and never came back.

"You're thinking about your dad," Reel whispered, looking down at me.

"How'd you know?"

"I just know." He shrugged. "He loved you. I remember."

"You sound like Grandpa," I said.

"How is Vince?"

"Not good. I spent the day with him last Tuesday. He kept getting me confused with Grandma."

"That's a compliment," Reel said, nudging me. "Remember that time she taught us kids how to build a go-kart?"

"The one you broke?"

"It was your grandma's idea to race it down Devil's Hill."

"And you were insane enough to try it. At least she made you wear your football helmet and pads."

"If I wouldn't have hit that big rock, I would've made it."

"I was scared to death, gripping Grandma's hand as we watched you zoom down the hill. You smiled the whole way down."

"Adrenaline. I think your grandma was an adrenaline junkie too."

"I know she was. She made me go zip-lining with her once. When it was over, I was puking and she was telling me to hurry up, because she wanted to go again."

Reel laughed. "She was a lot of fun."

"She was." I grinned, looking up at him. "What's gotten into you? You never laugh and smile."

Reel tossed his napkin onto his plate. "I think it's the job I just finished. Kelsey, the woman I was talking about, she's been through some really bad shit. And yet she's living her life, making the best of it. I want to be more like that. I want to be able to set the work aside and enjoy myself."

"Wow. How enlightening."

"Don't get too excited. I like being an ass too."

The front door opened, and Rod and Bart stepped inside. I waved at them, but when Rod saw me, he looked at Reel and scurried back out the door.

"Why did Rod have a swollen eye?" I asked.

"Must've walked into a door," Reel said before downing the rest of his beer and standing up. Pulling his wallet, he tossed cash on the table.

"That's too much," I said, looking at the money.

"It's fine," he said, holding his hand out to help me out of the booth. "Tansey works hard and could use the cash."

"In that case, what do you think about buying some of her paintings for your house? They're really good."

"Sounds fine with me."

I told Tansey we were going upstairs to check her inventory, and we exited through the back door. Climbing the exterior stairs, I was pulling my keys from my purse when I missed the step and started to take a nosedive. With my body inches away from smacking into the stairs, Reel caught me around the waist, swinging my body around to face him.

My hands instinctively braced the tops of his broad shoulders as I looked up at him.

"You okay?" he whispered. He placed his free hand on the side of my head, stroking his thumb across my cheek.

It took me a moment to process his question. And even then, I wasn't sure whether my voice would hold, so I only nodded. Pushing away from him, I put distance between us.

His eyes scanned down my body, stopping at my chest. His eyes lit with a curious humor, and he reached toward my cleavage.

I jumped another few inches away, looking down to see the note that Uncle Mike had wrote had jostled above its lacy hiding place.

Reel jerked the note out, opening it to read. "Show them what you're made of." Reel's eyes lifted to meet mine. "And what are you made of Deanna?"

I took another step back, handing him the keys. "Emotionally? Or physically?" I asked. "Physically, I think I'm made of mostly cookies and donuts."

"I bet you taste like sugar, too," Reel said, unlocking the door. He stepped inside the apartment, holding the door open for me. "Damn. This place is nice." Reel whistled as he looked around.

I made a beeline for the paintings on the far wall, hoping he wouldn't notice how blistering red my cheeks were from his sugar comment. "Uncle Mike helped Tansey fix it up. She did all the design work and decorating. You should've asked her to help you furnish your house. She has an eye for it."

"I think you're doing a great job," he said, as he joined me in front of several paintings leaning against the wall.

"I know there are a few paintings here that would go great with those curtains," I said, pulling the paintings out. "Tansey can get a discount on framing them too."

I pulled out several that I liked, and Reel nodded his approval. He leaned over and picked up a small oil painting. It was a portrait of me; my face was dusted with a layer of flour. Over the years, I'd been Tansey's guinea pig more times than I could count.

"She's good," Reel said, admiring the painting. "She even captured how your eyes dance when you're excited."

I laughed, finding another picture that I thought would look nice. "My eyes don't dance." I moved the pictures we selected to the other wall. "You can negotiate the price with Tansey later. She's pretty reasonable, though."

"What does she do with all these?"

"She sells some at local craft fairs. And there's a gallery in Cooper City that sells some."

"Does she have more?"

"Yup. The ones that don't sell are in a cedar storage room at Uncle Mike's."

"I might know some people who would buy these," Reel said, studying another painting.

"She'd appreciate the referral. There aren't enough people buying original paintings anymore."

Reel wasn't listening to me. He'd pulled out his cell phone and was taking pictures of the paintings. His phone made a noise as he sent them to someone. Within minutes, his phone beeped, and he looked back at the screen, smiling before pocketing his phone. "Let's go," he said, turning toward the door.

I realized he set the portrait of me along the wrong wall, so I moved it back over to the for-sale pile before hurrying to catch up with him.

Back downstairs, Reel told Tansey that he'd track her down the next day to get a price on the paintings and to arrange for them to be framed. He also let her know that he knew someone who might be interested in buying more. Tansey gave me a high-five and told me that she'd be sure to get my commission ready. I followed Reel out the front door.

Reel gave me a curious look as we crossed the parking lot. "You'd never charge Tansey a dime for a commission, so what was that all about?"

"Most people who send referrals her way get a free drink at the bar, but since I seldom drink, I get Snickers candy bars."

Reel snorted and opened the passenger door, placing his hand on my lower back as I climbed up inside the truck. He tucked my skirt to my thigh before closing the door. A minute later he swung into the driver's seat. "Do you still have time to go furniture shopping?"

"If we're back by five, yes. Uncle Mike's going to take a look at my car for me tonight."

"What's wrong with it?"

"I have no idea."

Reel turned his head and glared down at me, waiting for more information.

"Something's wrong with the gas pedal," I said, throwing my hands up. "It kept wanting to speed up this morning."

"That doesn't make sense."

"Well, that's what it was doing. I had to shut the car off and coast down the street."

He stared at me for a long moment before shaking his head in what appeared to be disbelief.

Connecting his cell phone to the docking station in his truck, he commanded the phone to call Rod.

Rod was a volunteer firefighter part of the week, but by trade, he was the town's only real mechanic. Sure, there were others who knew enough to work on their own cars, but if it was anything serious, it was up to Rod to fix it.

"What do you want?" Rod answered.

"Send a tow truck over to pick up Tweedle's car. Have the accelerator checked."

"What's wrong with it?"

"The pedal was sticking," Reel answered, looking over at me.

"What?"

"Just check it out."

"I'll send Bart over now. I can take a look at it this afternoon."

"Send me the bill," Reel said before disconnecting the line.

"I can't let you pay for my car repairs."

"Sure you can, but Rod won't charge me. He owes me a favor. And I owe you a favor since you're helping me with this shopping shit. So it all becomes one big bartering circle."

"I'll text Uncle Mike and let him know. He'll be happy that he doesn't have to deal with it. He was working a twelve-hour shift today."

"I noticed extra cars on patrol last night. Something going on?"

"The old Burgess house had a break-in. Someone was living there until they were spooked and ran off. And the party store out on Highway 6 was robbed after hours."

"High school kids?"

"No clue. Uncle Mike doesn't like to share the details. He just signed up for more hours and keeps calling us girls regularly to check in."

"Hmm. I'll get with him and see whether I can help. Usually my dad is the biggest trouble that this town has to deal with."

"Legally, yes. Trouble in general—my mother trumps Everett any day of the week."

As he drove, Reel reached behind my seat, pulling a bottle of water out of a cooler. He handed it to me, and I uncapped it, handing it back.

"What did your mother say about what happened at the carnival?" he asked, before taking a drink.

"That I'm a sexual deviant in need of therapy."

Reel spewed water all over the dash.

"What?" He laughed.

I just grinned.

Chapter Six

The furniture store was fun but somewhat depressing. Reel ended up picking out the couch I had had my eye on for months. He told me that I could visit it anytime I wanted. I slugged him in the shoulder before moving on to dining room furniture. It only took an hour to pick out the main furnishings.

"Are you poor yet?" I asked as he paid the large bill.

"No. Not even close," Reel said, tucking his wallet into his back pocket.

"Do the bedrooms have wood flooring too?"

"Whole house," Reel said, nodding.

I bit my lower lip, thinking.

"Why?"

"Well, you might want some rugs. The floor might get cold. I personally hate getting out of bed and putting my feet on cold floors."

Reel tipped his head back, looking painfully at the ceiling.

"Never mind."

"No, it's a good idea," he said, shaking off whatever thoughts he was having. "Where do we buy rugs?"

"There's a carpet store at the end of the block. We can walk there. The owner is a friend of mine."

"How do you know the owner?" Reel asked, opening the door for me. After he followed me out the door, Reel reached down and held my hand. He must still think of me as a little girl, worried I'd run into traffic.

Annoyed, I pulled my hand back. "My mother redecorates every year, remember? For years, she dragged me with her, telling the whole time I had terrible taste."

"I think you have great taste. Then again, I have no idea how everything will look when it's put together."

"You're going to let me see it, right? I mean, so I know how it turns out?"

"I was counting on you to tell me where everything goes," he said, grinning at me.

I turned into the carpet store, heading straight toward the back. Phil Farley, the owner of the carpet store and one of my favorite people, liked to dicker on prices as much as I did. We both viewed it as a serious sport to be mastered, so after selecting the rugs I thought would look the best with the furnishings, I crossed my arms and stared at Phil who stood waiting on the other side of the room.

He took his cue and walked over, crossing his arms in front of him, waiting for the war to begin.

"Two hundred for the three rugs," I said.

Phil shook his head in dismay. "Each?"

"Together."

"Not even close, sweetheart. That's a grand worth of rugs."

"That's fine," Reel said, pulling out his wallet.

Phil and I both glared at Reel.

"Or not," Reel said, sighing.

"Two-fifty."

"Seven and a half."

Reel groaned, rubbing a hand down his forehead.

I laughed and decided to end the deal early. "Four and a quarter. Final offer."

Phil glared down at me. "Four and a quarter and a kiss on the cheek."

I stepped up on my tippy toes to kiss Phil's cheek.

"Sold." Phil smiled, giving me a hug. "Haven't seen you around lately. How have you been, sweetheart?"

"Good. My friend Reel just bought a house. I haven't seen it yet, so I'm winging it. If the living room rug is too big, can he exchange it?"

"Sure. Sure. I'll make sure he gets your special pricing."

"Thanks."

"Can I pay now?" Reel asked.

Phil and I both laughed as Reel followed us to the checkout counter.

Five minutes later, we exited with Reel holding the door open for me.

"Are we done?" Reel asked, once again grabbing my hand.

"Sure," I answered, pulling my hand away again. *Damn it, I'm not a kid anymore. Ugh.*

Reel smirked but didn't look down at me. Instead he kept monitoring anyone who walked near us or drove by.

"At this point we need everything to be put together before we can work on lamps, knickknacks, and miscellaneous stuff," I said. "You'll also need kitchen utensils and more dishes, but Aunt Carol and I have boxes of extra stuff from garage sales. We'll sort some items out for you."

Something I'd said made Reel grin, but he kept his focus on our surroundings. I watched his eyes travel down the block, up the building windows, and then across the street.

"Habit?" I asked, looking at him.

A quick nod was his only answer before he opened the passenger door to his truck and helped me climb inside. As I pulled on my seatbelt Reel's phone chirped from the truck's cubby.

I pointed at the phone as Reel climbed in. "I think you have a message."

In no hurry to check it, Reel started the truck, cranked the air conditioning, and buckled his seatbelt. Picking up the phone, he tapped a few buttons, playing the message on speaker.

"Reel, get home. Something's up with Tweedle's car," Rod said on the voicemail message. "I called Mike to let him know. He wants you to take Tweedle to his house."

"What's that all about?" I asked.

Reel pushed the button to delete the message but didn't answer. His eyes swept a full 360-view before he put the truck in reverse and pulled out. As he put the truck in forward gear and drove away, his eyes continued to sweep the area.

"Reel?"

"Yeah."

"Why'd you get so quiet? And why are you looking around so much?"

"Rod didn't say what was wrong with your car. Instead, he said he called Mike, which means he didn't like what he'd found."

"As in what? Like someone took it for a joyride?"

"No. As in someone tampered with it."

"No way." I laughed, but I wasn't finding the thought very funny. "You've been working security too long. Who'd mess with my car?"

"I don't know. *Yet*." He glanced over at me, and I saw the cold distant glare that scared even me.

I'd seen that look before, though it had been many years. It was the same look he'd worn when I was sixteen and he beat my homecoming date to a bloody pulp. I'd been ready to punch my date myself before Reel had shown up out of nowhere, but the way his eyes had turned to rage was a memory I would likely never forget.

"You're scaring me," I whispered.

Reel reached out and held my hand. "You're safe. This is the shit I'm good at," he said, pulling my hand up and kissing my knuckles. His face didn't soften with the gentle words, though.

"What about Tansey?"

Reel commanded the phone to call Rod.

"Are you back in town?" Rod answered after only one ring.

"Twenty minutes away. Anybody have eyes on Tansey?"

"I'm at The Bar. She's getting her purse. I'll drive her to Mike's."

"Be there soon."

Chapter Seven

"I'm not staying here," I said for the fourth time.

"She can stay with me," Reel said.

"At your dad's house? No way." Uncle Mike said, shaking his head.

"I bought a house," Reel answered.

"The one that doesn't have furniture?" I asked.

"She's staying here," Uncle Mike said.

"She'll be safer with me," Reel said.

"Are you saying I can't protect my own damn niece?" Uncle Mike snapped.

"These are great paintings," Rod said, staring at one of Tansey's paintings hanging in the dining room.

I looked at Tansey, and she nodded, following me into the kitchen. Aunt Carol passed us our purses as we walked out the back door and started across the yard.

My rental house was on the next block over and three houses down. After entering through the back door, Tansey relocked it. We both sighed. Home sweet home.

"What's really going on?" Tansey asked.

We both tossed our purses on the entryway counter and moved into the kitchen. I got a large mixing bowl down as Tansey grabbed my measuring cups and the flour.

"I have no idea. But I think it's worse than they know."

"Spill. What don't they know?"

I liked to bake when I was stressed. Tansey settled onto a bar stool and waited for me to mix up cake batter, giving me time to collect my thoughts.

"I don't think the car was the first time someone tried to hurt me." I poured the cake batter into a pan and set the oven temperature to preheat. Moving to the sink, I started washing the bowl so I could reuse it.

"The Ferris wheel?" Tansey asked.

"Maybe. I mean, have you ever heard of one of those safety bars just popping open?"

"No, but how would anyone know which seat you would sit in?"

I lifted my hands in an *I-don't-know* gesture. "Maybe the carny who latched the gate did it."

"Do you remember what he looked like?"

"No, it's a total blank. I tried to remember, but when I was climbing into the seat, I was distracted by Sally Frasier getting groped by Buck Peaton."

"Eww."

"Right?" I snickered. "I was so repulsed I couldn't look away."

Tansey shuddered and then shook her head. "It's a big stretch that someone would get a job working at a carnival just on the off chance they'd get close to you. How would someone even know you'd be there?"

"Everyone knew I'd be there," I said, sighing. "It was the talk of the town. Six o'clock on opening day of the carnival, remember?"

"You think it's someone we know?"

"Not necessarily. It could've been someone who just overheard the gossip."

Every year on my birthday, a dozen roses were delivered. The card never had a name but always promised that someday he'd meet me at the summer carnival. Trying to make it easier on my anonymous suitor, every year I went to the carnival on opening night and rode the Ferris wheel. Except my suitor never showed. Years went by and each year the same delivery arrived with the same future promise.

Uncle Mike and Aunt Carol swore on a Bible that it wasn't them playing a trick on me. I made Tansey do the same, even though I knew it wasn't her. I had a pretty good idea who the mystery person was, but he never manned up to follow through.

"Someone tampered with your car *and* the gate on the Ferris wheel seat?"

"Maybe."

"What are you not telling me?" Tansey asked, with one eyebrow arched.

"I think someone's been in my house," I whispered, scooping out flour for a batch of biscuits.

"When?" Tansey asked, looking around.

"Last week. I came home from work and noticed little things out of place. And there was a dirt mark that looked like a footprint on the floor."

"Could it have been your sister? She would totally break in here to snoop, and she never takes off her shoes."

"No, the print was too big, like hiking boots or construction boots."

"Shit."

"Yeah." I sighed. "There's one more thing."

"Tell me," Tansey said, leaning her head down into her hands.

"Later that day, I found a snake in my bedroom."

"A *snake*?"

"A rattlesnake."

"*A WHAT*?" Tansey screeched, jumping up from her barstool.

"You heard me."

Tansey didn't say anything. She stood there staring at me, waiting for the rest of the story.

"After cleaning the dirty smudge on the floor, I decided to go ahead and clean the entire floor. That seemed to have jumpstarted a cleaning frenzy, and before I knew it, I was in the bedroom vacuuming when I heard a noise. I turned the vacuum off and got down on the floor to look under the bed, coming almost nose-to-nose with a rattlesnake."

"Holy shit. Holy shit. What did you do?"

"You are my best friend, so if I tell you what happened next, you have to promise to never tell another soul."

"Promise. Tell me! Tell me!" she said, sitting down again and gripping the edge of the countertop.

"I peed my pants," I admitted, sitting on my own stool.

"Obviously," Tansey said, rolling her eyes. "Who wouldn't? But what the hell happened with the snake?"

"I stayed frozen, not moving an inch for what seemed like forever. Eventually it slithered farther away, and I bailed out of the bedroom. I called Tucker, and he collected it for me. He was scratching his head trying to figure out how a rattlesnake would have gotten into my house, but he promised not to tell anyone."

"This doesn't make any sense. What could *you*, of all people, have done to piss someone off this badly?"

I shrugged, kneading the biscuit dough a little more roughly than what was required.

"Why didn't you say anything?"

"I figured it was all explainable," I thumbed the dough into the pile of flour on the counter. "That maybe Uncle Mike forgot to take his shoes off and was in my house to fix something. That the snake had somehow gotten in by some natural means. That I broke the Ferris wheel gate when I leaned on it."

"You are not half as big as you have in your head that you are." She walked over and pulled a beer from the refrigerator for herself and a bottle of water for me.

"We have to tell Uncle Mike."

"No way." I shook my head. "What if it was you? Would you tell him?"

"Hell, no," she admitted. "He'd chain me in the basement until the case was solved."

"See?"

"Let's compromise. They already know about the Ferris wheel incident. Let's stick the idea in their heads for them to investigate that."

I thought it over, eyeing Tansey's beer while I did. Alcohol sounded like a good idea, but I knew the beer would turn warm before I finished it.

"Fine," I muttered.

The cake batter had sat long enough, so I placed it in the oven before opening the cabinet above the stove, pulling out a bottle of vodka. "But I won't let them control my life. I'm staying here. You should stay with Aunt Carol and Uncle Mike."

Tansey smiled at the bottle of booze, getting out the orange juice. "Ha. Fat chance of that happening." Tansey made a call on her cell phone. "Aunt Carol, can you send the guys to the carnival to check out the Ferris wheel? And can you sneak us over some handguns?"

Tansey nodded several times, listening to Aunt Carol. "Yes, we remember how to use them. Uncle Mike drilled us for years." She rolled her eyes. "I know. Someday we'll get our permits." Then she was nodding again. "Okay. See you soon but drive over. Don't walk. And when you pull into the driveway, honk your horn."

Tansey glanced at me quickly before looking away. "No. There's nothing else I'm allowed to share at this time." Tansey hung up and smiled at me.

"You just tipped off Aunt Carol that something more was going on," I said, throwing a small wad of biscuit dough at her.

"Yeah," Tansey said, giggling as she picked the dough out of her hair. "But at least when I'm at work, I'll know that Aunt Carol will keep track of you. Besides, she won't rat you out. She knows how overprotective Uncle Mike can be."

I pretended to glare at her for a few seconds before flipping my biscuit dough in the flour. "Are you working tonight?"

"Nope. But I'm scheduled for a double shift tomorrow. Lunch until closing." Tansey pulled two glasses from the cupboard and handed them to me.

I filled both and passed one to her. She grabbed the vodka bottle and added another shot into hers.

We drank as we cut the biscuit dough into circles and moved them to cookie sheets. Fifteen minutes passed and Aunt Carol still hadn't arrived. Getting nervous, I called her cell number.

"I had to run to the store," Aunt Carol answered. "I'm almost there."

"I'll wait in the driveway for you," I said before hanging up.

When Aunt Carol got out, she started pulling bags out of her car, setting them in the driveway. Tansey and I hurried over to take them.

Carrying everything inside, Tansey relocked the door behind us.

"What is all this?" I asked, setting the bags on the counter.

"Booze and bullets," Aunt Carol said, chuckling. "Mike won't notice the guns missing because they're my guns, but he'd notice if a box of bullets disappeared. I drove to the hardware store to buy more. Then I decided that if you two needed guns, I needed alcohol."

"Cheers!" Tansey said, holding up her glass.

Aunt Carol smiled but then realized I also had a glass. Her face shifted to a frown. "Is it that bad? I haven't seen you drink since your twenty-first birthday."

"I've drank since then," I said, shrugging. "At The Bar I sometimes have a glass of wine."

"No, you don't," she said, shaking her head. "You order the wine and carry it around for a couple of hours, but by the time you leave, you've barely taken three sips."

I stuck my tongue out at Aunt Carol before picking up my glass and chugging the rest of my drink. Slamming the glass back down, I inadvertently cracked the glass. "See? I drink."

Tansey took the glass and placed it in the trashcan. "That's going to hurt in the morning. Tomorrow's Saturday. Don't forget how early you get up to make the donuts."

"Good point. I think I'll have just one more before I switch to water." I pulled a fresh glass from the cabinet as they both watched me.

Chapter Eight

I giggled, leaning too far over on the stool and almost falling before grabbing onto the breakfast bar. "He held my hand. Like I was five and needed supervision walking near traffic!"

Tansey and Aunt Carol looked at each other.

"What?"

"He doesn't see you like a kid," Aunt Carol said.

"Not even a little," Tansey said.

"Yes, he does," I slurred. "Believe me. I know. I tried to get him to see me like an adult a long time ago. He told me to behave and drove me home."

I could hear my voice and see my body moving, but my brain wasn't quite connecting what I was saying or doing. I reached for my water and knocked the glass over.

"Coffee," Aunt Carol ordered, grabbing the glass before it rolled off the edge of the counter.

Tansey tossed a dish towel over my head to Aunt Carol before starting a pot of coffee. I watched as Aunt Carol mopped up the mess I had made.

"You need to eat," Aunt Carol said, sliding the plate of biscuits toward me.

"I should eat salad. Or rice cakes. I tried to eat rice cakes once, but they don't have any flavor. Why would someone make food without flavor?"

"Biscuits. *Now.*"

Giggling, I tore a section of a biscuit off and popped it into my mouth. It tasted wonderful, still warm from baking. I didn't even remember pulling them from the oven. *Wait.* I didn't remember putting them into the oven.

Realizing that I had also been baking a cake, I looked around. The cake was sitting unfrosted on the far counter. "I should finish that."

"It's fine," Tansey said. "You can take it with you to work tomorrow and slap some frosting on it. I'll make sure it's covered before we go to bed."

"But it needs to be flipped while it's still warm and set up on a tray."

"You made it hours ago," Aunt Carol said, shaking her head. "Drinking really doesn't suit you."

I giggled. "It's the only time I get called a lightweight."

"What do you drink when you two go dancing in Cooper City?" Aunt Carol asked.

"I drink beer," Tansey answered. "She drinks ginger ale in a cocktail glass and tells people it's scotch."

The back door opened as Tansey was setting a cup of coffee in front of me.

Uncle Mike walked into the kitchen, followed by Reel, who was followed by Rod. I giggled, thinking of their nicknames. Uncle Mike looked at me and laughed.

Reel looked at me, and an eyebrow went up as he walked toward me and tipped my head up with a finger under my chin. "You're trashed."

"Just tipsy." I giggled again, unable to spot myself.

"How much did you drink?" he asked, smirking.

"I had TWO! Can you believe it? That's the most I've ever had." I held my fingers in front of him, showing him the two. He wrapped his hand around mine and lowered my hand, shaking his head.

"How much did she really have?" Reel asked Tansey.

"Four. We couldn't stop her. She was on a roll."

"I didn't have four," I said, shaking my head.

"You didn't bake a cake and biscuits either, remember?" Aunt Carol asked.

"What cake?" I asked.

"Okay. Time for bed," Reel said, pulling me up off the stool and wrapping an arm around me.

"But it's still light out," I said, swaying to the side.

"It will be morning before you know it," he said, picking me up and carrying me toward the bedrooms.

~*~*~

I DIDN'T REMEMBER MAKING IT to bed. I didn't remember falling asleep. I didn't remember anything after Reel carried me down the hall. The next thing I remembered was kicking away the blankets that were tangled around me and running to my bathroom to hurl.

As I sang to the porcelain gods, the bathroom ceiling light flickered on. Someone lifted my hair away from my face and rubbed my back. After puking everything I had in me, the dry heaves started. I was exhausted, and shooting pains scissored across my stomach.

"Try and relax," Reel's voice whispered behind me.

"Ugh. I thought Tansey was holding my hair," I moaned, flushing the toilet.

"Lean back against the tub. It will feel cool on your back."

He helped me slide over to lean against the tub before wetting a washcloth for me. He wasn't wearing a shirt, and his feet were bare. He still wore his jeans, but the button and zipper were undone, offering me a peek at his navy undershorts. The man had a spectacular body, rippled with honey tanned muscles and the faintest stretch of golden chest hair that trailed down his center and disappeared out of sight.

Reel squatted down with the cloth.

I focused on the ugly tiles on the wall as I used the washcloth to wipe my face before folding it to the inside and holding it to my forehead. "What time is it?"

"About 4:00. I was told to wake you by 5:00, so you can sleep for another hour."

"No," I sighed. "I like to get to the bakery early on Saturdays. We always have a lot of orders to fill. And I left early yesterday, so I might need to make more breads and pies."

Reel got some pills out of the medicine cabinet and filled a glass of water.

"Swish this and spit. Then take these pills."

I swished, spit, and took the pills. I didn't even ask what they were.

"Can you lend me a hand?" I asked, reaching up.

He pulled me up but didn't step back, so I was standing inches away from him. I could feel the heat from his body radiating onto my skin. His hands moved to my hips. I cleared my throat.

"Something you want to say?" he asked.

"I could use some privacy," I whispered. "You know, to take a shower and brush my teeth."

"Are you sure you'll be alright on your own?" he asked.

"Very sure," I nodded, my face flushing. "Thanks, umm, for the hair-holding bit."

"Anytime," he chuckled, kissing me on the forehead and stepping out of the bathroom.

I quickly closed the door and looked at myself in the mirror. I looked horrible. My face was pasty white except for the bright red blotches in the center of my cheeks. My hair was sweaty and matted. And, worse yet, not only did I look like I'd been run through the wringer, I was wearing one of my extra-girly, lace and satin nightgowns. I was pretty sure the image looking back at me was Pine Valley's version of a crack whore.

"Way to go, Sullivan," I muttered to myself.

"Did you say something?" Reel called from the bedroom.

"Nope. I'm good," I called back, quickly starting up the water to take a shower.

Twenty minutes later, I was clean and dressed and had brushed my teeth twice. I twisted my hair into a bun as I peeked into the spare room to check on Tansey. She was sound asleep in her pink flannel PJs, curled into Rod's shoulder. Rod smiled, motioning for me to be quiet.

I raised two fingers, pointed to my eyes, and then pointed at him with my most menacing glare. He just smiled wider.

Shaking my head, I walked through the living room and into the kitchen.

"I swear, if your brother makes a move on Tansey while she's sleeping—I'll cut him."

The corners of Reel's mouth curved in a grin as he sipped his coffee. He had a shirt on, but it was unbuttoned. I looked away.

"See something you like?"

I blushed and looked down, noticing a cup of coffee with cream and two slices of lightly buttered toast sat in front of me. "Yes, the toast. Thank you." I knew that my rosy cheeks were giving me away. Since when did I blush? "Did you guys find the carny who was working the Ferris wheel?"

I took a bite of my toast and chewed slowly. I wasn't positive I could keep it down, but so far so good. If I was going to puke again, I'd rather puke up food than have the dry heaves.

"No one could give a good description of him. He showed up earlier in the day and asked for a job running the Ferris wheel. Offered to work for cheap wages. The driver's license they copied was a fake."

I watched Reel's eyes turn cold as he looked out the window. I could understand why people thought he looked dangerous. It wasn't the size of him, though he was stacked with muscles on a lean frame. It was the intensity of his eyes. It reminded me of the time his mother, Loretta, dated a guy who made the mistake of hitting her. The guy moved out of town after Reel went to "talk" with him.

"Reel, I'm going to be fine," I said, leaning over the breakfast bar to place my hand over one of his.

He turned his hand over and grasped mine. Walking around the breakfast bar, he wrapped his arms around me.

"I know," he whispered, kissing the top of my head. "I won't let anyone hurt you."

"It's not your job to protect me."

"Yes, it is. Now eat your toast, and I'll drive you to work."

"I can walk."

He raised a scolding eyebrow at me. I sighed but focused on eating my toast like a good girl.

~*~*~

Arriving at the bakery, I found the display cases barren. I lifted the clipboard from the hook on the wall and scanned the catering orders. It was going to be a whirlwind day getting everything baked in time, so I ordered Reel to leave so I could focus. He wasn't happy, but after searching the bakery and ensuring the doors were locked, he agreed. I started baking my ass off to get caught up.

By the time Samantha arrived, I had the breakfast display case filled and was starting on breads and catering orders.

"You're amazing," Samantha said, jumping in to help. "I should give you a raise."

"Yes, you should," I said, though I knew I would never see one.

Over the years, Samantha had given me exactly a 2 percent raise each year on the anniversary of my employment. Twice, my raises were rolled into matching increases in the minimum-wage law. I sighed and pulled the cake pans out of the oven. Mrs. Denton had ordered an anniversary cake and would be picking it up in a few hours. By the time the layers cooled, we'd be opening the bakery for customers and I'd have to watch the clock to make sure it was decorated in time.

"You know I'd pay you more if I could," Samantha said.

I knew the bakery profits were enough to afford to pay me a higher wage. In fact, I made more money on my catering jobs. But for reasons Samantha never explained, she kept my pay low.

"Can you get a batch of brownies started?" I asked, changing the subject and placing the pies in the oven.

Samantha gathered the ingredients for the brownies, and we worked quietly for the rest of the morning.

~*~*~

BY FIVE THE LAST CATERING order was picked up, and I hung up my apron. Exhausted and in a poor mood, I grabbed my purse from the office and stepped out of the bakery and into the alley. I was disappointed when I saw the food I had set out was still in the grocery bag. I decided to leave it in case the mysterious teenager showed up later.

Walking out of the alley, I spotted Reel leaning against the door of my car.

"I can't believe you worked a twelve-hour shift with a hangover," he said. "You must be beat."

"I feel like folding into a puddle, but my day isn't over yet," I sighed. "Do you have the keys?"

"Where to?" Reel asked, walking over to open the passenger door.

"The church. It's the third Saturday of the month. I work the monthly sleepover party for the kids."

I slid into the passenger seat, not bothering to argue with Reel that I could drive myself three blocks to the church. I was bone tired.

"You just put in a twelve-hour shift, and now you're going to babysit a bunch of bratty kids while their parents go get drunk?"

I nodded with my eyes closed and leaned back in the seat.

"Why?"

"Money. It's all part of the Master Plan."

"How much do you make?"

"Usually around three hundred. Sometimes it's less; sometimes it's more. It depends on how many kids are dropped off. Usually it's around thirty."

"Thirty kids? Are you insane?"

"Probably."

"What if I just pay you to go home and sleep?"

"Then the parents won't have a sitter, and Tansey loses out on the extra tip money. She makes double what I make on the third Saturday of the month."

Reel chuckled. "You started the church-sleepover program, didn't you?"

"Yeah." I looked over at him. "It originally started in my living room, but when it got too big, we moved to the church. I have a couple of seniors who hang out and play cards so I can meet the adult-to-kid ratio."

"Sneaky. So how do you keep thirty kids in line?"

I didn't have time to answer as we had pulled into the church lot. Amy Story was standing distraught in the parking lot, wringing her hands as her three-year-old twin girls screamed their heads off in the back seat of her old Volvo. I pulled the first girl out of the car and passed her to a surprised Reel. The child wailed even louder. I grabbed the second girl and the diaper bag and closed the car door.

"*Run!*" I said to Amy as I shuffled with her screaming child through the side entrance of the church. I could hear the car's tires peeling out of the parking lot as Reel closed the door behind us.

"Good evening, Reverend!" I yelled over the screaming toddlers.

"Evening, Tweedle!" the reverend yelled back, grinning as he laid some mats on the floor.

I set the girl I was carrying on one of the mats and took the other screaming child from Reel and set her beside her sister. Both girls continued to scream.

"Enough!" I yelled at them.

Both girls froze midwail and looked up at me with huge eyes.

"Aunty Tweedle has had a bad day so you two will be good or it's bedtime." I pulled a sandwich bag out of my purse and handed it to Reel. "Give them each a half-slice of banana bread."

Walking over to the far wall, I kept an eye on the twins and watched Reel carefully sit on the floor beside them and hand the girls the bread. They smashed their half-slices in their faces and between their fingers as Reel leaned back, looking repulsed.

I laughed, walking away to sign in the rest of the kids who were rapidly being deserted by stressed-out parents. A few of them I suspected had already started drinking. You could see the desperation in their eyes, just before they fled for freedom.

I had been asked several times to change the program to twice a month but had refused. Master Plan or not, it wasn't worth the money to go through this twice a month.

"Figured you could use an extra set of hands tonight," Aunt Carol said, walking in with two more toddlers in tow.

"I'll happily split the profits with you," I said, leaning over to kiss her cheek before she turned away to corral the toddlers onto their designated mat.

"I'm bored," one of the regular preteens, Ariel, complained.

"You just got here," I said, rolling my eyes. "Besides, Mrs. Z said that Tommy was coming tonight."

"Really?" the girl squealed, her eyes lighting up. "I better check my makeup." She ran off toward the bathroom as the front door opened again and Tommy strutted through.

"I'm bored," he grumbled.

"Ariel's here."

Tommy's eyes lit up as he casually glanced around the room.

"She's in the restroom. Make yourself useful and start setting up the sandwich table."

Tommy jogged over to the table to start pulling the breads out of the bag. I knew when Ariel came back, she'd get the meat and cheese trays out and start helping the elementary school kids make their sandwiches.

"Free labor?" Reel said, draping an arm over my shoulder.

"Young love," I said, watching Ariel run over to help Tommy. "Are you staying or going?"

"Staying, unfortunately," Reel said. "I thought your uncle gave in a little too easily when I told him I'd watch you tonight. Now I know why."

Uncle Mike had volunteered to help me once and only once. I was sure right about now he was kicked back in his recliner, having a good laugh at Reel's expense. "Make yourself useful then. Get plates of food for the toddlers. Ariel can tell you what you need. I have to get the tables and highchairs set up."

"You're going to give those twin girls more food? They mashed the bread I gave them everywhere. It's even up their noses."

"They'll eat it eventually," I said. "They usually pick it off each other."

"Gross."

I nudged him toward the food table.

~*~*~

By midnight, I had settled baby Aaron back to sleep for the third time. I looked around the room. Reel was sitting on the floor, leaning against a wall, sleeping. Aunt Carol had made a bed between Tommy and Ariel and was sleeping as they whispered to each other over her. The rest of the kids were lights out. Some of the toddlers were sleeping on top of each other, and I pulled them off, lining them up. They had food stuck all over them, but I learned a long time ago it was a waste of time to clean them until just before their parents picked them up. Most of the kids were shuffled from the rec room into Sunday service here in the same church, so after we cleaned them, they changed into their Sunday clothes.

"You need to sleep," Reel whispered from the far side of the room.

I walked over and sat down beside him. "Baby Aaron doesn't sleep for more than an hour or two at a time," I said. "He's teething."

"I'll get up when he wakes. Go ahead and sleep for a while."

Reel wrapped an arm around me and pulled me into his shoulder. For such a firm body, he was comfortable to lean into. My eyelids dropped, no longer able to stay open.

~*~*~

I woke, lying on one of the floor mats, wrapped in a blanket. The sound of kids laughing and playing nearby caused me to sit up abruptly, afraid of what I would find.

Reel was sitting cross-legged on the mat in the center of the room with baby Aaron nestled in a makeshift bed on his lap. He was rinsing a rag out of a big bucket of water before using it to mop down the next toddler in line. Water ran in several directions, soaking the rubber mat and the kid's clothes.

"This isn't how Aunt Tweedle does it," Ariel complained, as she dried off one of the drenched toddlers.

"But it's fun to watch," Tommy said, keeping the toddlers in line to wait for their turn and not run off.

Aunt Carol snorted as she re-dressed one of the toddlers in clean clothes.

I looked over and saw that the elementary kids were lined up with their duffle bags, waiting for their turn in the bathroom to change into their Sunday clothes.

I looked up at the clock. Sunday school would start in half an hour, and the rest of the kids would be picked up around the same time. I went back to sleep.

Chapter Nine

After dropping Reel off at his truck, I drove first to the bakery. I was glad to see that the grocery bag I'd set out yesterday was gone. I set the bag of leftovers from the church in the same spot before driving home.

I opened the back door but stopped, stepping back immediately. One smell a baker knew to always be aware of was the smell of gas.

I dropped my oversized purse in front of the door to prop it open and walked around the side of the house to the propane tank. Turning the dial, I closed the valve on the tank and stood trying to decide what to do next.

The smart thing to do would be to call the fire department. But then Rod would call Uncle Mike and Reel. And then I'd have babysitters again, after spending the past twenty minutes arguing with Reel that I didn't need a babysitter.

Decision made, I returned to the backdoor, dropping my phone on top of my purse, and carefully walked into the house. The smell of gas was intense in the kitchen, and I held my breath as I opened the kitchen windows. I moved into the living room, then throughout the rest of the house and opened the rest of the windows as I went. Walking over to the thermostat, I turned the air conditioner off.

Needing to breathe, I hurried out the back door, grabbing my phone on the way. Pulling a lawn chair out of the garage, I settled into it before I called Skip, the local handyman.

"Good morning, Miss Tweedle," Skip answered.

"Morning, Skip. Can you spare some time to swing by today?"

"Sure. But Sundays are overtime rates. Do you want me to put you on the schedule for tomorrow instead?"

"No, it can't wait. I have a gas leak. I turned the propane off and have the house airing out, but I don't want to take any chances."

"I'll be there in five minutes. You're not in the house, are you?"

"No. I'll wait outside."

Even the best planning can lead to unwanted results in a small town where everyone knows everyone. I had barely hung up before I heard the firetruck's siren blaring from two blocks away, heading my way. Uncle Mike's patrol car beat them to the house, lights flashing and skidding to a stop. Reel's pickup screeched to a stop right behind the firetruck as everyone raced to get to the scene. I leaned my head back and closed my eyes.

I ignored the chaos and focused on the warm morning sun as I stayed stretched out in my lawn chair. It wasn't until a shadow blocked the light that I finally opened my eyes.

Tansey stood grinning down at me. "I hear Tucker's strawberry patch is growing like mad and ripe for the first picking."

"Did you park far enough away that we can sneak off?"

"Sure did."

I climbed out of my chair and grabbed my purse. The men were too busy arguing about some connector on my oven to even notice Tansey and me slipping around the corner of the house and climbing into her Subaru. As Tansey drove us away from the scene, I found some country-rock music and turned the dial up.

Off-pitch, we belted out the familiar song as we turned down Ole Hickory Lane. Just as Tansey finished the turn, I caught a glimpse of a vehicle in the side mirror.

Expecting to see Reel or Uncle Mike following us, I looked out the back window and froze. A black SUV with tinted windows was barreling toward us.

"Shit!" I yelled, a second before the monster of a vehicle slammed into us.

"Holy mother!" Tansey yelled as she tried to control the Subaru.

"Gun it! He's coming again!"

Tansey floored the old Subaru, but there was nowhere to turn. Cornfields stretched to the edge of the road on both sides of us for at least a mile. I dug in my purse, pulling my phone out. I nearly dropped it as the SUV rammed us again.

Phone on speaker, we were still screaming when Tucker answered.

"*Tweedle?*!!" Tucker yelled.

"Tucker!! Tansey and I are on our way to your house, and some maniac is trying to make us crash!"

"You on Hickory?"

"Yeah—in the straightaway."

"Have you passed the big maple tree?"

"No."

"Get to the maple and make a sharp right. Follow the two-track to the house. I'm on my way. Whatever happens, just keep driving!"

"That track is barely wide enough for a four-wheeler!" Tansey yelled.

"Unless you want to be roadkill, take the damn turn!" I yelled as we approached the maple and the SUV behind us slammed into us for the third time.

We started skidding on an angle into the center of the road, turning sideways. Tansey took her foot off the gas as we slid past the maple. Just past the tree, she practically stood on the accelerator with both feet as the tires gripped the road and launched us into the cornfield and onto the two-track. We were half on, half off the two-track lane.

I looked out the back window and watched the SUV slam on its brakes, sliding past the maple down the road.

"Go! Go! Go!" I yelled, watching the other driver reverse and then turn on the two-track.

"Fuck it," Tansey yelled, not bothering to try to stay on the trail, but driving wherever the Subaru bounced into the five-foot stalks.

The green stalks slapped at us through the windows. The Subaru had old crank-style windows, and I rolled mine first, before leaning over Tansey's lap and rolling hers up as far as I could manage it. The Subaru bounced up and down like it was driving over a never-ending set of railroad tracks as we crossed the field diagonally.

"Is that the house up ahead?" Tansey yelled.

I leaned forward in my seat for a better look, seconds before the corn parted. In front of us, directly in our path, was Tucker on his tractor. Tucker swerved, but the tractor was moving slower than we were. Tansey leaned toward me, using her weight to pull the steering wheel with her. I screamed as we breezed past Tucker with inches to spare.

I was still screaming when the Subaru launched out of the cornfield and into Tucker's backyard. Tansey slammed on the brakes, but we were moving too fast. Knowing we didn't have time to stop before we'd crash, I reached over and dragged the steering wheel away from the house, aiming for the shed instead.

Slamming into the shed, the Subaru turned the old wooden structure into kindling around us. Debris crashed through the windshield as Tansey and I both leaned over in the seat gripping each other for dear life and screaming into each other's ears.

Barreling out the other side, the Subaru bounced off an old oak tree, and the inside of the vehicle seemed to recoil as the airbags slammed into us with enough force to ricochet us into our seats.

Neither of us spoke as we knocked the airbags away. The radiator hissed. The radio continued to blare *Old Time Rock 'n' Roll*.

Tansey reached a shaky hand out and shut the radio off.

I looked over at her and laughed. "I hope you have insurance on this thing."

"Don't laugh. You're going to need to carpool with me for a while."

I laughed anyway as I shook glass off my arms and legs.

"How am I going to get my fat ass out of here, anyway?"

We both tried our doors, but they were a crumpled mess. Tansey slid over the seat into the back before turning to pull my arms and help drag me over too. It was a narrow fit with the damaged roof, and when I finally slid through, I ended up wedged between the front seat and the back seat with Tansey flattened beneath me.

"Can't... breathe..." Tansey muttered from under me.

I rolled enough to the side to get a foot under me and pushed myself over the back seat and into the cargo area. I heard Tansey grunt as I flipped over and rolled. Someone opened the back tailgate, and I rolled right out of the Subaru and onto the dry prickly grass with a loud thump and whoosh, as the air was knocked out of me.

"Praise Jesus," Loretta said, standing above me and looking down. "Thought for sure you girls had met your maker when I saw you crash."

As I crawled out, dropping to the grass, Loretta reached in to help Tansey out. She flopped down beside me.

I looked at her, and she looked at me.

"Nice driving," I said, nodding to the car.

"Did we really just live through that?" Tansey asked.

"If nothing major's broken, I suggest you girls get your asses up and into the house," Loretta ordered, pulling us each up by an arm.

The sound of a shotgun coming from the cornfield registered in my head, and I jumped up, dragging Loretta and Tansey with me as we limped in a jog across the yard, up the back porch, and into the house. I locked the door behind us.

"You girls find a safe spot. I've got an itch to put some lead in someone's ass," Loretta said as she removed a rifle from the rack beside the door.

Tansey and I followed her up the narrow steps to the second-floor bedroom. I stepped over Tucker's undershorts and peeked out the window as Loretta knelt in front of it, aiming the rifle. I was standing too close, and when Loretta fired, her shoulder knocked into my thigh, knocking me back on the bed.

"Dumbass," Tansey said, laughing in front of the other window.

"Did you get him?" I asked Loretta.

"Got the passenger side window. He's turning off, heading away. Who the hell is it? I don't recognize the SUV."

"We didn't stop for introductions," I said before trotting back downstairs.

"Someone's trying to kill Tweedle," Tansey explained as they followed me.

"*Why?* You burn someone's favorite cookies? Steal the blue ribbon in a baking contest?"

"Ever since Myrtle Brighton threatened to set her hair on fire, Tweedle won't compete in baking contests anymore," Tansey said as she pulled glasses out of the cupboard.

"Probably smart," Loretta said, getting lemonade out of the refrigerator. "Heard Reel's back in town, but I haven't seen him yet. You been keeping him busy, Tweedle?"

I moved the well-worn cookie jar from the counter to the kitchen table and we each pulled out a chair.

"He's in overprotective big-brother mode at the moment. Feel free to find another project to keep him occupied," I said, rolling my eyes.

Loretta and Tansey looked at each other and both shook their heads. I decided not to even question their silent conversation.

Loretta was Rod and Reel's mother, though the family resemblance wasn't easily noticed with Loretta's fire red hair, slim build, and the light twang in her voice when she spoke or laughed. She and Everett had never been more than the one-night stand that left her pregnant with the boys. And she was okay with that. She'd stayed single for the most part, other than a few short relationships, until she began dating Tucker about two years ago. And while she still owned the house a few doors down from Aunt Carol's, she spent most of her days and nights with Tucker.

"You living here yet?" I asked, snagging a second cookie.

"Live with Tucker? Nah. I might not be the brightest bulb, but even a country bumpkin like myself knows Tucker's got too much hillbilly in him for me to deal with twenty-four-seven. God knows I love him, but by the fourth time in any given week I have to pick up his dirty underwear, I know it's time to grab my purse and head home for a break."

"Absence makes the heart grow fonder," Tansey nodded.

~*~*~

I WAS ON MY THIRD cookie when the cavalry arrived. Tucker led Uncle Mike, Reel, and Rod into the kitchen, and Uncle Mike stole what remained of my cookie.

"Hey, Mom." Rod greeted Loretta with a kiss on the cheek.

"Hey, Mom." Reel smirked, kissing her other cheek. "Heard you shot out the guy's windshield."

"Would've gotten the driver, but the truck bounced at the last second," Loretta pouted. "How long you been in town?"

"Few days. Meant to head this way but got distracted."

"I bet." Loretta smiled, patting his cheek.

"You owe me a few crates of corn," Tucker grumbled.

"Trade you baked goods?"

"I want zucchini bread. And lemon cookies. Lots of lemon cookies," Tucker nodded.

"Deal," I said. "Rod, think you can take a look at Tansey's Subaru? Seems to be something wrong with it."

"Like a tree in the front seat?" Uncle Mike asked.

"Could just be some corn stuck in the wheel-well," Tansey said, smirking.

"You girls hurt?" Uncle Mike asked.

"Mostly just bruises," I said. "But Tansey has a cut on her arm she hasn't noticed yet."

Tansey looked at her arm. Her face whitened and she wobbled as her eyes fluttered closed and her knees buckled. As she fell, Rod and Reel reached out to catch her.

Rod tore her shirt sleeve open to look at the cut. "It's not deep. I'll get her patched up before she wakes."

Reel pulled me upward, out of my chair, inspecting my arms, legs, back, and face.

"I'm okay. See, just bruises."

He gently kissed the knot forming on my forehead before leaning into me and resting his hands on my hips as he purposely took slow easy breaths in and out.

"Where the hell am I going to park the tractor now?" Tucker yelled, looking out the kitchen window.

"That tractor shed was falling apart," Loretta barked back. "They did you a favor. Now the insurance company will pay for a new one."

"I had tools in there!"

"You had nothin' but piles of junk in there. Who you try'n' to fool?" Loretta said rolling her eyes.

I felt Reel chuckle before he stepped back and kissed my forehead again.

"Come on, Tucker. I'll help you salvage your tools while you tell me about the SUV you saw."

"Plate number was QH7 TL8," Loretta said, as she refilled the glasses with lemonade. "Out-of-state license plate. Had some kind of cloud or something on it."

"I'll run the number," Uncle Mike nodded, stepping out on the back porch.

Tucker followed Reel outside. I rinsed the bloody rag out that Rod had used to clean Tansey's arm as he finished bandaging it. After rinsing it, I took the rag to the freezer and filled it with ice to hold on the knot forming on the side of my forehead.

"If you hit your head, we should get it checked out," Rod said to me.

"Been knocked around worse than this. If I have any symptoms of a concussion, I'll get a ride to the ER."

"Remember that time you fell down the stadium bleachers at the homecoming game?" Loretta laughed. "That was one hell of a show."

"Not likely to forget," I said, rolling my eyes.

TANSEY WAS BACK ON HER feet and settled into the kitchen chair when Aunt Carol stomped in through the front door.

"Is it really too much to ask to get through a Sunday service without interruption? First, I hear there's a gas leak, but it's under control. Then I hear you were both in a car accident. I swear, you two are the reason that I never had children of my own!"

She gripped my chin, tilting my head to look at my bruised forehead. She huffed, then turned to Tansey to pull her arm over, making sure the bandage was sealed and clean. "What were you two doing out this way, anyway?"

"I'm guessing they heard the first strawberries were in," Loretta said, filling another glass of lemonade.

"Everbearing strawberries?" Aunt Carol asked, suddenly curious.

Loretta nodded.

"I'll take six quarts," Aunt Carol said, pulling her cash pouch out.

"I wanted a dozen, but I'm not sure where my purse is," I said, trying to remember whether I saw it after the accident.

"It's still in the Subaru, but I couldn't reach it," Reel answered, walking back inside the house. He pulled his wallet and handed some cash to Loretta, way more than the cost of a dozen quarts of strawberries. Loretta smiled, kissed him on the cheek, and stuffed the money in her bra.

"Classy, Mom," Reel sighed.

"I'll get the containers," Tansey said, limping to the back porch.

~*~*~

Everyone except Uncle Mike picked strawberries, eating as many as ended up in the wooden containers. Around thirty quarts, we quit picking and started dragging the overflowing wagon back to the house.

Reel shook his head as he passed some more cash to Loretta and looked back at me. "You making your shortbread later?"

"Ooh, I want angel food cake," Tansey said, licking the strawberry juice off her fingers.

"I can make both. I don't have any catering jobs today."

"Your oven is out of commission," Rod said. "You need a new regulator for your gas line. Skip can't get one until tomorrow morning."

"Dang. I forgot about the gas leak."

"You mean the gas-filled house that you walked into instead of calling the fire department?" Rod asked.

"I shut the tank off before I went inside. And I was only in there long enough to open the windows."

"You should have turned the power off to the house first. Then you should have let the back door air the fumes out some before going in to open the windows. And you should have had protective gear on."

"How was I supposed to know?"

"You weren't," Reel grumbled, rubbing a hand down his face in frustration. "You were supposed to act like a normal person and call 911."

"We all love Tweedle to pieces, but she'll never be *normal*." Loretta chuckled. "And thank the Lord for that gift because normal is boring."

"Amen," Aunt Carol said.

I sucked the juice from another strawberry.

"The SUV was reported stolen in Kentucky," Uncle Mike said, meeting up with us halfway back to the house. "Deputies just found it parked in the next county over. No sign of the driver."

"Damn it, Mike. What the hell is going on?" Reel yelled.

"You tell me," Mike yelled back. "My niece was perfectly safe before you came back into town."

"No, I wasn't," I sighed, rolling my eyes. "It started weeks before Reel came back."

I pulled the wagon over to Aunt Carol's car, and she popped the trunk. Everyone had become quiet as I moved the quarts. *Shit. I just told on myself.*

I glanced back at Tansey. She was super focused on her nails, trying to feign innocence. Rod threw an arm over her shoulder and crooked her head in his arm, pulling her closer. "What don't we know?"

"I have no idea what you're talking about," she said, looking up at me.

"You still haven't told them 'bout the rattlesnake?" Tucker chuckled.

"Damn it, Tucker," I mumbled, placing the last quart of strawberries in the trunk.

"What rattlesnake?" Reel asked.

I ignored them and got in the back seat of Aunt Carol's car. Tansey slid in beside me and slammed the door shut. Aunt Carol got behind the wheel and started the car.

"You girls are in big trouble," Aunt Carol said, pulling out of the driveway.

We could hear Reel and Uncle Mike yelling as we drove down the road.

"Where to?" Aunt Carol asked.

"Let's go to my apartment," Tansey answered. "I want to change into some clean clothes. Tweedle can bake her stress away while I get some painting time in."

"What will I do?" Aunt Carol asked.

"I heard they were having a back-room poker game this afternoon at The Bar," Tansey said.

Aunt Carol didn't say anything, but I felt the car accelerate. Tansey and I shared a grin before relaxing into our seats.

Chapter Ten

"I can't believe I lost three hundred bucks in poker," Reel grumbled before taking another giant spoonful of strawberry shortcake.

"I can't believe you were stupid enough to play against Aunt Carol," Rod said, smirking over at Reel from the chair beside him.

Tansey and I were both cleaning out our purses, tossing the demolished items into the trash. I had a lip gloss that had exploded shimmering goo all over everything. Tansey had purple eyeshadow that now accented all her belongings. Both of us were just happy to have our cash and driver's licenses back.

Aunt Carol walked through the door of Tansey's apartment with a big smile.

"How'd you do?" I asked.

"It will make a nice deposit in my Master Plan account."

"You too?" Reel chuckled. "What are you saving for?"

"I have no idea," Aunt Carol said. "I wanted to own a small café, but if Tweedle opens a bakery, I don't want to compete against her."

"Or we could open a bakery that's also a café," I said. "We could be partners."

"Make sure there's room for my art gallery," Tansey said.

We grinned at each other as Aunt Carol openly counted her winnings in front of Reel.

Rod looked at each of us. "You know, you three tease each other, but if you pooled your money, I bet the three of you could pull it off."

"We still wouldn't have enough," I said. "Not yet, anyway."

"We could get a loan for the rest," Tansey said. "Something to think about at least."

"Think about it later," Reel said. "Right now, we need to figure out how to keep Tweedle safe."

"She can stay with me," Tansey said. "She works a short shift tomorrow, and then it's our night out in Cooper City."

"Too dangerous," Reel said. "You both need protection, and now is not a good time for a night out in the city."

"Now is the perfect time for a night out," I mumbled.

"Tweedle—"

"Stop, Reel," I said, pointing at him. "You don't get to come back to town and start bossing me around." I tossed the rest of the items from my purse into the trash. "I have an uncle that fills the bossy role quite well. And if we ever needed a night out, it's now, more than ever. I'll stay here tonight. After work tomorrow, Tansey and I will go to Cooper City as planned. You don't get a say in the matter. So either shut it, or get out."

Aunt Carol paused her counting and looked up at me in surprise. Tansey snorted. Rod laughed, grabbing a cookie from the platter as he got up to leave.

"Come on, bro. We better give Tweedle some space before she snaps for good."

Reel was pissed. He picked up his plate and silverware and let them drop loudly in the sink as he stormed out of the apartment.

"About time you put him in his place," Uncle Mike said, leaning back in his chair while eating another cookie. "But you both need to stay at our house tonight."

"Out!" I yelled, pointing toward the door.

Uncle Mike sighed but got up and lumbered out the door.

"Well done, my dear," Aunt Carol said.

"Bravo," Tansey said. "But are we really staying here tonight without protection?"

"Please," I said, rolling my eyes. "The two of them are discussing how to manipulate us into compliance while the third one runs inside to buy a couple of beers. My guess is Rod runs in for the beers," I said, as I pulled a bundle of carrots out of the refrigerator.

Tansey ran over to the windows and looked down.

"How'd you know?"

"Overbearing alpha males," Aunt Carol muttered. "How long before they come back upstairs?"

"About the time the mosquitoes start nipping at them," I sighed. "Or they get hungry again, whichever comes first."

"I'll give them time to drink their beers, but then I'm dragging your uncle home. I trust Rod and Reel to keep you two out of too much trouble."

"Think Uncle Mike will argue about leaving?" Tansey asked.

"Argue with Aunt Carol?" I shook my head. "He wouldn't dare."

Aunt Carol's eyes twinkled as she hid her poker winnings in the bottom of her purse.

~*~*~

THE VEGETABLE BEEF STEW WAS done about the same time Rod and Reel snuck back inside the apartment. Tansey filled a bowl for each of us. They sat at the table, silently eating while they watched us. Tansey and I ate at the breakfast bar and afterward, settled on the couch to watch a chick flick we had seen a million times.

"Isn't this the one where the woman hires a male prostitute to pretend to be her boyfriend for her sister's wedding?" Rod asked, as he sat on the floor in front of Tansey.

"No," Reel said, sitting on the floor in front of me. "This is the movie where the woman is writing an article on how to get a guy to break up with her."

"How do you know that?" I laughed.

"Our mom used to play these movies all the time," Reel said, tilting his head back to look at me. "I'm man enough to admit it."

"Oh, yeah? Then what's your favorite part?"

"Mine's when the woman wears the dress without a bra and she's perky from the cold air," Rod said.

Tansey knocked him over with her foot. He grabbed both her feet and pulled her down on the floor next to him. Reel got up and took her place on the couch.

"Still waiting," I said, looking at him, waiting for his answer. "What's your favorite part?"

"When they sang *You're So Vain* on stage." Reel pulled me off to the side so he could lie down, then tugged me to lay next to him.

I thought about moving away, but I decided I was too comfortable. I adjusted my head to use his arm as a pillow and relaxed.

Chapter Eleven

After searching the bakery for any signs of danger, Reel agreed to leave. Mondays weren't all that busy, but I had Tuesdays off so I needed to make enough pies and breads for two days. I was running at full speed by the time Samantha arrived.

"You're late," I grumbled.

"Please," she snorted. "We both know that you do most of the work. You only need me to deal with the customers."

"Well, today I'm sore and not moving as fast as normal, so strap on an apron and start helping."

I nodded to the bushel of peaches, and Samantha took the hint and started cutting them up.

"Why are you sore? Have some man fun last night?" Samantha asked, wiggling her eyebrows.

"No. Tansey and I were in a car accident yesterday. Every muscle in my body hurts today."

"Oh, no. Sorry. I didn't hear about any accident. Is Tansey okay?"

"She's bruised and has a cut on her arm, but she'll be fine."

"What happened?"

"No time to explain. I need those damn peaches done. Then I need you to start boxing up the donut orders for the morning pickups."

Samantha didn't say anything, but sensing my foul mood, she kept busy and out of my hair. I wasn't really sure why I was taking out my frustration on her. Or why I was frustrated in the first place. Maybe it was because someone wanted me dead. Maybe it was because I'd woken up in Reel's arms, and the sad reality was that I'd liked it. Maybe I was just tired and needed everyone to give me some breathing room. The reasons why didn't matter. I was, beyond a doubt, cranky as hell.

An hour or so later, I slammed the bread I was kneading into a pile of flour, creating a white cloud to explode over the front of me. I sighed, dropping my chin to my chest, trying to force myself to relax.

"Samantha!" I called out.

"Yeah?" she asked, peeking her head in through the door.

"I'm sorry I'm being such a brat. I've had a few shitty days, and I'm taking it out on you—and the bread."

"No worries. I think you're allowed one bad day." Samantha grinned, slipping back to the customer counter.

"Samantha!" I yelled again.

"Yeah," she chuckled, sticking her head back in the door.

"I need a favor," I said, walking over to the refrigerator and taking the plastic container of leftover vegetable soup out and grabbing a plastic spoon. "I promised Reel I wouldn't leave the bakery. Can you walk this out to the end of the alley and leave it there?"

Samantha raised an eyebrow but took the soup and walked out the back door. When she returned a minute later, hand on hip, she said, "Should I be worried?"

I shook my head. "Teenager was looking for food the other day in our dumpster. I've been setting food out, and it's been disappearing regularly."

"Damn. Anything I can do?"

"Nothing else can be done until he's willing to trust someone."

She nodded, looking back toward the door, before she went back to the service counter.

~*~*~

At 3:00, Tansey walked through the back door and declared it was time to get out of Dodge.

"You girls have fun but be safe. No more car accidents," Samantha said, pulling my apron off me and shoving me toward the door. "And I'll set some food out in the morning for your new friend."

"Thanks. Last four pies are in the oven. Keep an eye on them."

"Got it. Go," Samantha said, snapping the apron at me.

"Gladly," Tansey said, shoving me out the door where my VW Bug was waiting to whisk us away. "Who's the friend she was talking about?"

"A homeless kid has been in the neighborhood," I said, sliding into the passenger seat and strapping on my seatbelt.

"Another one? I swear, you are like a magnet for those in need. They always seem to find you," Tansey said, shaking her head. "Well, what's the plan? Pool some money for him? Gather blankets?"

"He's too skittish. Leaving food is about all we can do for now and Samantha is covering that, so let's get out of town while we can."

"Don't look, but Rod's car is at the other end of the street. They followed me over here."

"That's okay. I don't mind them being close by with everything that's happened lately."

"You sure? I can lose them when we hit the interstate if you want me to."

"Nah." I yawned. "It's not worth it."

"You're exhausted. Do you want to cancel?"

"I won't promise to keep up with you on the dance floor, but I definitely need a night away from this town. Hopefully Rod and Reel are the only ones that follow us."

"Reel will spot anyone trying to tail us," Tansey nodded. "And my muscles are so bruised I doubt I'll be dancing the night away either."

"Until you drink a few shots and get your superpowers," I said, giggling.

Tansey grinned, turning up the radio as she turned onto the highway.

~*~*~

WHEN WE GOT TO COOPER CITY, Tansey passed our turnoff to the hotel. "Where are we going?"

"Don't get mad."

"Why would I get mad?"

"Because Reel got us rooms at a bed and breakfast. He agreed to give us space but said it would be safer if they were close by. The boys have rooms on the first floor, and we have rooms on the second floor."

"And the bill is paid?"

"Paid in full," Tansey said, taking the next exit and turning down a side street.

A mile or so down the road, she turned left down a long drive and pulled up in front of a large Victorian house with an oversized front porch.

"If this place has a pool, we're staying in tonight."

"No pool. But there's a hot tub out back that is calling for me and my stiff muscles."

~*~*~

TANSEY AND I SOAKED IN the hot tub while eating off the platter of grilled kabobs that Reel had ordered for us. The boys were keeping their distance on the other side of the patio, eating their own kabobs, but had stayed within sight.

"I feel weird in this skimpy swimsuit," I whispered to Tansey, leaning further into the water. "Reel keeps staring at me."

"He should stare," Tansey said. "You look hot in that bikini."

"I'm too big to wear a bikini."

"Nonsense. You have curves, and he obviously likes them."

"I'd rather have your long legs and perky tits."

Tansey looked down at her boobs and pushed them up once, then twice. Rod groaned, leaning his head back and stretching out his legs, adjusting his shorts.

"Rod looks uncomfortable," I said, giggling. "Maybe you should play with yourself again."

"I think we better go back to the room and change," Tansey said, laughing as she stood and stepped out of the hot tub.

I quickly followed her out, grabbing a towel to cover myself as I hurried inside. I wished I'd thought to bring a coverup.

I was almost to my door when Reel caught up with me and stopped me.

"Let me check the room," he said, pulling me to a stop and entering before me.

I stood in the doorway and watched him search the closet, behind the curtains, and in the private bathroom.

"All clear," he said, sauntering back to the door.

I cinched the towel tighter around me as I slid past him.

"I'm going to regret this," Reel grumbled, turning to push me against the wall as his body pressed into mine. And then he kissed me and the world spun.

His hands, stroking hot against my skin, dove under the towel as he massaged his fingers into my hips and back, before sliding under my swimsuit bottom to grip my bare ass. He lifted me, pinning me between the wall and his body. I could feel his erection through his jeans as he rubbed against me. His kiss grew deeper, more passionate, as his tongue stroked mine.

My head swam at the overall sensations as my own hands dragged instinctually over his body. And just as he was pulling me toward the bed, I remembered the words he had said: *I'm going to regret this.*

He didn't want me. Not really. In a weak moment, he was willing to sleep with me, already knowing he would regret it. I pushed away from him, separating myself from his touch.

I stood motionless, panting, but watchful of his every move. "Get out," I whispered, turning away from him so he couldn't see the tears that had broken free.

"Deanna?"

I felt him reaching toward me, and I stepped farther away.

"*Get out! Get out of my room!*" I yelled, throwing the hairbrush from the table at him. "Get out!"

The bedroom door swung open, and Tansey, wearing only a short skirt and a bra, ran past Reel and grabbed hold of me.

"Reel Thurman, I don't know what you did to my best friend, but I suggest you get out of this room," Tansey said, as she pulled me into a hug and held me.

I crumpled into my friend's shoulder, not even caring that I was making a scene as I cried.

Chapter Twelve

By the time I stopped crying, I was mad. I was so mad I was practically spitting as I applied another layer of mascara and switched my sensible pumps for my slutty heels. I stepped back and looked in the mirror. Sure, the girl looking back had a few extra pounds, breasts that were a bit too big, and a booty that bounced, but I'd be damned if there weren't men out there who would want me—men who wouldn't regret later being with me.

Even I had to admit I looked good in the short baby-blue dress with the plunging neckline and the flared skirt. My hair, shining bright and clipped up on the sides, was layered in curls down my back. I turned to check my backside in the mirror and grinned.

Happy with my appearance, I tossed my makeup in my purse and turned to the door. Tansey was standing there, leaning up against the doorjamb, smirking.

"Damn, girl. You're on fire."

"I'm pissed. Let him have his regrets," I said, as I stomped past her.

She hurried to catch up with me. "Take it easy," Tansey snorted, grabbing my arm and walking down the stairs beside me. "You've only worn those heels once, and I do believe the last time you tripped on the courthouse stairs."

"Why do sexy shoes have to be so dangerous?" I whispered, clinging to the rail on the other side.

"Two more steps," Tansey said.

"Hi there," the girl from the check-in counter greeted us at the bottom of the stairs. She was obviously off the clock, having changed into a cocktail dress and heels. "Remember me? I'm Bridget."

"Hi, Bridget," Tansey said.

"I heard you guys were going out dancing. Can I go? Please? I don't have any plans tonight." She bopped up and down on her toes, which I would have thought impossible to do in her four-inch heels.

"Sure, but our car doesn't have a very big back seat," Tansey said.

"No, problem. I have my boyfriend's Escalade," Bridget said, skipping to the door.

"Is she on drugs?" I whispered to Tansey.

"If she is, I hope she shares," Tansey said, leading us out.

~*~*~

BRIDGET DROVE US TO THE club and convinced the first guy she ran into to buy us a round of drinks. Normally, Tansey and I wouldn't allow someone to buy drinks for us, but he escorted us to the bar and had the bartender give us our drinks directly. He seemed like a good-ole boy from a western movie. A bit out of place in a dance club, but he seemed genuine. He told me he thought it was smart that I was drinking ginger ale and bypassing the real stuff.

Tansey snorted and downed her shot before grabbing her beer and towing me to the dance floor.

Bridget followed, bouncing up and down in excitement and looking at everyone and everything around her like she had never been clubbing before.

"I love dancing," Bridget shouted, as she threw her hands up and gave into the music.

"Where's your drink?" I asked, careful not to spill my own as I danced.

"I left it with Wayne. The guy who bought us our drinks," she hollered back over the music.

"That's not smart," Tansey said, shaking her head.

"It's okay. He's one of my boyfriend's friends," she said, jumping up and down to the beat of the music as she spun in a circle. "If you run into any trouble tonight, find Wayne. He'll kick anyone's ass that messes with you."

She turned and started dirty dancing with the guy behind her, totally oblivious to the blonde who was trying to get the same guy's attention.

"Damn, I like her," Tansey said, downing her beer and handing her empty bottle to one of the bouncers.

The bouncer sighed, passing the bottle to a waitress passing by, never taking his eyes off Tansey as she moved her lean body to the music.

I turned to the guy behind me and danced with him. No way in hell was I playing the wallflower tonight.

~*~*~

HOURS LATER, TANSEY WAS FEELING no pain as she danced with some hottie. I went back to the bar to get another ginger ale. I slid into an opening in front of the bar and nodded to my empty glass. Seconds later the bartender was sliding a new drink in front of me and waved me off when I tried to pay. I took a long sip of the cold liquid. The club was packed, and it was hot enough without all the dancing. My feet were killing me in the stupid heels. I was desperately missing my cute pumps.

"Hey, sexy," a guy purred, sliding in beside me at the bar and resting one hand loosely on my waist.

"Hey there," I said, smiling up at him, careful to set my drink on the bar so I didn't spill it down the front of either of us.

"I've seen you here before," he said. "You always look hot, but damn—tonight, babe, you look mouth-watering."

"Have we met?"

"Never had the balls to talk to you. You always had too many men chasing after you."

"I think you're mistaking me for someone else."

"I didn't say that you ever noticed the trail of men following you," he said with a cheeky grin before shrugging. "Figured you were married. You never showed much interest."

"Until today, I may have been distracted. I'm not anymore," I flirted, picking up my glass and taking another long sip.

"Tweedle? You good?" Wayne asked from beside me, glaring at the guy I was flirting with.

"I'm good. No worries," I said, half turning and looking up at him.

When I turned my attention back, the guy was gone. I looked back at Wayne and glared. "How the hell am I going to get laid tonight if you scare the men away?" I grabbed my glass from the bar and took a long drink.

"Didn't know sex was on your agenda," Wayne said, scratching the back of his head.

"Well, it is," I snapped, stepping around Wayne.

I stumbled, losing my balance, and Wayne reached out to catch me.

"Tweedle?"

My blood ran cold as the room tilted and swayed. I looked down at my drink, carefully setting it on the tall table that was next to me.

"Tweedle?" Wayne called again, still holding my arm.

I had to find Tansey. But I had lost sight of her.

The bathrooms... We always said if one of us was in trouble, we would meet near the bathrooms. I looked back at Wayne. He was glancing across the room and saying something barely audible. I looked over and spotted Bridget with a tall man, dark features, and a look of rage in his eyes.

We were tricked. They'd been watching us the entire time.

Pulling out of Wayne's grasp, I turned sideways and barreled through a group of people watching the dance floor. Ducking to hide, I pushed my way toward the bathrooms as fast as I could. The floor seemed to tilt to one side and then the other as I moved, causing me to recklessly bump into people. I didn't dare stop moving, though. I knew Wayne had slipped something into my drink and would follow me. My only hope was to find Tansey.

Stepping out of the crowd into the short hallway, I found Tansey leaning against the wall. Her eyes were half closed, and she was swaying. She saw me and reached out but almost fell. Throwing her arm over my shoulder, I tried to drag her weight back toward the crowd, when I heard Wayne call out my name. Swiveling the other way, I dragged Tansey with me into the kitchen. Seeing a walk-in cooler on the far wall, I kept going past the surprised kitchen workers toward the cooler, opening it with my free hand, while my other arm held Tansey around her waist and dragged her inside with me.

Setting Tansey roughly on the floor, I threw the contents off a wire-rack shelf before tipping it forward and wedging it behind the lever door handle and the door frame to keep the door from being opened.

"Tweedle!!" I heard Wayne yell as he pounded on the door.

"Shit, shit, shit," I said, sitting next to Tansey and pulling her limp body so her head rested on my lap.

She was completely out of it, but she was breathing. I had to get us help.

I fumbled in my purse, pulling out my phone. My hands shook as I hit the dial button.

"Help me. We're locked in the cooler in the kitchen. Some guy named Wayne drugged us," I whimpered over the phone.

"Deanna, you're okay," Reel said, though I could hear him running. "Rod and I are almost there."

"Hurry. Tansey's really out of it."

"I'm here, babe. I'm here. The door won't open. I need you to unlock it."

"What if you think you're here, but when I open the door, you're somewhere else?"

Loud pounding vibrated the door, and I could hear Reel yelling both through the door and the phone to unlock the door.

"Okay, okay. Give me a minute," I said before setting the phone down and sliding out from under Tansey.

Wedging the door in place proved easier than unwedging the door. It took me three tries, but I finally had the rack lifted enough to yell to Reel to open the door. When the door opened, he used one hand to push the rack back upright as he pulled me close to him with the other.

"Rod, get in here! Tansey's unconscious!"

Rod was already pushing us out of the way as he picked Tansey up and carried her into the kitchen. "She's breathing, but I need to get her to the hospital."

"I'll drive," Bridget said, leading the way out the side door.

"No! They tricked us. They've been watching us the whole night!" I screamed, trying to stop Rod from leaving with Bridget.

"Deanna! Look at me! Stop," he said, grasping me by the shoulders and preventing me from running after Rod and Tansey. "I hired them! They are part of the security team I work with. They were hired to keep an eye on you."

"Are you sure? That's Tansey!" I said, pointing toward the back door. *"That's my Tansey!"*

"I'm sure," he said, holding the sides of my face. "Were you drugged too?"

He was watching my eyes, and while I was far better off than Tansey, the floor and walls kept moving. Wayne moved a chair over and Reel settled me on it as he squatted in front of me and took my pulse and checked my eyes.

"I'm okay," I sniffled. "I want to see Tansey. I'm worried about Tansey."

"Found the fucker," the tall man with the dark hair and dark eyes said as he stormed into the kitchen and threw the guy who had been flirting with me down on the floor next to Reel.

"Yeah, that's the one," Wayne glared, as he stepped up next to him. His grin didn't diminish the wicked look in his eyes as he stared down at the guy.

"He's mine," Reel said, as he grabbed the guy by the collar with one hand and started dragging him out the back door. "Keep your eyes on Tweedle."

The guy was screaming in fear, but Wayne, the tall drink of dangerous, and the kitchen staff just laughed.

"He's going to kill him. You have to stop him," I said, looking up at Wayne.

"Fucker deserves a beating," the tall dark man said. He got out his wallet and tossed a wad of cash to the manager, nodding at the cooler.

I stood and moved toward the door, my legs shaking.

"Whoa, little lady. Where do you think you're going?" Wayne said.

"He's going to kill him. I have to stop him," I said, trying to push past him.

"No, he won't," the tall man said. "Ryan is the most level-headed guy we work with."

"*LISTEN TO ME!* Reel will hurt anyone who threatens me. He's protected me his entire life. He's going to *kill him*!" I yelled.

I must've finally said something that made sense to them because Wayne ran out the door. The tall guy latched onto my arm and shifted us to the doorway, watching outside.

Reel was indeed going ape-shit on the guy who was now lying in the alley in the fetal position. Wayne did his best to drag Reel off, but the tall guy left my side to help.

It took both men to move Reel to the far brick wall, and Reel was still straining for freedom.

"Reel! Reel—look at me," I said, running over to grasp his face. "Stop it. Listen to me. I'm okay. I'm right here. Look at me!"

"Tweedle, maybe you should step back," Wayne said, struggling to control Reel as he pushed away again.

I latched my arms around Reel's neck and did what any sensible woman would do—I jumped up, wrapping my legs around his hips.

Holding him close, I whispered calming words in his ear as I rubbed his back with one hand and held on with the other. I felt the rage slowly seep out of him before his arms moved around me to hold me against him. I kept talking to him as he leaned his head onto my shoulder.

"Are you with me? Are you back with me again, Reel?"

He nodded into my shoulder, and I kissed his cheek.

I leaned back, looking at him. "Good, because if anyone gets to hurt this punk, it's me."

Reel nodded, letting me slide down his body to stand on my own. He leaned his head down, briefly resting it on my shoulder and taking a deep breath. When he leaned back, he nodded again, "Yes, ma'am,"

I turned to the man on the ground. "Hey, asshole." I placed my spiked heel on his chest, just under his chin. "I think you should explain to me why you drugged us before I jam my heel into your eye."

"You heard her," Reel growled from behind me.

Wayne and the other guy stood beside me, arms crossed.

"Some guy paid me to drug you and lead you outside. I swear, it's the truth. He said he was your boyfriend and was trying to teach you a lesson on being safe. He had a picture of you and him together. I swear, I'm telling the truth. I wouldn't have hurt you or your friend."

"Something you want to tell me, babe?" Reel asked.

"Do you have the picture?" I asked the guy on the ground, but he shook his head no. "Why drug my friend then?"

"She was watching you like a Doberman. I couldn't get to you without her seeing. She was only pretending to drink all those beers. The bartender was filling them with water. I had to drug her."

I leaned over to pull his wallet. Taking his driver's license out, I tossed the wallet at him. "You better hope my friend is okay. If she's not, you'll be seeing me again."

I turned, walking down the alley toward the parking lot. I needed to see Tansey. I needed to know she was okay.

"Damn," Wayne chuckled as the boys followed.

"That's my girl," Reel chuckled proudly behind me.

"She has a nice ass too," the tall guy chuckled.

I heard the *ooof* as the air left his lungs.

Chapter Thirteen

When the glass doors slid opened to the ER, I could hear Tansey screaming from somewhere beyond the swinging doors. The security guard was busy arguing with Rod, trying to keep him in the waiting area, as I ran around them, following the terrified shrieks. Down the hall, around the corner, and into the first curtained room, I followed the screams, finding Tansey.

"Get back!" I yelled, as I pushed past a nurse and climbed up onto the bed, pinning Tansey down. "Tansey! You're safe! I'm here!"

"Get me out of here!" she cried, straining to sit up and pull her arms free.

They had strapped her to the bed. While holding one of her shoulders down, I pulled the buckle beside me to release one arm. Once freed, she gripped it around me. Rod raced in and hurried to the other side to unstrap the other arm.

"What the hell are you doing to her!?" he yelled.

"She needs the restraints," the doctor said. "She was aggressive and trying to pull out her IV."

"She's scared to death of hospitals!" I yelled as Tansey's other arm was freed and she clung to me, sobbing. "Reel, get a wheelchair."

"On it," Reel said, before disappearing down the hall.

"Rod, unhook the IV bag from the stand. We need to move her outside."

"She can't go anywhere," the doctor argued. "We don't even know what she was given yet."

"But obviously she's responding. She's awake."

"Her heart rate is escalated," one of the nurses warned.

"Her mother attempted suicide several times before finally succeeding. The last trip to the hospital, Tansey was covered in her mother's blood. She's terrified. We need to move her outside."

"Shit," the nurse said, before moving a monitor to the end of the bed and releasing a latch so the bed would move. "Hold on."

She swung the bed out and toward the hall, with me still sitting partially on top of Tansey as her nails dug into my skin and her small frame trembled.

"Wait a minute," the doctor stammered.

"I suggest you step out of the way," Rod glared, getting between Tansey and the doctor.

The doctor quickly stepped back, and Rod helped push the bed down the hall.

"Guess you don't need the chair," Reel said, ditching the wheelchair in the walkway and grabbing the other side of the bed. "Clear a path, Wayne!"

Wayne and the tall guy cleared people out of the way through the waiting room and to the sliding doors.

"Almost there," I whispered to Tansey, rocking her back and forth.

"Her blood pressure is coming down," the nurse nodded.

They swung the bed out into the cool air and off to the side of the walkway.

"BP 110 over 90," the nurse told another doctor who had followed us out.

"What's the story here?" the other doctor asked, looking at the chart.

"She was drugged at a nightclub earlier this evening. When she became alert, she started panicking," the nurse answered. "Appears she has some post-traumatic experiences from being in emergency rooms."

"Smart to move her outside," the doctor nodded. "Do we have the toxicology report?"

"No, but I think it was some type of sedative," the nurse answered.

I was listening to them but focused on Tansey. We were counting together. "52, 53, 54, 55…"

Rod reached out and held one of her hands and counted with us. "60, 61, 62, 63, …"

"I'm okay," Tansey nodded, taking a deep breath.

"Yes, you are," the nurse said, smiling. "BP 100 over 80. Pulse 110. I'm going to get you a blanket. I need you to promise not to disappear, okay?"

"I'll stay with her," the doctor said.

"Doctor, Deanna was drugged too, but doesn't seem to have ingested as much," Reel said, resting a hand on my shoulder.

"Well, while you're right here," the doctor said, checking my eyes with a flashlight. He checked my pulse too, then unhooked the blood pressure monitor from Tansey to check mine.

I rolled my eyes, and Tansey giggled.

"Blood pressure is a bit low, but nothing to be concerned about," the doctor said, placing the cuff back on Tansey. "Do you feel dehydrated or tired?" he asked me.

"I'm good," I shook my head. "What about Tansey? Can she go home tonight?"

"Let's run the IV for a while and keep an eye on her. But if she's still doing good in an hour, we can let her go as long as she's monitored the rest of the night."

"Oh, her ass will be monitored," Rod said, his eyes not leaving Tansey.

She tilted her head and smiled up at him.

"You need me to look at those hands of yours?" the doctor asked Reel.

Reel looked down at his hands before shoving them in his pockets. "No."

The doctor nodded. He left when the nurse returned with a blanket. "I brought a couple. Seems you ladies didn't remember your coats tonight."

I passed one to Bridget as Reel wrapped one around my shoulders. I was still sitting, straddled over Tansey. I stumbled around some until I was beside her with my legs hanging off the side of the bed. Reel took the corners of the blanket and draped them over my lap.

"Wayne, I'm sorry I thought you were the bad guy," I said, looking over at him.

"Hell, little lady, I don't blame you. You knew I'd been standing next to you and that I was pretending to be someone I wasn't. I told Ryan it was a stupid plan." Wayne chuckled.

"I was totally impressed with the cooler move!" Bridget giggled, bouncing up and down.

"What cooler move?" Tansey asked.

"I locked us in a cooler and dropped a rack over the handle so they couldn't open the door," I answered.

"How did you think of that so quickly?" the tall guy asked.

"If you tell me your name, I'll answer your question."

"Sorry. Deanna, this is Bones. Bones, this is Deanna," Reel said, pointing between us. "And she knew that trick because when we were kids, Tansey and Deanna were playing in the bakery's cooler when they accidentally knocked the rack over, lodging the door shut."

"At least the fire department didn't have to blowtorch the door open this time," I said.

"Eh-hmm." Wayne cleared his throat. "This is probably bad timing and definitely none of my business, but I can't shake the thought from my head." He shifted his weight from one foot to the other before looking back at me. "At the B&B, we heard you yell at Ryan to get out of your room. Then at the bar, you said you were trying to get laid."

Ryan stiffened, placing a hand on my thigh while glaring at Wayne.

"I'm sorry," Wayne said, holding up his hands to Reel before looking back at me. "I need to know if Ryan stepped out of line."

"None of your damn business, Wayne," Reel growled.

"You made it our business when you hired us to protect her," Bones said, crossing his arms over his massive chest.

"It's fine," I said, pushing Reel's hand off my lap. "Reel and I have been friends since we were kids, but tonight he said, well, uhm…" I took a deep breath, pushing down my emotions. "He said *I'm going to regret this*, then he kissed me. It made me mad, like really mad."

Tansey rubbed my arm, comforting me.

Bridget stepped back and punched Reel in the lower side of his back.

"Shit," Reel cursed, stumbling forward and leaning over. "Damn it, Bridget. The kidney? Really?"

"That was cruel," Bridget said, glaring.

Rod leaned his forehead against Tansey's shoulder, laughing. "Reel, you're such a dumbass."

Bones and Wayne were laughing too.

"Why the hell did that piss you off?" Reel asked me.

Bridget pulled her arm back again, but Bones dragged her a few feet away.

"You were going to regret kissing me?" I glared. "Like I was an embarrassment?"

Reel looked down at me with a look of surprise. He cradled my face in his hands. "No, Deanna. I was going to regret it because I wouldn't want to stop. I knew that if I gave into kissing you, it would make it even harder to stay outside in the car while you danced the night away with other men in that club."

I looked at him, watching his face. I could tell by his smirk that he was telling the truth.

Tansey giggled beside me.

"Well, I didn't know," I mumbled.

"Well, now you do," Reel said, leaning in to kiss me gently on the lips.

Chapter Fourteen

Aunt Carol and Uncle Mike had called three times before I was able to convince them that we were fine and would drive back in the morning. It was late by the time I got Tansey changed and settled into bed. Rod strolled into the room and curled up beside her, propping himself up and promising to keep an eye on her. It was just as well. My eyelids were heavy, and the adrenaline had worn off hours ago.

I stumbled out of her room and into the next one over to sleep in my own assigned bed. On top of the comforter, fully dressed, Reel slept peacefully. He must have fallen asleep while he was waiting for me. Part of me wanted to curl up beside him. I had been in love with Reel Thurman since we were children, and he always made me feel safe and loved. But it was for that exact same reason that I knew I needed to protect myself. I couldn't trust him to stay. To be part of my life.

I turned and walked out of the room and down the stairs.

Bones and Wayne quietly played cards in the parlor. Wayne lifted an eyebrow but didn't say anything as I walked past them to one of the sofas and curled up. Bones left the room, returning a few minutes later with a pillow and blanket for me.

"Thanks," I said, tucking the pillow under my head as he draped the blanket over me.

~*~*~

Keeping baker's hours was just part of who I was. Before dawn could blink on the horizon, I was up, tiptoeing past Wayne who slept on the other couch, and startling Bones in the kitchen.

"Everything okay?" he asked, looking around.

"Just have a routine," I said. "That fresh coffee?" I asked, nodding toward the coffee pot as I opened up cupboards.

I had never stayed in a hotel, motel, or inn that had complained when I borrowed their kitchen to make homemade biscuits or other baked goods. This was my first time in a B&B, but I figured they would be like-minded.

I pulled out several mixing bowls and found the baking supplies.

"Cream?" Bones asked, after pouring me a cup of coffee.

"Yes, please. Any particular bakery favorites?"

"What's your specialty?"

"Everything," I said.

"Apple strudel?" Bones challenged, pulling out some apples along with the cream.

I nodded and got to work. By the time the cook arrived at 8:00, she pulled out a stool and drank coffee while sampling the baked goods. She definitely didn't mind having the morning off, and I'd kept Bones busy cleaning the dishes, so the kitchen was cleaner than she had left it the day before.

"I thought I smelled something," Bridget said, bouncing into the room.

Bones held out his half piece of apple strudel, and she latched onto it like a shark.

I slid the platter to their end of the counter.

"I should have known," Reel said, shaking his head as he sauntered in.

"Oh, good, Goldilocks vacated my bedroom." I took off the apron. "Pull the pie in eight minutes," I said, passing Reel the apron.

"Me?"

"I got it," the cook said, taking the apron from his hands.

I escaped from the kitchen and climbed the stairs. Back in my room, I tried not to look in the mirror while I stripped off my dress from the night before and dug through my ratted hair to remove the hair clips. Moving into the private bathroom, I stepped under the steamy spray of water, letting it melt the prior night off my skin and out of my mind. The scent of lavender soap filled the air as I lathered up.

I stayed in the shower until I was feeling guilty for hogging the hot water and finally turned the valves off. Wrapped in fresh towels, I rummaged through my duffle bag, disappointed to find Tansey had packed my yellow skirt with a blue shirt. It wasn't even the blue shirt with yellow flowers, so it wasn't coordinated. Luckily, I had my white sweater and sandals, so it would do until I got home. I was ready to go downstairs when my phone rang.

After looking at the display, I sighed and answered, "Hello, Mother."

"Deanna, dear, the gossip has died down. I think it would be socially acceptable for us to meet for breakfast this morning. Actually, brunch is more fashionable. Say, 11:00 at the country club?"

Pine Valley didn't have a country club, but townsfolk called the expensive restaurant up at the lake just that. I had no understanding of how my mother could afford to eat there. To my knowledge, she had never worked a day in her life, and it wasn't like my father was sending her money. I probably didn't want to know how she managed it.

"I'm out of town. We'll have to meet another day," I said, looking around the room to make sure I had packed everything before zipping my bag closed.

"Where are you? You couldn't have gone too far."

"Goodbye, Mother," I said, before hitting the end button.

I grabbed my duffle and turned to leave, seeing Tansey just inside the doorway grinning at me.

"You look back to your old self again."

"I feel like I slept a week. Maybe I should get drugged more often."

"Let's not," I said as I looped an arm through hers and turned her out the doorway. "Baked goods galore downstairs. You hungry?"

"Starving. Is that baked apples I smell?"

"Apple strudel. I let Bones pick the specialty this morning."

"Which one is Bones again?"

"The tall, dark, and dangerous-looking one."

"As opposed to the bulky badass cowboy and the twins who look like street fighters?" Tansey asked with a cocked eyebrow.

"Lots of testosterone, that's for sure."

"You sneaking out?" Tansey nodded to my duffle bag.

"Do you mind? I want to go see Grandpa and need some alone time."

"Go but watch to make sure no one follows you. I'll tell the others you're still upstairs."

I kissed Tansey's cheek and slipped out the front door while everyone was in the kitchen.

Sliding behind the wheel of my VW Bug, I threw it in neutral and let it coast down the drive. When I was far enough away from the house, I popped the clutch and started it up.

I sped off down the road, a grin on my face and my eyes watching the mirrors for anyone following me. *Freedom*, I thought as I rolled down the windows.

Chapter Fifteen

My grandpa, once sharp as a tack and as confrontational as a grizzly, walked around the house in his bathrobe, looking lost and mumbling to himself. I tried to talk to him, but it only made him agitated. The live-in nurse, accustomed to my Tuesday visits, escaped for a reprieve as soon as I arrived. She wouldn't return for a few hours, and I couldn't say I blamed her, though I didn't particularly like her either. Hell, I didn't even know her name.

Grandpa's housekeeper had quit a few weeks before, and I sighed as I looked around at the disastrous state of the house. Knowing it wasn't the nurse's job to keep the house clean, I still cringed at how anyone could live somewhere with dust coating the furniture and dirty dishes stacked everywhere. My grandmother, bless her heart, would come back to haunt us all if she knew how disastrous her house looked.

I picked up a pile of clean laundry from the living room floor and decided to use a pair of my grandpa's boxers as a dust rag. I traveled from room to room, tossing misplaced belongings into a clothes basket. After I made the first trip through, I went to the laundry room and started the washer. In the kitchen, a groan escaped when I saw the pile of dirty dishes. It was obvious that the nurse had stacked everything to wait for my Tuesday visit. The top-of-the-line dishwasher sat untouched.

I filled the dishwasher, washing what remained by hand, before scrubbing everything else in the kitchen. As I cleaned, my grandpa brought me an assortment of things, one by one. Some were dirty dishes or silverware, but most were oddball knickknacks from around the house that needed cleaning. I'd wash and dry them and then he'd disappear with each item to God knows where. I doubted they'd end up where they belonged, but it was keeping him settled, so it didn't matter.

I finished cleaning the kitchen, including the floors. I washed, dried, and took care of three loads of laundry, intentionally leaving the nurse's dirty clothes in a pile. After vacuuming, dusting a second time, and moving various knickknacks back into their original rooms, I sat in a chair in the foyer, exhausted. Looking up the grand stairway, I willed myself to get up and clean the second floor. I just didn't have it in me, though, to see what was up there.

I decided to look for my grandpa. The house was quiet, too quiet. I found him in his den, behind the massive mahogany desk, sitting in his leather chair.

"Hey, Grandpa." I sat in one of the guest chairs.

He looked at me before turning his head toward the other room. I heard a car pulling up outside and was about to stand when Grandpa reached a hand out and grabbed my arm with such force that I knew I was going to have bruises.

"Don't let the Martians get you, Tweedle-Dee. Run!"

With that, he jumped from his chair and ran from the room with his terry cloth robe flapping behind him.

I sighed. He was getting worse, and I needed to make better arrangements for him. It was obvious the house needed more attention, and the lawn was looking pretty shabby as well.

"Where's the old dude?" the nurse asked, stepping into the room.

"The old dude's name is Vince," I snapped.

I wanted desperately to fire her and send her packing, but my grandpa's attorney handled the estate, and I didn't have the authority. I only held his medical proxy.

Fuming, I grabbed the rolodex and looked up the attorney's number again. Getting his voicemail, I demanded he call me immediately. I slammed the phone down in its cradle and went in search of Grandpa again. I found him asleep in his bed and decided to slip out before he woke.

KNOWING I WAS IN TROUBLE, I drove to Uncle Mike's house to face the music. Wayne and Bones were leaning against a black Escalade a few houses down when I pulled up.

Wayne walked over and opened my car door, grinning. "Ryan's pissed."

"Good for him," I said. "I'm more worried about my uncle."

"Ryan texted us and said your uncle knew where you were but wouldn't tell him. We've been listening to them yell at each other for ten minutes and decided it wasn't a good time for introductions."

I snorted and made my way inside.

"Where the hell have you been?" Reel yelled.

"Why?"

"*Why? Why!?* Because some nut job has been trying to kill you and you ditched your security detail. That's why!"

"So? Everyone knew where I was. I was perfectly safe." I tossed my purse atop the counter and gave Aunt Carol a kiss on the cheek. "Uncle Mike, why aren't you at work?"

"Got suspended for twenty-four hours," he snorted.

"Why? What happened?"

"I told the chief he was an idiot. He didn't take to kindly to my honesty. He wanted to fire me, but I'm the only one with any real training, so he suspended me without pay for twenty-four hours."

"Well, at least you finally have a day off," I said.

"How's your grandpa, dear?" Aunt Carol asked.

"That's where you were? You should have told us. It wasn't safe for you to go alone."

My temper spiked, and I turned on Reel to unload. "Get this through that thick skull of yours—I didn't ask for a babysitter! I am not your responsibility. And I don't need or want for you to be bossing me around all the time. I will do-go-see whomever I damn well please!"

Bridget snorted from the doorway. "She reminds me of Kelsey."

"She's usually not as stubborn and cranky as Kelsey," Reel grumbled. He rubbed his hands over his face and stepped closer to me, placing his hands on my hips. "What's wrong? You only yell when you are upset about someone you care about."

"It's her grandpa," Uncle Mike sighed. "Old man isn't doing so well."

My lower lip started to tremble, and I tried to turn away, but Reel pulled me into his embrace. I sobbed into his shoulder, trying to come to terms with the fact that my grandpa would never again be the man I had known him to be.

When I settled, Reel steered me over to the kitchen table and sat me down.

"I'm sorry. I know how close you are to him," he said, pushing my hair out of my face.

"Once upon a time, you were close to him too."

Reel nodded. "I was going to visit him when I got back into town, but someone has kept me busy lately." He wiped my tears away.

"Is he eating? Taking his meds?" Aunt Carol asked, placing a hand on my shoulder.

"I don't know if he's taking his meds, but I know he's eating," I said, nodding. "I also tried to call his attorney again. If I don't hear from him by tomorrow, I'll drive to the city to track him down."

"Then what? You going to put him in a headlock?" Reel asked, chuckling.

"If that's what it takes," I said, raising my chin.

"Come on. You need some fresh air." Reel pulled me up from the chair and steering me toward the door, leading me outside and down the walkway to the west.

I stopped walking and tugged on his hand to get him to stop. "Let's go the other direction. Toward town."

"I want to show you something. We need to go this way," he said, pulling me along.

I followed his lead, down one block and then the next. Wayne and Bones stayed on the walkway behind us, giving us some privacy, but close enough if trouble arose. As we crossed the next block, my steps slowed, moving barely a few inches at a time as my legs trembled.

"Deanna, come on," Reel said, pulling me to hurry.

As we passed the big evergreen, my knees locked, and I was frozen, staring at the house across the street.

"Deanna?"

"Brother, something's wrong," Wayne said, as he stepped beside me.

Bones stepped protectively in front of me. "Tweedle?" Bones asked, scouting the perimeter. "What's wrong?"

"The house, the blue one at the end of the road," I said, leaning into Wayne to hide it from my view.

Bridget's black Escalade screeched to a halt beside us, and Tansey jumped out of the passenger seat. I threw myself at her, and she wrapped her arms around me while ushering me toward the Escalade.

"What the hell is going on?" Reel asked.

"She's terrified," Bones answered.

"Of what?" Reel asked, trying to stop me.

"The blue house?" Wayne answered as Tansey opened the back door and helped me inside.

"But she adores that house," Reel said. "That's why I bought it for her."

"*You bought that thing?*" Tansey yelled. "Are you insane?

"She used to stare at it for hours when we were kids. I'd find her almost every night at the end of the block looking at it."

"Because it has haunted her since she was a little girl. She used to have nightmares about it. Her sister used to tease her about that house coming to get her!"

"Shit! Why didn't anyone tell me?"

"You should have known!" Tansey yelled, slamming the car door and getting in the front passenger seat.

Bridget accelerated down the road, and Tansey started counting with me, 11, 12, 13, 14…

The counting faded as my brain fogged over.

~*~*~

THE CRACK-SLAP OF A HAND AGAINST my cheek fired my brain back to life as a burning sensation lit my skin.

I reeled to the side, cupping the side of my face as I fell to the floor. I looked up at a wide-eyed Bridget, standing over me.

"What the hell happened?" Tansey asked, running into the room and kneeling on the floor beside me.

"Your method of coaxing her out of her trance wasn't working," Bridget said, shrugging. "I thought I'd try something else."

"You hit her?"

"My best friend, Haley, has had to give me a good whack once or twice." Bridget said, moving over to sit in an accent chair. "You with us now?" she asked me.

"Was I not with you before?" I asked, crawling up from the floor and back onto the couch. I was startled when I realized I was in my own house.

"You've been in a trance for about an hour," Aunt Carol said, walking into the room and setting out a platter of cheese, crackers, and grapes. "Nicely done, Bridget."

Both my eyebrows shot up. "She hit me!"

"Yes, dear. But nothing else was working," Aunt Carol said, sighing. "You once went a whole week without talking to anyone, only eating when forced. You barely even slept. You were like the walking dead. I'm all for Bridget knocking you around if I don't have to go through that again." Aunt Carol turned back to the kitchen.

Tansey rolled her eyes. "I barely remember that. We were so young."

"When did that happen?" I asked.

"We were in kindergarten or somewhere before kindergarten," Tansey said. "I don't remember much, other than you were like a zombie. Then one day you showed up my house ready to go for a bike ride."

"Was she at the blue house before she went into shock?" Bridget asked.

"Drop it, Bridget," Tansey said with a glare. "Or I'll return the favor of smacking you around."

I giggled, watching my best friend. "You're such a badass."

"Only when my girl needs some protecting," Tansey said, hugging me.

I heard an odd mix of yelling and laughing outside in the front yard. Aunt Carol rushed over and looked out the front door.

"Oh, dear. Tweedle, you may need to intervene," Aunt Carol said, wringing her hands.

I walked over to the door to look out, laughing at the scene in front of me. Bones and Wayne were on the porch, also laughing.

Reel, on the other hand, was yelling loudly as my sister chased him around the front yard, calling him Rod.

"You should go help him," Aunt Carol insisted.

"Why? He was the idiot who bought the blue house," I said as I watched the game of tag play out.

"You'd think that after all of us growing up together, Darlene would be able to tell Reel and Rod apart," Tansey said from beside me.

"She was too busy looking in the mirror."

"Where is Rod, anyway?" Aunt Carol asked.

"He was outside," Tansey said, as we all pressed our noses closer to the glass.

"He's in the bushes," Bridget said, pointing from a side window.

I opened the door, and Darlene stopped chasing Reel long enough to look at me.

"That's Reel," I said, pointing to Reel. "That's Rod," I said, pointing to Rod, who poked his head up out of the bushes.

"Damn you, Tweedle!" Rod yelled as he took off running down the street.

Darlene chased after him in her heels, pulling the skimpy leather skirt down every few paces.

"That was evil," Tansey said, laughing as she threw her arm over my shoulders.

"You both need to repent," Aunt Carol clucked, turning back to the kitchen.

Chapter Sixteen

I spent the rest of the day in my room, reading and sorting my closet. Aunt Carol and Tansey checked on me occasionally but sensing I needed time alone, left me in peace. I knew everyone else was somewhere nearby, but I didn't care. I was upset with Reel for buying that damn blue house. I was upset that, after several more phone calls, I was still unable to get ahold of the lawyer.

I went to bed early, and by the time I woke in the morning, I felt like I hadn't slept at all.

Entering the kitchen after dressing, Reel greeted me with a to-go coffee and insisted on driving me to work in his truck.

When we arrived at the bakery, I was ordered to stand beside the door while he completed a thorough search. After he gave the all-clear, I moved to the center of the kitchen, starting up the four ovens and the deep fryer.

"What can I do to help?" Reel asked.

"Make a pot of tea? Coffee isn't working for me this morning."

Reel heated a kettle and made a pot of coffee for himself. I mixed up a batch of muffins and started them baking before making a batch of donut batter. I showed Reel how to fry the donuts and started mixing up biscuits.

"Damn it! How do you do this without burning yourself?"

I shrugged, rolling out the biscuit dough. "I've been making them for so long now that either I learned how to magically make them, or I'm immune to burning my hands. I probably have permanent nerve damage. Here, trade me jobs."

I set Reel to work cutting out the biscuits while I took over making the donuts. I kept catching him watching my hands, trying to see whether I was splattered with hot oil. He finally shook his head and gave up trying to figure out what the trick was.

"What's next?" Reel asked.

I looked at the table and grinned. "Did you think we'd just throw out the extra dough?"

"I guess not," he said, rolling it into a ball.

He didn't cover his hands in flour and ended up with biscuit dough sticking everywhere. I cooked the last plain donut before going over and covering my hands in flour to finish the biscuits.

"You make this look easy," Reel sighed, going to the sink to wash the sticky dough off his hands.

"It is after this many years. Sit. Drink your coffee. I need to finish a few more things, and then I'll put you to work peeling apples."

Reel pulled out a stool. After pulling the muffins, I filled three of the ovens with biscuits.

"Why do you cook them all at once?"

"It's easier to smell when they're done."

"You don't use a timer?"

"With a timer, you can't be sure whether the oven is running a little hot, or whether your biscuits were too big or small. But with smell, you always know."

I poured more hot water into my teacup before mixing up a batch of apple fritters, using the last of my precut apples. I set out a new bushel for Reel to peel.

Checking the front storage cabinets and the catering orders, I took inventory and made a mental list of everything that needed to be prepped and baked. I had the cooling racks half filled by the time Samantha arrived.

"Bless you." She smiled. "Inventory got pretty low yesterday."

"I saw that," I said. "Okay, Reel. You can leave now. Samantha's here."

"I don't think so," he said, focused on the apple he was peeling.

Truth be told, I could have peeled all the apples in about ten minutes, but it was keeping him out of my hair.

"Seriously. We open at seven anyway. Go home. You have furniture and rugs being delivered today."

"What's going on?" Samantha asked, hanging up her purse.

"Somebody is trying to hurt Deanna," Reel said, tossing the half-peeled apple into the bowl.

"Why on Earth would anyone want to hurt Tweedle?"

"I wish I knew," I said. "I'm really curious how I pissed someone off this much."

"Is it your sister? She's evil."

"No. I know that at least three of the occasions it was a man," I answered as I dropped another fritter into the hot oil.

"Three?" Reel's voice growled.

Shit-shit-shit. I just tattled on myself!

"I mean, I assume the second time was a man. Everybody knows there are more guy mechanics than girl mechanics."

I could feel Reel approaching, but I didn't turn to face him. Samantha's eyes expanded to twice their normal size as she walked backward.

"Turn and face me if you're going to lie to me, Deanna," he said, standing right behind me.

"I have to watch the fritter," I said, looking into the fryer.

He didn't say anything. But he didn't move away either.

I stood watching the fritter as it got browner by the second.

"You going to take it out or let it burn?"

"What are the chances of you being distracted by a kitchen fire?"

"Set the place on fire. You're still going to face me when the smoke clears."

"Fine!" I said, pulling the strainer up to remove the fritter. "Someone was in my house last week. They left a muddy footprint on my floor. And, unless the chick has really big feet, it was a man."

"Are you sure it wasn't your uncle?"

"It could've been," I admitted.

Reel put his hands on my shoulders and turned me to face him. Using his finger, he lifted my chin, so I was forced to look up at him.

"But you know it wasn't your uncle. How?"

"It was the same day I found the snake in the house."

"The rattlesnake? And you didn't think the footprint was a clue that someone put it there deliberately?" he asked with a raised eyebrow.

"Holy shit!" Samantha squealed. "Did you pee your pants?"

"No, of course not," I lied, hoping that she didn't see my face turning red or my fingers crossed behind my back. "I'm not stupid, Reel. I suspected someone put the snake in my bedroom."

I never stopped looking at Reel. His intense blue eyes appeared to darken to a deep purple. He was beyond angry.

"Reel, I was fine."

"Someone broke into your house and left a poisonous snake, and you didn't tell anyone? You did what, exactly?"

"Hoped it was all a big misunderstanding?" I lifted my hands in an I-don't know gesture. "I mean, who'd want to hurt me? I'm a baker! It sounds crazy!"

"And after the Ferris wheel?"

"I was a little more concerned, but not worried. Then the car started acting up, and I might've gotten a bit nervous then, but worse things could've happened."

Reel stepped away and started pacing. "So it takes three threatening situations for you to get nervous. Good to know."

"I suppose when someone tried to run you off the road, that made you what...? Slightly concerned? How about when someone tried to kidnap you? And, oh, the gas leak that could have blown you to bits?

Were you even scared then? Do you understand how serious this is?"

"Sure," I agreed.

"Sure? *Sure?* Someone is trying to *kill you*, Deanna!"

I laughed. "But they're not very good at it."

Samantha snorted, and Reel turned his glare at her. She stammered some incoherent words and ran out of the kitchen, into the serving area.

I laughed again.

"This is not funny," Reel snapped.

"Actually, it is. I think you've just had too much coffee."

"What if someone comes after you and I'm not around? What are you going to do then?"

I reached behind my back and pulled out the revolver I was wearing clipped to my pants under my shirt. "I don't want to, but if I have to, I'll shoot him."

Reel shook his head and rolled his eyes. "You really think you could kill someone?"

"Hell no," I said, shaking my head. "But I'm a really good shot. I could shoot a pinky toe or something, so I had time to run away. Some scientists say that due to evolution, the human race no longer needs the baby toe. Based on that theory, I wouldn't be maiming anyone."

From the other side of the kitchen door, we heard Samantha snort.

"Samantha, get in here!" Reel ordered.

Samantha peeked in the door, and when she saw where Reel was standing, she skirted away from him to the other side of me.

"What about you? Do you know how to shoot?"

Samantha reached under the prep table, pulling out a shotgun to lie on the table. Crossing to her purse, she pulled out a gigantic handgun that looked like it should be in an over-the-top action movie.

"And if someone is coming after Deanna?"

"I won't be aiming for his foot," Samantha said. "Someone tries to hurt Tweedle when I'm around, they leave in a coroner's van."

I looked back at the shotgun and then looked under the table. Sure enough, there was a recessed cubby made to fit the shotgun perfectly.

"How long has that been there?" I asked Samantha, pointing to the shotgun.

"About fifteen years," she said.

"You've worked above a shotgun for ten years and never noticed it?" Reel yelled. "And you wonder why I worry about you?"

"Reel, you need to calm down. You're getting awfully worked up."

Reel slammed his hands on the table. Samantha took a protective step in front of me, still holding her handgun.

"He won't hurt me, Samantha," I said, walking around the table to stand next to Reel. "Look, I should have told you or Uncle Mike about the snake, but I was hoping it was all a coincidence. But as you can see, Samantha has the action-hero thing down, and I'll be fine for the rest of my shift. Go walk off your anger, and we can argue later."

Reel glared down at me for a few seconds, then leaned his head back and stared at the drop ceiling for another minute. After a big long sigh, he asked, "What time do you get done?"

"We have some late afternoon orders, so I'll be done around five. I can call if we get done earlier."

Reel was watching me to see whether I was fibbing. Eventually nodding, he looked back at Samantha.

"I got it. Shoot to kill," she nodded.

"And, you really know how to use that?" Reel asked.

"Tucker's my great uncle. He taught me how to shoot."

"You swear that you won't hesitate?"

"It won't be the first time I shot someone," she said.

"Really?" I asked, surprised.

"Don't repeat that," Samantha said, giving me the stare down.

It was Reel's turn to snort. "Fine. I'm heading home for a nap before the furniture is delivered. Don't leave the bakery unless you're with your uncle or me."

"Yes, sir."

"I mean it."

"I know," I sighed.

Reel hesitated for several long silent seconds as he stared down at me. Finally, he released the breath he had been holding. "Be safe," he said, pulling me by the back of the neck into him for a brief kiss before leaving through the back door.

"Damn. I always heard the rumors, but I never actually thought they were true. No offense," Samantha said.

"What rumors?"

"About you and Reel."

"What about me and Reel?"

"That he's in love with you and you're oblivious to it." Samantha smirked.

"He's not in love with me," I said, rolling my eyes. "Geesh. We've been friends since grade school. He thinks of me as a kid sister."

She laughed. "He most certainly does not think of you as a sister."

"Whatever. We don't have time to argue. Finish the fritters so I can finish the apples."

"Trade. I'll do the apples. I always burn myself with that deep fryer."

I shrugged, starting another batch of fritters.

"Hey, the food I set out yesterday was still in the alley this morning. I replaced it with a fresh bag, but I think your teenager took off."

"Hopefully he went home or to a shelter," I said, chewing on my lower lip.

Chapter Seventeen

It was busier than normal. We didn't stop baking all day, and by 3:00 we still had special orders to bake. We were way behind schedule. Samantha was calling some of our customers and rescheduling their pickup times while I baked.

I had nine pies in the oven, nine more ready to go in, and was mixing up a devil's food chocolate cake when Samantha yelled for me to come up front.

"What's up?" I asked, walking through the door.

"You whore!" Darlene screamed at me, coming around the counter and stalking me toward the window. "Don't think that I didn't hear that *both* the Thurman brothers have been sleeping at your house. I warned you to stay away from Rod!"

"You're my sister, but you better shut the hell up, right now."

"Or what? What are you going to do, you little slut?"

I reached into the dessert case, pulled what was left of the lemon custard cake and mashed it into her face.

It felt good. So, good in fact, that I mashed the rest of it into the top of her head, grinding it in for good measure.

She screeched in horror.

I laughed so hard, I had to lean over and brace myself with my hands on my knees.

Uncle Mike rushed into the bakery and froze.

He stared first at Darlene and then at me. A slight smirk appeared before he cleared his facial expression, stepped around the service counter, and steered Darlene through the dining area and out the door. He followed her as they walked down the sidewalk out of view.

The customers all cheered and clapped.

"For the record—I did *not* sleep with either one of the Thurman brothers!"

Several of the women, including Samantha, booed. Even Mrs. Crookburn, who was enjoying her afternoon tea and pastry, booed. I shook my head and went to pull the pies out of the oven.

After rotating the pies and using the last oven to start the cake, I went out with a broom and mop to clean up the mess I had made. Mrs. Crookburn was just leaving, and I rushed over to open the door for her. Sarah Temple was bouncing her baby girl on her hip, talking to Samantha by the register, while Sarah's five-year-old son Bradley ran circles around one of the tables. Two local hunters sat on the other side of the room at one of the small tables drinking coffee. Everyone else had cleared out. *We should be good to close by 4:00 except for the late pickup orders*, I thought.

Hearing a loud roar behind me, I turned and saw Mrs. Crookburn's car racing toward the storefront window.

"Run!" I yelled, diving toward little Bradley, who was still doing laps around the table.

Reaching him as the car crashed through the window, I tossed his little body toward the back hallway, toward the bathrooms. He was still airborne when I felt the car slam into me, rolling me on top of the hood.

~*~*~

"Deanna!"

"Tweedle!"

"Deanna!"

I heard them calling but my ears were fuzzy.

No wait, my whole body was fuzzy.

Nope, that wasn't right either. My head was fuzzy. My body—*hurt. Everywhere.*

"Here," I called out, but it sounded muffled.

"*DEANNA! Where are you?*" I heard Reel scream.

"Here," I tried to say again, but it wasn't much louder.

"She's over there," a man's voice called. "I can see her leg. The car must have thrown her under the table."

"Tweedle," Uncle Mike yelled, standing over me. "Hang on. Don't move."

"Bradley? Is Bradley okay?" I asked, rolling onto my back.

"Don't move," Reel ordered, climbing over what appeared to be parts of a table to kneel where I was lying.

"Bradley?" I asked again.

"He's okay. He said the crazy baking lady threw him. I assume that was you," Reel said, stroking the side of my face.

He might have been grinning, but his eyes were ice cold as he surveyed my body.

"That bad, huh?" I coughed.

"Your leg might be broken. And you have a couple deep cuts, but you're going to be just fine," he said, leaning over to kiss my forehead.

"You don't know that." I continued to cough and realized I was having trouble breathing.

"Get this car out of here!" Reel yelled. "Rod! We need to get her out!"

"We can't pull the car out. It's supporting one of the walls," Rod yelled from somewhere.

"Reel," I said, reaching up to his face. "Get me out."

"You could have broken bones. A neck injury. A spine injury."

I coughed another round, gasping for air in between spitting up blood.

"Screw it," Reel said, reaching under me. "This is going to hurt. Just hang on."

My leg screamed in pain as it was shifted around and banged into things. Uncle Mike tried to follow to brace the leg, but he wasn't able to keep up with Reel through all the debris. And Reel wasn't waiting for him. For the first time, I saw real fear flash across his face as he watched me struggle to breathe.

"Are you nuts?" Rod yelled.

"She can't breathe!" Reel yelled back.

"Shit. Get the backboard!"

"Is she okay?" a woman called out as I was moved out into the sunlight. "You saved my son, Tweedle. Thank you! You saved my son!"

I was laid on a backboard at the same time it was being lifted to a gurney. Everything around me was spinning. I could no longer pull a breath into my lungs, no matter how hard I tried. I looked up at Reel as he wiped tears from my cheeks. I didn't even know I was crying. I wondered whether he knew that he was crying too. I passed out.

Chapter Eighteen

"You should go home and get some sleep," Uncle Mike said.

He sounded close by, but my eyes refused to open.

"*You* should go home and get some sleep," Reel said.

"I'm family. If anyone's staying, it'll be me," Uncle Mike snapped. "Besides, you were the one who was supposed to be keeping an eye on her."

"I'm not likely to forget. But you're the one who didn't even know she was in danger, long before I got back into town."

"If you really cared about her, you'd quit your job and find something local."

"Like what? Construction? What exactly do you expect me to do?"

"Then find someone else!"

"Not happening, Mike. I already told you. I'm not waiting any longer. I've waited eight years. It's her choice now."

"What choice? To become a widow or a lonely wife whose husband is never home? Is that really the life you want for her?"

"You think she isn't lonely already? How many dates has she been on in the past eight years? How many times has she fallen in love?"

"She's dated!"

"Three times! And, she never went on a second date with any of them! I might not have been around, but I've kept an eye on her. I've always been here when she needed me."

"You'll break her heart," Uncle Mike whispered.

"I'd kill myself before I ever hurt her," Reel whispered.

I drifted back to sleep.

~*~*~

"I'm not leaving," Reel said.

"Me neither," Uncle Mike said.

"Both of you, *out!*" Aunt Carol ordered. "Go to the bar. Go home and shower. Go swim in the lake. I don't really care. You stink. You're scaring the staff. And I'm sick of the constant bickering. The doctors said she'll be fine, so *go!*"

I heard some huffing and puffing, followed by some shuffling of feet. A minute later, it was quiet in the room except for Aunt Carol's soft humming.

"Are they gone?" I asked. My voice was scratchy. I raised my arm to my throat, but I must have been on some good drugs because my hand came flying up at warp speed, and I smacked myself in the face.

Aunt Carol came over and held up a cup with a straw poking out the top. She gently helped me sit enough to drink before settling me back down. "They're going to be pissed when they find out that you woke as soon as they left. I swear they were having a standoff to see which one could sit the longest in those uncomfortable chairs."

"I woke up once before, but they were arguing. I decided I was too tired to deal with it, and I went back to sleep."

"Smart girl. They're both being alpha idiots."

"Alpha idiots," I repeated, grinning before remembering the bakery crash. "Samantha? The other customers? Was everyone else okay?"

"You were the only one hurt bad enough for an ambulance. One of the other customers needed stitches, and everyone had a few bruises except the baby and Bradley. I hear you launched Bradley like a football." Aunt Carol giggled.

"Good thing he doesn't weigh much."

"Tansey's been in and out. You know hospitals are hard for her, but she's stopped in twice a day since you were brought here."

"Call her and tell her I'm good, but she can keep her distance. I'll be home soon."

"I'll text her, but I don't think she'll listen." She tapped out a text message. "Tansey will need to see you awake with her own eyes."

"Why couldn't I breathe?"

"One of your lungs collapsed. They blew it back up, or whatever they do. You have a couple bruised ribs, some stitches, and you smashed the shit out of your leg. But nothing that won't heal."

"Mrs. Crookburn's car?"

"It was an accident. Mrs. Crookburn thought she was in reverse and didn't realize she had the accelerator pedal all the way to the floor. She's promised to never drive again."

"You mean that mailboxes will once again be safe in Pine Valley?"

"The hardware store already has big signs all over town that a new selection of mailboxes and posts will be available by tomorrow."

"What day is it?"

"Friday. They gave you the good drugs, so you'd sleep for a few days. They didn't want you moving around much."

I nodded, and Aunt Carol helped me take another drink of water before she started jetting around the room cleaning. She picked up trash, folded blankets, and then started dead-heading the flowers.

"Aunt Carol?"

"Hmm?"

"Did my mother come to check on me?"

"Not that I know of. I don't think your uncle or Reel would have let her near you if she did. She probably knows that."

"She really does hate me, doesn't she?"

"I don't think so. No. I think your mother just doesn't know how to love anyone other than herself," she sighed. "Your sister seems to have inherited the same trait. But I heard through the grapevine that you taught her not to mess with you," Aunt Carol winked.

"The lemon cake!" I chuckled, clutching my ribs as they protested. "I forgot."

"Betty Fergin was coming out of the beauty shop when your uncle was leading Darlene away. Betty took pictures of Darlene with her phone and sent them to me. I'm going to get one of them blown up and framed. Hang it over my toilet."

"Ooh. That's mean," I said, trying not to laugh.

"She deserves it," Aunt Carol said. "Besides, I need something for the wall in there, anyway. I think the yellow color of the lemon cake has a nice pop to it with Darlene's blue dress as the backdrop. It will go well with my towels."

"Remind me to never piss you off."

I looked around the room at all the flowers. I noticed the room was large with a full-size couch and two recliner chairs.

"How'd I get such a fancy room? My insurance isn't going to cover this. Hell, I'm not sure my insurance will cover anything."

"Reel had your room upgraded. I have no idea how much it was, but he wrote a check, and the administrator ran off in the other direction holding it in a death grip."

"I'll have to clean out my savings to pay him back."

"He doesn't expect you to. And your uncle doesn't know about it, so I'd keep it on the DL."

"Oh my God! You really are alive!" Tansey screeched from the doorway, throwing her purse and a teddy bear on the floor as she ran to me and covered my cheek with kisses. "Shit! You scared the hell out of me!"

"*You* were scared? I was the one running from a crazed Buick!"

"I assure you, the experience was much worse for me."

"Was that my teddy bear that you dumped on the floor?"

"Oh, yeah." She ran back and picked up her purse and the bear. "It's like the sixth stuffed animal

I've bought. I couldn't think of anything else to buy. You weren't awake so Klondike bars wouldn't work."

"Take the bear back for a refund and buy me a Klondike."

"Gladly."

"You really should work your way up to normal food before eating chocolate and ice cream," Aunt Carol said.

"Why?" Tansey and I asked at the same time.

Aunt Carol rolled her eyes and went back to freshening up the flowers.

~*~*~

Tansey snuck over to the corner store to buy Klondike bars, and after that, the news spread fast through Pine Valley that I was awake. My hospital room was crammed with friends, family, neighbors, customers, and even my mailman, which was a bit odd. And everyone brought Klondike bars. I doubted there was a single box of Klondikes for sale in the county.

Little Bradley stepped up beside the bed and started to cry when he saw my cast. But the tears quickly disappeared when Reel found a marker so he could sign it. Bradley proudly printed his name in big letters. His mother, Sarah, stepped over and kissed my cheek. She was too emotional to say anything, and I just nodded, looking back at the sweet little boy. I was glad I was able to get to him fast enough too.

"Alright, everyone," Aunt Carol spoke up. "I'm afraid visiting time is over. Our girl needs some rest.

And please take the Klondike bars with you. We don't have a freezer here, and she hasn't eaten solid food in days."

Everyone quickly signed my cast, said their good wishes, and departed. Only Tansey, Rod, Reel, Aunt Carol, and Uncle Mike remained.

"The rest of you need to go home too," I said. "I'm just going to be sleeping. There's no point in staying."

"Your accident might have been only an accident, but we still don't know who was trying to hurt you before that," Uncle Mike said.

"He's right. We'll need to set up shifts," Reel nodded.

"I've got the first shift then," Wayne said, stepping into the room.

"And just who the hell are you?" Uncle Mike demanded, standing to block Wayne's path.

"You must be the protective uncle," Wayne nodded. "Nice to officially meet you. I work with Ryan doing security. We also served together."

"I called Wayne because we need help keeping the girls safe while we figure out who's been trying to hurt Deanna."

"Smart. Be sure to tell me how much the bill is," Uncle Mike nodded.

"No bill, sir," Wayne said. "Most of us are on personal leave, taking a break after a big case. We're volunteering on this one. We owe Ryan a favor or two."

"It's weird to hear people call you Ryan," I said to Reel.

"Think how hard it would be for me to keep my professional image if they knew about the nickname."

"Holy shit," Wayne said. "Ryan knows how to smile." He shook his head. "Is it the pretty lady, or is it the nickname?"

"Shut it, Wayne," Reel said, chuckling.

"I'll let it go for now," Wayne said, nodding sideways at me. "I heard when I entered that it's time for this little lady to get some rest. Everyone can go home and sleep in their own beds. I'll stand guard outside the room."

"I appreciate it, but I don't know you," Uncle Mike said honestly.

"I do," Reel said. "I'd trust Wayne with Deanna's life. That said, I'd still feel better sleeping here on the couch while Wayne stands guard."

Uncle Mike wanted to argue, but one scolding look from Aunt Carol kept him from saying anything.

"I'll take Tansey home," Rod offered.

"But I drove," Tansey argued as Rod steered her toward the door.

"I don't care," Rod said.

"I'm not leaving Tweedle's car here. What if someone steals it?"

"No one in their right mind would steal Tweedle's car. Everyone in town knows it's hers."

"Someone who didn't have a car might," she argued, as they disappeared into the hall.

"Call us if you need anything," Uncle Mike said, kissing my forehead.

"He means it, and so do I," Aunt Carol said, kissing my cheek.

Aunt Carol weaved her arm through Uncle Mike's as they left.

"I'll be right outside the door. I'll warn you if any of the medical staff need to come in," Wayne said, stepping out and closing the door after him.

"Hey," Reel said, leaning over me. "You really okay? Do you need any pain pills? Anything?"

"I'm good. I'm just tired."

"Then go to sleep," he said, kissing my forehead.

My eyes drifted shut as he stroked my hair away from my face.

Chapter Nineteen

"I WANT OUT OF HERE," I snapped. "I'll sign whatever it takes, but I'm leaving. Even if I have to shoot my way out."

"Now there's a woman I can respect," Bridget said as she skipped into the room.

"Bridget, you're not helping," Reel grumbled.

Bridget winked at me.

"Miss Sullivan, you really need to stay at the hospital and rest for a few more days," the doctor explained.

Bridget and I both snorted.

"Let me guess," Bridget said, turning to me. "Nurses checking on you every two hours, doctors doing their rounds at 5:00, monitor alarms constantly going off."

"I'm exhausted. I want out."

"Doctor, does she need anything other than rest?" Bridget asked.

"No," he sighed. "She's healing well, and her lungs sound good."

"Then get the release papers. I'm kidnapping her in twenty minutes," Bridget said, grabbing the suitcase Aunt Carol had left in the corner of the room and setting it on the end of the bed.

"Don't tell anyone she's checking out," Reel ordered the doctor.

The doctor nodded and rushed out.

Bridget made a phone call. "Hey, Bones, Tweedle is being wheeled out in twenty." There was a pause before she spoke again. "I don't know. Just figure it out!" she snapped before hanging up. She rolled her eyes at the phone and stuffed it in her back pocket. "Do you want me or Ryan to help you get dressed?"

I blushed, unable to answer. Reel chuckled before walking out of the room.

"Ah," she said, opening the suitcase. "He hasn't seen your naked booty yet."

"Not since all of us went skinny-dipping when I was eight."

She helped me untie the back of the gown, then turned away while I put on a bra. Aunt Carol had packed a comfortable oversized flannel button-up shirt instead of a T-shirt, so I didn't have to raise my arms up over my head. My muscles were still sore.

A nurse came to remove the catheter and helped me get my underwear and shorts over my cast. The shorts were soft stretchy cotton and felt like pajama shorts. I glanced at the inside label and smiled. They were pajama shorts.

"That's an interesting outfit," Bridget said with one eyebrow cocked.

"I don't care what I look like. I just want to go home."

"Oh, I didn't say you could go home," Bridget said as the nurse left and Reel entered.

"Music to my ears," Reel said. "I thought you'd finally lost it, Bridget."

Bridget rolled her eyes. "I'm not stupid, but she's not going to get any rest here. Where can we take her? Do we need to move her out of town?"

"Wait, what?" I asked.

"She can stay at her uncle's house or my house. But if she stays at her uncle's, I'd be concerned with putting her aunt in danger."

"Why can't I go home?" I asked.

"To the house where someone broke in and left you a rattlesnake?" Bridget asked. "The house where someone broke a gas line, hoping you would die in an explosion?" She patted my arm like I was a child. "Don't be silly."

"It was only the two times," I muttered.

Reel walked to the other side of the bed and leaned over. "No. You can't stay at home."

"Fine. I'll stay with Tansey," I said, glaring while crossing my arms over my chest.

"Fine," Reel said, crossing his arms over his chest. "If you can make it up her two-story exterior staircase with that cast and the crutches, then I'll tell the security team that they have to stand outside, in the open, for days on end, protecting your ass."

"That's just mean."

"And you're being difficult for no reason," Reel said, grinning at me.

"Woah," Bridget said with wide eyes. "Wayne warned me that Ryan smiles around here, but I didn't believe it."

"It's a new thing he just started doing," I told her. "I think it's still in a trial phase for him. And around here, like it or not, he goes by Reel, not Ryan."

"Good to know." Bridget nodded. "Wait…" She pointed at Reel. "Isn't your brother's name Rod?"

"It has to do with fishing," Reel said, shaking his head. "Don't ask."

"Like one of the locals isn't going to offer up the story?" I said with a raised eyebrow.

"Do we have a location?" Wayne asked, strolling into the room.

Bridget and Reel both turned to look at me.

I smiled wide. "Yes. 4235 Birch Street."

Reel shook his head. "You're impossible."

"Whose house is that?" Bridget asked, seeing Reel's reaction.

"Her grandpa's house. Vince has Alzheimer's."

"Dementia, not Alzheimer's," I said. "Two birds, one stone. I can help keep an eye on Grandpa while everyone else keeps an eye on me. And the house is private with six bedrooms."

"Sold," Wayne said.

"Is there a pool?" Bridget asked, hopping up and down.

"Nope, sorry."

"Fine. We'll stay at your grandpa's. It'd be good to see the old coot again, even if he doesn't remember who I am."

"Let's roll," Wayne said, moving a wheelchair over to the bed.

Reel helped me off the bed and into the chair, carefully placing my leg into the leg-rest.

"I need my purse," I said, looking across the room to the stand.

"I can carry it," Bridget offered, retrieving the purse.

"No, thank you," I said, taking the purse.

I opened it up to confirm Aunt Carol had slid the revolver inside.

"You've got a gun?" Bridget asked.

"I borrowed it. Just in case."

"But she won't shoot anyone except in the foot, so she'll have time to run away," Reel said, rolling his eyes.

Bridget and I looked down at my broken leg.

"Maybe aim for the kneecap," Bridget said.

"Do you think that would give me enough time?"

We looked to Wayne and Reel for an answer, but they just shook their heads.

~*~*~

As they wheeled me down the hall, I heard loud clomping ahead. I leaned over to look around Wayne's large frame. I sighed loudly at the same time as Reel.

"You know her?" Wayne asked.

"Unfortunately," I muttered.

"Want me to get rid of her?" Bridget giggled.

"Yes, but she's my mother, so that's not very nice of me to say."

Wayne looked back at me surprised. Reel snorted.

"Mother, I was just leaving."

"No one told me you were being released today," she said, acting insulted to be kept out of the loop.

"I was unconscious for days, and you didn't care, so why would you care to know when I'm leaving?"

"Honestly, Deanna, you must learn to be a bit less self-involved. I have obligations. They don't change just because you got into a fender-bender."

"I was run over by a Buick."

"Whatever. I bought you flowers."

She tried to pass me the flowers, but Wayne intercepted. He inspected the miniature gift shop bouquet before passing them to me. I pulled the card but didn't take the flowers. The card was a standard get-well card, unsigned. How thoughtful.

"I don't want them," I said, tossing the card at my mother. "I'm done. I've been disappointed by you for the last time. Stay out of my life."

Wayne handed her back the small vase, and Reel steered the wheelchair around her. No one spoke until the elevator door closed.

"You okay?" Reel asked, with a firm hand on my shoulder.

"I'm a bit disappointed. I thought there would be a lot of fireworks when I finally ended it with her."

"Like how you ended it with your sister?"

"I don't know what you're talking about."

"Whenever she comes into town, people start loudly asking each other whether they can smell lemons. She runs off in the opposite direction."

Bridget and Wayne turned with raised eyebrows, but the elevator doors opened. They stepped in front of me again as they led us down a side hall. Wayne directed us through the kitchen cafeteria and out an employee-only exit where a black SUV was sitting with the engine running.

"Wayne, can you drive my truck? It's in the east lot," Reel asked, passing him the keys.

"As soon as you guys are safely off," Wayne nodded, taking the keys and turning his back to the SUV to survey the area.

Bridget opened the back door, and Reel lifted me up and into the SUV, shutting the door behind me. He opened the back latch of the SUV and tossed the wheelchair in before jogging to the other side of the SUV and sliding inside. Bridget was already in the front passenger seat, seatbelt on, and fidgeting with the radio stations.

"Let's move," Reel said, grabbing my hand.

Bones was behind the wheel and quickly maneuvered around the parking lot and down a deserted side street. He turned the radio off for the second time as he turned right, then down two blocks he turned left. At the next right, he shut the radio off for the third time, and Bridget looked around the seat at me and winked.

"It's clear," Bones said, reaching over to slap Bridget's hand as she reached for the radio. "Bridget, stop. We're on a job."

"Oh, and I suppose there's some rule about not listening to the radio?"

"Yes," Reel and Bones both answered.

"Oh," she pouted. She peeked back at me again. "I'm only a trainee."

"Barely even a trainee." Bones snorted. "Grady and Donovan haven't agreed to hire you yet."

"I'm sure Tweedle will give me a good reference," Bridget said.

I gave her a thumbs-up and laughed.

"Head four blocks south and then six blocks east," Reel said. "And thanks for staying in town, Bones."

"I owe you," Bones nodded in the rearview mirror. "And I find Tweedle entertaining." He winked in the mirror.

"Sorry for causing all this trouble."

"Not a problem," Bones said, looking over at Bridget. "I'm used to hanging out with women who get themselves in trouble."

Bridget whopped him in the arm. He laughed but rested an arm on the center console to fend her off if needed.

"You better call Tansey and your aunt," Reel whispered. "If they go to the hospital and find you gone, they'll worry."

"Not to mention Uncle Mike will be pissed."

"That too. I don't need another fight with him right now. Your aunt and uncle practically raised all of us on some level. But with you girls, he needs to cut the umbilical cord already."

"Should I tell him you said that?"

"Are you trying to get me killed?"

"You're afraid of my uncle?"

"Not afraid," Reel said. "More like respectful."

"Bullshit."

Call. Your. Aunt.

Bridget and Bones chuckled from the front seat, obviously listening to us. Reel sighed and leaned his head back into the headrest.

I called Aunt Carol, and she agreed to get ahold of Tansey and Uncle Mike. She would make sure Tansey had an escort over to my house to pick up some more clothes for me. She also offered to go grocery shopping to stock-up on food for Grandpa's house.

"That would be great but take the money out of my checking account. I don't want you or Uncle Mike paying for it," I said.

"But you're saving for that couch. I'd rather not spend that money."

"It's fine. Someone already bought the couch," I fake-glared at Reel. "Spend whatever's in there. I already paid my rent for the month."

"If you're sure," she said.

"Positive. Thanks, Aunt Carol."

We ended the call, and Bridget turned around in the seat to face me.

"I don't want to offend you or anything, but you don't have to empty your bank account."

"It's fine, really. Aunt Carol's a bargain shopper, and I get paid in two days."

"What she's trying to say is that she knows that Reel and I can afford to buy a grocery store's worth of groceries, and we wouldn't even miss the money," Bones said. "Bridget's already learned that it's not worth the energy trying to keep a scorecard of expenses going, especially with Reel."

"Why especially with you?" I asked Reel.

Reel smiled but didn't say anything.

"Because he hasn't taken much time off since he started. I doubt he's spent a dime more than food or rent since he got out of the service."

"Well, he spent a ton of money on Friday. Almost three grand."

They all laughed.

"That's a new suit for Bones," Bridget said, rolling her eyes.

Reel looked over at me. "Until I bought the house, I saved everything I made. I paid cash for the house, and it didn't even dent my account. Don't drive yourself into bankruptcy worrying about us."

I pouted, thinking that I was the epic underdog. I hadn't traveled like they had. I didn't make much money. And now I was the one putting everyone in danger and couldn't even afford to cover the extra expenses.

"I'm looking forward to eating baked goods for the next few days," Reel said, nudging me with his shoulder. "We're going to be eating like royalty. My mouth is watering just thinking about biscuits for breakfast, followed by the cream puffs for midmorning, homemade pies for lunch, cookies for an afternoon snack, garlic cheese bread or French bread with dinner, and chocolate eclairs for dessert."

"And forty-five pounds later," I said, laughing.

"Not for me," Reel said, slapping his waistline.

"Yeah, that's what Uncle Mike used to say."

"You wouldn't love me if I got fat?" he joked.

"Donovan would fire your ass," Bones said, chuckling.

Reel continued to grin at me as I tried to imagine him being overweight.

"You can't see it, can you?"

"No." I shook my head. "Maybe it's the perfect hair. Maybe when you start to lose the hair, I'll be able to imagine you with a big gut."

"I'm not going to lose my hair," he said.

"Your father has a combover."

"He lost his hair because of the alcohol, though."

Bridget turned in her seat and looked at me, then at Reel.

"Right?" Reel asked, sliding a hand through his thick dirty-blond hair.

"Alcohol can contribute to hair loss," I said, nodding along. "Sure."

He exhaled a big breath, relaxing. Bridget quickly turned to face forward again, but I could see her shoulders shake as she silently laughed.

"The house at the end of the road, the big colonial, is my grandpa's," I directed Bones.

"The house hasn't been maintained. The yard either," Reel said, leaning forward in his seat.

"It looks worse each time I visit. I keep calling the damn attorney, but he's not calling me back. I'm worried that the medical bills are depleting Grandpa's accounts. I hope he doesn't have to sell the house."

"I'll make a few calls and see what's what," Reel promised before slipping out of the SUV and getting out the wheelchair.

I opened the door on my side, but when Reel came around, Bones was carrying the wheelchair, and Reel lifted me out of the seat.

"What are you doing?" I asked startled.

"Carrying you up the front porch."

"But the ramp is still out back, from when Grandma needed it. Surely you remember; you helped build it."

"I remember," Reel said and walked across the drive to the front porch.

"You're going to hurt yourself. I weigh too much."

"I bet Reel can bench-press twice your weight," Bridget said. "Look, his muscles aren't even flinching."

Sure enough, I looked, and Reel's biceps seemed completely relaxed. He smiled as he climbed the stairs, two at a time.

Grandpa abruptly answered the door before we knocked. He was wearing a pair of pink boxers and an oversized Metallica T-shirt. Both must have come from the spare bedroom where I kept some clothes.

The final touch was his old-fashioned tube socks with the thick red stripe at the top. The socks were stretched nearly to his knees.

"Vince," Reel nodded, carrying me past Grandpa and into the house.

"Reel," Grandpa said. "I was hoping you'd visit. But you shouldn't have brought Tweedle with you. It's not safe."

Everyone froze and looked at Grandpa.

"Why isn't it safe, Vince?" Reel asked, still holding me.

"Well, the Martians, of course," Grandpa snapped, before stomping up the main staircase.

"He's not supposed to go upstairs anymore. Where the hell is his nurse?" I grumbled, as Reel settled me in the wheelchair.

"I'll go check on him and see whether I can get him to come back downstairs."

"I'll look for the nurse," Bridget said, wandering off toward the kitchen.

"I'll stay with you until one of them comes back," Bones offered.

"I have my gun. I promise to shoot someone in at least a kneecap if they try to hurt me. I'd rather you walk through and make sure all the first-floor windows and doors are locked before someone has a chance to figure out where we went. Or, worse, my grandpa decides to run away."

"The kneecap?"

"Don't ask," I sighed.

I pulled the gun out of my purse, resting it on my lap. Bones nodded and started with the front door, following along the wall and locking all the windows and patio doors. From the living room, he entered my grandpa's office. When he came out again, he shook his head but didn't say anything. He walked back to the foyer and turned down the hall.

I was curious, so I rolled my chair to the office doorway. Grandpa's office, always immaculate without a scrap of paper out of place, furniture shining so bright it would blind you, was utter chaos. Papers littered the desk and floor. Filing cabinets were emptied with the drawers still open. A desk lamp lay shattered on the floor.

"What the hell?" I said to myself.

"How long has it been since you've been in the office?" Reel whispered from behind me.

"I was in here Tuesday. I spent the day cleaning the house. Everything was perfect when I left."

"Were you upstairs?"

"No." I shook my head. "I was too exhausted by the time I finished downstairs to see what kind of mess was up there. Why?"

"Dee," Reel said, walking around the chair and squatting in front of me. "It looks like someone's been taking things from the house. Furniture, paintings, your grandmother's jewelry."

"No," I said, not wanting to believe it. "But we hired a nurse."

"I found the nurse," Bridget said, walking into the office and looking around. "She's passed out drunk in one of the upstairs bedrooms."

"Either drag her down here, or I swear I'll crawl up the stairs to get her myself."

"Give me a minute," Bridget said, turning out of the room.

"I think we need to call the lawyer again," Reel said.

I nodded and pointed to the rolodex laying on the floor. "Scott Barons."

As expected, when Reel called the phone number, he was prompted to leave a message.

He did. A very stern message.

Next, he made another call, asking whoever had answered to run a background on Scott Barons.

I waited until he hung up before saying, "He's been my grandpa's lawyer for decades."

"But your grandpa used to be a man whom most feared and everyone else respected enough to never cross."

I nodded my agreement but still hoped that whatever was going on, Scott Barons wasn't involved.

A loud scream echoed from upstairs, and Grandpa came running down the stairs.

"I didn't do it. I didn't hurt anybody," he said, shaking in fear, his eyes begging me to believe him.

"It's okay, Vince," Reel said. "A friend of ours was just waking up your nurse. Your granddaughter wants to have a word with her."

"Oh," Grandpa said, trying to understand. He scratched his head, thinking hard.

When Bridget dragged the alcohol-reeking, soaking-wet nurse into the living room, Grandpa ran off toward the kitchen. Bridget had either dumped a bucket of water on the woman or dunked her in a lake. Water was running off her like it was raining, pooling around her.

"What the hell is going on around here?" I yelled at the woman.

"Vince was taking his nap, so I took one too," she tried to explain as she rubbed her eyes, smearing her mascara across her face.

"You're drunk. And the house is a disaster. And my grandpa is running around unmonitored."

"You fired me," she said, shrugging. "It's not my job anymore."

"What do you mean you were fired? I didn't fire you. Who told you that?"

"Yesterday the man in the fancy suit showed up. He said I no longer worked here and to pack up and leave. Then he went into the office and started going through all the papers. Made a real mess of things, too."

"What man in a suit? What was his name?"

"I put the card in the drawer." She crossed to the entranceway table.

I rolled my chair over so I could watch her as she opened the drawer.

"It's gone," she said, pulling the drawer all the way out and looking in the empty cubby. "But who would have taken it?"

"Do you remember his name?"

She shook her head no.

"You said 'the man in the fancy suit,'" Bridget interrupted. "Not 'some man' in a suit. Had you met him before?"

"Sure," she said. "He started coming around a few months ago. That's when I put his card in the drawer. At first, he'd just walk through the house and check on Vince, said he was checking to make sure that everything was in order. About a month ago, he showed up with some moving guys and had them haul out some of the upstairs furniture. He told me he was liquidating some things to cover Vince's new medicine."

"What new medicine? Grandpa isn't on any new medicine."

"The yellow pills," the nurse said. "He gave me a bottle of pills and told me to give them to Vince three times a day. I tried to look them up, but he said they were from a medical trial and you already signed off. He showed me the form with your signature."

I handed Reel my gun and dumped the contents of my purse into my lap. I barely heard the knock at the front door as I pulled my phone out and called my grandpa's doctor. My hand shook as the phone rang on the other end. I watched Wayne and Aunt Carol walk through the door as Bones held it open for them.

I felt Reel's hands rub back and forth on my shoulders. I took a deep breath just as the receptionist answered.

"Yes, I need to speak to Dr. Wilson," I said.

"He's with a patient right now. Can I take a message?"

"No. It's Deanna Sullivan calling regarding my grandpa. Please interrupt him and tell him it's an emergency."

"I can wait for him to come out if you like and see if he can take your call."

"Go pound on the damn door and get him on the phone!"

I was promptly put on hold, but it didn't last long.

"Tweedle?" Dr. Wilson answered.

"Dr. Wilson, did you prescribe my grandpa new medication without speaking to me?"

"No. I couldn't if I wanted to. You have his medical proxy."

"Someone showed up and told the nurse to start giving him some type of yellow pill."

"I don't know anything about yellow pills. Is he okay?"

"No. I thought his dementia was accelerating. But what if it was from the drugs?"

"I'll cancel my appointments and be there as quick as I can. Try to track down those pills."

I nodded but couldn't say anything before he disconnected the line.

"Dee," Reel whispered from beside me.

"No," I said, shaking my head. I couldn't afford to break down and cry. My grandpa needed me. "Aunt Carol, can you get Uncle Mike over here?"

She nodded and dug out her phone. The groceries that Wayne had helped her carry inside were already forgotten. Looking back at my own phone, I took a deep breath and called my mother.

"Why are you calling me? I thought you said you never wanted to see me again," my mother said, by way of answering.

"I just called to apologize, Mother. It's been a rough few days, and they had me on all these drugs. I'm sorry I was acting so selfish. I was hoping you could join me for lunch at my grandpa's house. We're having filet mignon for lunch."

I saw Reel roll his eyes and heard Aunt Carol choke on a snort.

"Well, that does sound lovely. I suppose I could squeeze you in. What time?"

"An hour? Does that work?"

"Have I taught you nothing? Do you know how rude it is to invite someone for dinner on such short notice? Oh, never mind. You will never understand. I'll be there. Tell the cook that I like mine cooked to medium. And some red wine would be lovely," she said, before disconnecting.

I stared at the phone.

"It's not her, is it?" Reel asked, studying my face.

"She said to have the cook fix her steak to medium and to pull a bottle of red wine."

"I was in the wine cellar. It's almost empty," Bones said.

"So it's not her, right?" I asked Reel.

"It doesn't hurt to still question her. Maybe she hired someone to drug your grandpa, but they are raiding the house without her knowledge."

"Maybe," I nodded.

"Is Vince alright?" Aunt Carol asked.

"He's running around saying it's dangerous, that the Martians are coming. He's wearing my pink boxers."

"Oh dear. Which direction did he go?"

"Toward the kitchen," Reel answered.

Wayne followed Aunt Carol to the kitchen, carrying the groceries.

Reel's phone rang, and he stepped away to answer it.

Bridget leaned down in front of me and grabbed my hand. "Don't do that."

"Don't do what?"

"Blame yourself. You are not at fault. You didn't know."

"He's my grandpa," I said, my lower lip trembling.

"But playing the blame game will make you an easy target."

"Who should I blame? I was the one responsible for him," I said, glaring back at her.

"You tell us who's to blame," she said. "You're the one who knows everyone. Figure it out. That's how you protect your grandpa."

I nodded but didn't say anything.

"That was the background check on the lawyer, Scott Barons," Reel said. "He died three months ago."

"What? Why wasn't I notified?"

"Apparently, all the clients were notified by letter. They must've sent the letter to Vince directly."

"Is your uncle a big, pissed-off cop?" Bones asked, looking through the sidelight window.

A loud banging on the front door echoed through the foyer.

"Yup," I answered.

Bones opened the door, and Uncle Mike barreled past him straight to me.

"Are you okay? Carol called and said to get over here. She wouldn't tell me why."

"Someone's trying to hurt Grandpa and steal his money." My lower lip started to tremble, and I looked down, trying to prevent the tears.

"What?" Uncle Mike yelled.

"Move out of the way," Reel ordered, as he lifted me out of the wheelchair.

He held me close as I wrapped my arms around him. He sat us on the couch and extended my leg cast onto the next cushion.

"It's going to be okay, Deanna," he whispered into my hair as he rocked me back and forth. "I'm here."

I clutched him tighter, afraid that he'd vanish if I didn't. I wasn't sure how much more I could handle. I was a simple baker, living in a simple town. The craziness surrounding me seemed unreal.

Chapter Twenty

"Your mother just pulled up," Uncle Mike said, shaking my shoulder gently. "How do you want to handle this?"

During my mini-cry fit, I must have dozed off. Releasing my grip on Reel, I turned back to the room. At some point Tansey and Rod had arrived, and Tansey sat dutifully on the floor, waiting to see if I needed her. I reached down and grasped her hand. She was crying too. Rod sat on the floor behind her, with a comforting arm wrapped around her.

"What happened to the nurse?"

"I questioned her and then had her transported to the precinct," Uncle Mike answered.

"Good. I need everyone to go into the kitchen. I need to face my mother alone," I said, turning and moving my cast under the coffee table so I could face forward on the couch. "Bridget, can you pretend to be the nurse and let her inside?"

"I like that," Bones said to Bridget. "Later you can pretend to be my nurse."

"Only in your dreams," she said, walloping him in the gut before she turned to me. "For you, I'll play nurse or maid or whatever. But won't she recognize me from the hospital?"

"My mother would have considered you beneath her attention. If you had a green wart growing off the end of your nose, she wouldn't have noticed."

"My mother's just as bad," Bridget said, giggling.

Everyone except Bridget, Uncle Mike, and Reel moved toward the kitchen. Bridget moved to wait by the front door.

"I think one of us should stay," Uncle Mike said.

"No," I shook my head. "She won't drop her guard with either of you in the room. I need to talk to her alone."

"She's right. I don't like it, but she's right," Reel said. "We're not going to the other side of the house, though. Mike and I will be in Vince's office. She won't see us, but we will be able to hear everything."

"Fine but hurry up."

"Ten seconds," Bridget called as they both hurried into the den.

When the doorbell rang, Bridget winked at me before answering.

"Mrs. Sullivan?" Bridget said in a horrid imitation of a British accent. "Ms. Deanna Sullivan is waiting for you in the main living room. Please come in."

Bridget stepped back and waved her arm with a great flourish in my direction. I had a hard time watching her without laughing. Mother didn't even look at Bridget as she raised her head and walked into the living room like she owned every square inch of the place.

"Deanna," Mother nodded at me. "The lawn is atrocious. Your grandpa needs to hire a new landscaping company."

"I'll be sure to mention it. Please, have a seat. Lunch will be a few more minutes."

"Is Vince joining us?"

"No. He was feeling tired and went to rest."

"Good," mother said, taking a seat in the Queen Anne chair. "That man drones on about the most useless things."

My grandpa in his heyday could talk about finances from sunup to sundown. I agreed it could be a bit boring to listen to, but it was far from useless.

"Would you like some tea, ma'am?" Bridget asked me in her fake accent.

"Yes, please," I said, trying to hid my smirk. "Mother?"

"I'll have a glass of chardonnay. One of the better bottles, please," my mother said, addressing me, not sparing a glance at Bridget.

Bridget rolled her eyes and turned toward the kitchen.

"I'm glad you could join me on such short notice. I was hoping to ask you some questions."

"What sort of questions?"

"About Grandpa's lawyer," I sighed. "I keep trying to convince him he should get a new attorney."

"Is he still with that bore? Oh, what's his name," she said, snapping her fingers.

"Barons?"

"Yes, that's it. Scott Barons out of Cooper City. He hit on me after your father left us, you know. If he'd had more money, I might have considered it, but thankfully he didn't. He yapped nonstop about fraudulent tax filings."

"Why was he speaking to you about tax filings?"

"Oh, your grandpa insisted that I use him to file my taxes after your father took off. I never did understand whatever Mr. Barons was saying. I told him to handle the matter, and I signed the documents when he brought them to me a month later."

"Were you trying to commit fraud?"

"I really don't remember what the situation was, Deanna. I don't waste my energy paying attention to those types of things," she said, inspecting her manicure. "Is that really the question you wanted to ask?"

"No. I wanted to know if you were stealing from Grandpa."

"What on Earth are you talking about?" she asked, standing up.

"Stealing. Oh, and attempted murder, I suppose. Are you involved?"

"Did your grandpa accuse me of this? I know we don't see eye to eye, but I'd never be stupid enough to betray him. I learned that lesson soon after you were born."

"What do you mean?"

"Well, the checks of course," she said, looking around the room.

"What checks? Does Grandpa send you money?"

"It's really a private matter between your grandpa and me," she insisted, realizing that I didn't know what she was talking about.

"Well, I'm in charge of his estate now, so you can either tell me or grandpa's lawyer can," I said.

"I'd be more likely to maintain the arrangement if you admitted everything openly, though."

"It's really no big deal," she said as she twisted her ring nervously. "Your grandpa found out that Darlene wasn't your father's child and that I tricked your father into marrying me. But by then, I was pregnant with you. After you were born, your grandpa had a paternity test done to confirm it. He agreed to send me a monthly payment if I never told anyone that Darlene wasn't a Sullivan."

"Does Darlene know?"

"Of course not." She shook her head. "I wasn't even allowed to tell your father."

"And after all these years, you're still getting paid?"

"It was a lifelong commitment," she snapped.

"What did you mean that you learned never to cross Grandpa?"

"He cut me off for a few years after your father left." She shrugged. "He said I wasn't using the checks for what he deemed appropriate. He stopped sending me the money and paid the bills directly. He even had his housekeeper buy my groceries. It was so embarrassing. I couldn't even afford a salon haircut for two whole years."

"Oh dear," I faked empathy.

"Yes, I know. Now enough of this nonsense. I'm famished. Is lunch ready? And where did that harpy go to get me the chardonnay?"

"There's no lunch Mother. I needed information, and if I would have just asked you, you wouldn't have come."

"No filet mignon? Are you sure?"

"I'm sure."

Mother's face shifted to something between a pout and disdain. "And are you going to resume sending the monthly payments?"

"They stopped?"

"Yes," she said surprised. "I assumed your grandpa was cross with me and when you called, I was hoping he had changed his mind."

"His lawyer died."

"The boring guy?"

"Yes, Scott Barons."

"Yes, right. So why didn't your grandpa set up the payments with his new attorney?"

"No one knew the lawyer died. Unless you did."

"Why on earth would I have known that? Really, Deanna, you need to stop mixing socially with the common folks around here. You're no longer making sense."

"I'll look into the payments, but no promises." I moved to stand but remembered my broken leg. "You'll have to show yourself out, Mother. With my broken leg, I'm not that mobile."

"That's poor manners, Deanna. I taught you better than that," Mother snapped, exiting the room and showing herself out the front door.

As her tires peeled out of the driveway everyone reappeared.

"Did she really say you were lacking in manners for not being able to walk her to the door?" Bridget giggled.

"She sure did," I said. "What was the fake accent all about?"

"What? I thought it was pretty good."

"Why would you think someone would have a British employee around these parts?" Reel asked while he and Uncle Mike chuckled, shaking their heads.

"Well, I don't know," Bridget said. "It's a fancy old house."

"It's a colonial," Bones said.

"Whatever," she said, rolling her eyes.

"Dr. Wilson arrived," Bones said, changing the subject. "We had him enter through the kitchen door. He and your aunt are with your grandpa now. And we found some of the yellow pills to show the doctor."

"Good. How's Grandpa doing?"

Tansey shrugged. "He's still saying the Martians are dangerous. But Dr. Wilson gave him a light sedative, so he's running around less."

I nodded, looking toward the front windows. Reel sat down beside me and rested a hand on my knee.

"Is your mother involved?" Tansey asked.

"No," I said, shaking my head. "She's still trying to stay on Grandpa's good side. She doesn't even know about his condition."

"What about your sister?" Rod asked.

I shook my head no. "Do you know why I got nicknamed Tweedle-Dee?" I asked, looking at Rod.

"No clue, actually," he said, placing his hands on his hips and turning his head as if trying to think it out.

"Because I was Tweedle-Dee and Darlene was Tweedle-Dumbass," I answered, pointing at Uncle Mike.

Uncle Mike's face turned pink. "What? I never said it in front of her. Or anyone else except for you and Tansey."

"Isn't she your niece too?" Bridget asked Uncle Mike.

"And, my sister is my sister, but that doesn't mean she's not a bitch," Uncle Mike said.

"The point is, Darlene isn't smart enough to work a con like this. She's too greedy and can't keep a secret to save her own ass. The whole town would've known about it."

"She's right," Tansey said. "Darlene got hammered Saturday night and admitted to one of her slutty friends that she made out with Eric Mickers in the bathroom. She said it loud enough for everyone to hear, including Eric's girlfriend."

"That wasn't the best part." Rod laughed. "It wasn't *Eric* she made out with."

We all turned to Rod and waited for the punchline.

"It was his dad. She was too drunk to tell them apart."

"Noooo," Tansey squealed.

"Afraid so. Eric's stuck between throwing his dad under the bus for the crime or letting his girlfriend think he cheated on her."

"You men are so stupid," Tansey said, pulling her phone out of her back pocket. She called Eric's girlfriend and explained that it wasn't Eric who played around with Darlene but that no one wanted to rat out the other guy because he was married. She said a few *uh-huhs* before hanging up. "Eric has a girlfriend again."

"Just like that?" Rod asked.

"Well, she wouldn't have believed you or Eric, but she knows I have no reason to lie to her."

"While this is all very entertaining, can we get back to the real crimes happening in this town?" Uncle Mike complained.

"I can't think of anyone else," I said.

"Who stands to inherit if your grandpa dies?" Bones asked.

"I have no idea what his will says. I never worried about it. He could be giving it all to charity for all I know."

"We need to find his will," Reel said.

"He wouldn't keep it here," I said, shaking my head.

"What about a safe deposit box?" Bones asked.

"No. Grandpa was too cheap to rent one. I tried to convince him once that they'd give him one for free at his bank, but he said he didn't trust bankers."

"Wasn't he a banker?" Rod asked.

"No, he was a financial adviser. He hated it when someone referred to him as a banker."

"Where would his will be then? With the dead lawyer?" Uncle Mike asked.

"No," I said. "With his best friend, the other lawyer."

"Bingo," Reel said, smiling as he leaned back on the couch.

"Tucker?" Rod asked.

I pulled my phone and called Tucker.

Tucker was a farmer and weekend coon hunter, who also happened to be a great lawyer. He and my grandpa grew up together, running wild and stirring up trouble. Later in life, when my grandpa needed to hire a full-time attorney, he asked Tucker to take the job, but Tucker declined. He didn't want their friendship damaged by business. Tucker also didn't want to spend too much time in a suit, and Grandpa would've insisted he wear one.

"Who's this?" Tucker said, answering the call.

"It's Tweedle. You got a minute, Tucker?"

"Not really. I'm still trying to clean up the mess you made from your last visit."

"Sorry about that. But I need your help. I have a feeling that someone's searching for Grandpa's will. I'm trying to figure out who that someone is and why they'd be looking for it. I also have a feeling you can get your hands on that will."

"Maybe," Tucker said. "What's your grandpa say about all this?"

"He's not making much sense at the moment, being that someone tried to kill him by switching his meds. Dr. Wilson is with him now. But his regular lawyer died a few months back, and someone has been pretending to be in charge of the estate and coming over and stealing from the house."

"I'll be over as soon as I can. Loretta went back to her place for a few days, so it may take me awhile to find a pair of pants," Tucker said before hanging up.

"He's on his way over."

"He'll put on pants, right?" Uncle Mike asked.

"He said he'd look for them. Your guess is as good as mine on what happens if he can't find them."

"Tweedle," Dr. Wilson said, walking into the living room. "I think your grandpa should be admitted to the hospital. I'd like to get him on an IV and monitor his vitals."

"It's not safe," I said, shaking my head. "I don't know who's trying to hurt him."

Reel stood and pulled his wallet, handing a card to Aunt Carol. "Call that admin lady at the hospital and tell her I'll pay for whatever Dr. Wilson says Vince needs to be delivered here at the house."

"Reel, I can't let you pay," I said.

"No offense, Dee, but it's not up to you. Your grandpa set up my financial accounts and helped me manage them for years. Your grandmother taught me how to build go-karts and how to fistfight. Your grandpa might not be my blood relative, but he's my family too."

"Your grandpa taught me how to fix cars," Rod said, nodding.

"Grandma taught me how to make a martini," Tansey said, grinning. "And Grandpa paid for my art classes." She pointed to one of her earlier oil paintings that hung on the wall.

I understood what they were saying. My grandparents were generous people who shared their time with all of us as we grew up. But I still felt helpless, and I hated the feeling. I leaned over, resting my head in my hands.

"You need to sleep," Reel said, sitting back down and pulling me over to lean into him. "You just got out of the hospital this morning."

"I have to talk to Tucker when he gets here."

"She's right," Uncle Mike said. "That old coot is particular about client-privileged information. He won't talk to any of the rest of us about the estate."

I tried to stay awake. I really did. But my eyes slipped closed for just a minute as everyone's voices drifted away.

Chapter Twenty-One

I woke to the sound of snoring. A lot of snoring. Opening my eyes, the first thing I saw was Bridget sitting on the floor in front of me, bouncing.

Yes, bouncing. Like a little kid waiting for their parents to wake on Christmas morning. "Finally," she said. "I'm so bored. I thought this security stuff would be fun, but so far it's just a bunch of waiting around for something to happen."

"You don't seem like the bodyguard type," I said, yawning.

Bridget shrugged. "Thought I'd give it a spin. Donovan and Grady said they'd consider letting me join the training program if I did well shadowing on this job. But it's not shaping up to be all that exciting. I think working retail is a lot more entertaining."

I looked beside me to find Reel sleeping with his head tilted back, snoring. Looking to my other side, Uncle Mike was sleeping in a similar position. Across the room, Grandpa slept in a hospital bed. On both sides of him were recliner chairs, tilted back, occupied by Wayne and Tucker. Tucker had three toes sticking out of his ripped sock, but I was glad to see he was wearing pants.

"Help me up," I whispered.

Bridget soundlessly moved the coffee table over and handed me a crutch before pulling me up from the couch. From there, I followed her into the kitchen.

"Where is everyone?"

"Bones is outside patrolling the yard. *Boring.* Rod is out mowing the lawn. Aunt Carol and Tansey are in your grandpa's den, trying to sort all the papers and get them back where they belong."

"What have you been doing?"

"I gave myself a pedicure and cleaned one of the upstairs bedrooms for me to sleep in tonight. But then I didn't feel like cleaning anymore."

"Why didn't anyone wake me when Tucker got here?"

"They were going to, but then Tucker said he could use a nap too," she said, shrugging. "Do you want to go do something?"

"Like what?"

"We could go dancing."

I looked down at my leg in its big white cast.

"Right," she said, looking at my leg. "It's too early in the day, anyway. Maybe we should go to that dead lawyer guy's office and break in to get your grandpa's files!"

"Hate to break this to you, Bridget, but I wasn't too skilled at the B&E stuff before I broke my leg."

"I'll go," Tucker said, walking a bow-legged strut into the kitchen. "I made a few phone calls and couldn't find anyone in charge of getting us the papers the legal way. Besides, it's been a while since I broke in anywhere. Sounds like a hoot."

"But I need to talk to you about Grandpa's will," I said.

"Best wait on that until your grandpa wakes and we see whether he's regained his senses."

"Sweet." Bridget bounced. "I'll go get my supplies!" Bridget ran up the back stairs two at a time.

"Are you really taking her to break into that office?"

"Shucks, why not? If we get caught, I can talk my way out of it. Besides, I watched that minx snitch five wallets earlier with no one the wiser. She's good."

"She stole everyone's wallets?"

"I wouldn't say stole," Tucker said, chuckling. "More like relocated them. They're in the big vase in the foyer."

"Why would she do that?"

"Practice, I suppose." Tucker shrugged. "She didn't get mine though." He grinned, slapping his back pocket. His grin faded, and he used both hands to pat down his pockets. "Little minx!" he grumbled, walking back out.

I saw a crockpot on the counter and got out a bowl. I knew it was Aunt Carol's chili simmering in there before I pulled off the lid. I looked for bread but didn't find any. I sat and ate the chili without it.

"Good, you're eating," Aunt Carol said, carrying a garbage bag into the kitchen. "How was your nap?"

I looked up at the clock. "Long. Was I really out for three hours?"

"Everyone else was just as tired," Aunt Carol nodded. "And Dr. Wilson sedated your grandpa so he'll be asleep the rest of the night. He said we'd have to wait for the drugs to wear off to see what his mental state is like."

"I feel guilty."

"No reason to," Aunt Carol said, shaking her head. "If your grandpa had given you the information you needed to handle things, then he wouldn't have found himself in this position. But he decided to keep you in the dark and let his lawyer handle everything."

The kitchen door swung open, and Loretta walked in, slamming her purse on the counter. "How come I wasn't invited to the party?"

"You are always welcome, no invitation needed." I accepted her open-arm hug.

Bridget bounced back down the stairs wearing black heeled boots, tight black pants, a black V-neck top and carrying a small black backpack. Bones entered the kitchen from the porch door right as she jumped off the last step in a bouncy hop.

"No," Bones ordered, giving her a stare down.

"I wasn't asking for your permission," she said, skipping out to the foyer.

Bones sighed before glancing at me sideways. "Is she going to get arrested?"

I shrugged. I had no idea.

"Is she going by herself?"

"Nope. Tucker agreed to take her."

"The hillbilly?"

"The hillbilly attorney," I corrected.

"What's the gig?" Loretta asked, curious.

"B&E at a lawyer's office," I answered.

"It will be fine," Loretta said, waving off Bones' concern. "If they get caught, I give Tucker fifty-fifty odds of talking his way out of it. If that don't work, the old coot has plenty of money to bail them out."

Bones shook his head. "Is there more chili?"

"Of course," Aunt Carol said, filling a bowl to the brim. "Would you like a glass of milk with it?"

"Yes, ma'am. That would be great."

Bones was a bad boy in black leather with long black hair. Sitting next to him eating chili while he drank a tall glass of milk was, well, *weird*.

"Is there any bread?" Bones asked.

"No, sorry," Aunt Carol said. "With Tweedle always baking, I haven't bought bread in years. I didn't even think about it."

"If you get everything out for me, I can bake some bread. As long as I stand in one place, I should be okay."

Loretta helped Aunt Carol pull ingredients and dishes, stacking them next to me. I balanced on one leg, measuring the flour.

"How long do I have to wear this cast, anyway?"

"I have no idea, dear," Aunt Carol said, pulling supplies faster.

Loretta looked at me, and we both raised an eyebrow at Aunt Carol.

"Aunt Carol, what aren't you telling me?"

"I need to go check on Tansey. She was expecting me to come right back." Aunt Carol swung through the door and was gone.

"She's not very good at lying," Bones said, chuckling as he scooped another spoonful of chili.

"Ha, that woman amazes me." Loretta chuckled, shaking her head. "She has the best poker face in town but can't look her own niece in the eye when something sly is going on."

"Bones, can I borrow your phone?" I asked.

Bones slid his cell phone across the countertop toward me. I called information, having the call connected to Dr. Wilson's house phone.

"Hello," Dr. Wilson answered.

"Dr. Wilson, sorry to bother you again. I was wondering whether you could get the medical information on my leg and then call me back. I have a feeling I'm not getting the whole story."

He asked me a few questions regarding my doctor and then said he'd call back as soon as he could. Pine Valley was a small town, but the hospital was centrally located between several other towns and had a large staff. Dr. Wilson's practice was a mix between a walk-in clinic and house calls, so he seldom had the need to go to the hospital.

Bones' phone rang less than five minutes later.

"You're going to be pissed," Dr. Wilson said with a sigh.

"It's not broken, is it?"

"It was twisted and bruised badly, but it's not broken. You don't need that cast, but I figure you already know that. From what I could gather, the only thing that Reel and your uncle agreed on while you were in the hospital was to put a cast on your leg so they could keep an eye on you."

"Bastards."

"They love you."

"Bastards." It was worth mentioning a second time.

"If you can get to my office sometime this week, I'll get it cut off for you."

"I'll take care of it. Thanks, Dr. Wilson."

We both disconnected, and I slid the phone back to Bones.

"They didn't," Bones said, pocking his phone.

"Oh, yes, they did."

"Oh mercy, those boys better run," Loretta said, grinning.

Turning, I threw open the back door and walked peg-legged onto the porch and down the stairs.

"Where are we going?" Bones asked, jogging to catch up with me.

"To the woodshed."

The woodshed was really my grandpa's woodworking and mechanics room. It was also where the landscaping equipment was stored.

Rod was shutting down the riding lawn mower when I arrived. "Why are you walking on that leg?"

"Because my uncle and your brother faked how bad the injury was. I don't even need the damn cast!"

Rod laughed.

"It's not funny!"

"It kind of is. They're such control freaks when it comes to you."

"I need to cut this damn thing off. Where's that small spinning saw thingy?" I asked as I opened the door to the woodworking room.

"Since you just called it a spinning saw thingy, why don't you let me cut the cast off for you." Rod found the tool in question and cut a shallow line down both sides before pulling it open.

"Thanks," I said, pulling my leg out. Except for the massive purple bruises, the leg seemed to be in one piece. I tested standing on it. My muscles were sore, but overall it seemed fine. "Bastards."

"That's the third time she's called them bastards. Should we be worried?" Bones asked.

"Nah," Rod shook his head. "She won't hurt them. But she'll get even."

"Nothing wrong with that," Bones said.

I noticed a blanket laying on the floor in the corner. It looked like one of my grandmother's crocheted blankets. *What in the world would it be doing out here?*

I walked over, spotting the homeless teenager hiding on the other side of the metal cabinet.

Spooked, he darted for the far door, but Bones was faster, grabbing him and pinning him off his feet against the wall.

"Whoa!" I yelled. "Everyone, settle down."

"What are you doing in here?" Bones asked, getting in the kid's face.

"He was living in here," I said after looking at the meager belongings piled in the corner. "Release him, Bones."

"No," Bones said.

"I wasn't asking. *Release him,*" I said, walking up to stand beside him. "He's just a kid."

Bones lowered the teen to the floor but still held onto his shirt.

I rolled my eyes. "Okay, kid. It's time to come out of hiding. I can't let you live in a shed. I won't turn you in, but we can do better than this."

The kid's eyes darted from me to Bones, then over to Rod.

"I'm guessing you're the cause of the recent incidents around town. Sleeping in the Burgess house? Breaking into the party store on Highway 6?"

The kid looked back at me, guilt showing in his eyes, but he didn't answer.

"Anything worse than that? Did you hurt anyone?"

He shook his head, looking down at the floor.

"All right then. I can make a few calls and make sure everyone drops the charges. In exchange, I need you to agree to stay here for a while. Can you do that?"

The kid looked at me, waiting for the punch line. It would take him some time to realize there wasn't one.

"Let's go. We'll get you some clothes and a room to sleep in. I suspect you're hungry too," I said, leading the way out of the shed.

The kid hurried up beside me, seeming to think I was the safer choice than staying behind with Bones and Rod. "They won't hurt you. They're good men."

He snorted, glancing back.

"I'm Deanna. But everyone calls me Tweedle."

"Why?" the kid asked, looking at me, confused.

"Short for Tweedle-Dee, of course."

He nodded, but I could tell he was still confused. "I'm Colby."

"Nice to meet you, Colby. I'm going to refrain from shaking your hand until you've showered, though," I nudged him, grinning sideways at him.

A small grin touched the corners of his mouth as he opened the back door for me.

"Loretta, could you take my new friend Colby upstairs and find him a room to use? He'll also need a shower and some clean clothes. Seems he's a bit displaced at the moment."

"Sure, darlin'. Hey, Colby, follow me. We'll get you squared away in no time."

Colby looked back at me briefly, and I nodded. Loretta was already disappearing up the staircase, so he ran to catch up.

I walked down the hall to the bedroom that was being used by my grandpa. It had also been the room that my grandmother had slept in during the last few months she was with us. I'd always intended on going through her old medications to get rid of them, but never had. Luckily as I discovered when I opened the medicine cabinet, neither had anyone else.

I found the little blue pills I was looking for and took them back to the kitchen. I smiled, remembering how loopy the pills used to make my grandmother. Dumping them into a cup and filling it with warm water, I let the pills dissolve. Grabbing a bowl, I started throwing ingredients together from memory.

Rod, Bones, Aunt Carol, and Tansey all stood silently watching me.

Loretta joined the group ten minutes later.

Half an hour later, Colby, freshly showered and wearing a pair of my old sweatpants and one of Bones' black T-shirts, joined us. I was just taking the cookies out of the oven.

I slapped the homemade frosting on two dozen and set them aside, my audience eagerly grabbing for them. With the last dozen, I dumped the dissolved pills into the remaining frosting, stirred, and started covering the cookies.

"What was in that cup?" Colby asked.

Loretta laughed. "That there was a cup of Tweedle-Dee whoop-ass. Make sure you don't eat that batch of cookies."

"What if we confuse which cookies are which?" Aunt Carol asked, looking at the cookie she was currently eating.

"Good point," I nodded. "Tansey, grab out the cinnamon candies in the cabinet next to the stove. Reel and Uncle Mike love those damn candies."

Tansey helped decorate the tainted cookies with cinnamon candies while Rod and Aunt Carol used the green sprinkle candies on the untainted ones.

When we were done, I looked at everyone, sharing a grin.

Colby's eyes bugged out, and he reached out, grabbing Tansey's wrist.

Her finger was an inch from her lips with a dollop of the tainted frosting on top. She looked down at her finger. "Dang, kid. Thanks." She got up and walked over to the sink.

"Didn't mean to scare you," Colby said, looking down at the floor nervously.

"You did good, kid," Bones said, throwing an arm over his shoulder and jostling him a bit. "Maybe you should come work with me in security. Course, we'd have to beef you up a bit."

"How about he finishes high school before you try to recruit him," I suggested.

My leg was aching, so I slid onto a bar stool to give it a rest. "Tansey, can you run up to the attic and get the costumes?"

"Sure. Colby, mind giving me a hand?"

Colby shadowed her up the stairs. A few minutes later, they had all the costumes out of the attic, piled up on the dining room table. We emptied the boxes until I found what I was looking for.

"I'm going to go find Grandpa's video camera," Tansey said, giggling as she jogged out of the room.

Bones shook his head, watching Tansey leave. "I'm going to take another walk around the perimeter before the games begin."

Chapter Twenty-Two

I had three loaves of bread rising by the time the boys woke from their naps. Everyone else had eagerly returned to the kitchen to wait for the show. I moved behind the breakfast bar, grabbing the crutch to use as a prop so the missing cast wouldn't be apparent.

"Something smells good," Uncle Mike yawned, taking a seat.

"Is that bread?" Reel asked, sitting next to him.

Wayne walked in, scratching his head and sitting in the last seat.

"It is, but it won't be ready until dinner. Here. Have a cookie," I said, sliding the plate with the cinnamon candies in between Uncle Mike and Reel. Tansey slid the other platter which was half gone in front of Wayne.

"These are good," Reel said, eating almost an entire cookie in one bite. "Who's this?" Reel asked, nodding at Colby.

"This is Colby. He moved to Pine Valley a while back," Loretta smoothly lied. "He's going to stay a few days while his parents are out of town."

"I don't recognize you, kid. Who are your parents?" Uncle Mike said.

"He's one of my sister Patty's grandkids. You know how my sister's family is," Loretta said, rolling her eyes.

Uncle Mike chuckled, nodding his head. Loretta's sister Patty had a high accidental-pregnancy rate. Her offspring seemed to follow in her footsteps, and there was a constant stream of relatives moving in and out of the house that Loretta and Patty had inherited. So many, in fact, that Loretta signed off her rights to the house two decades ago because she wanted to distance herself and the boys from the insanity.

"Damn, Tweedle, these cookies are good. I love cinnamon candies," Uncle Mike said, picking up his third cookie.

Rod was silently laughing and dragged Tansey with him out of the kitchen. Aunt Carol started acting twitchy and said she still had work to do in the den, leaving abruptly.

"What's with everybody?" Reel asked, as he grabbed another cookie.

"Aunt Carol is tired. I'll make her rest soon."

"I'm glad you got some sleep," Reel nodded. "You needed it."

"I was indeed tired. When I woke up, it was like everything was much clearer."

Bones choked on his coffee and turned away. Colby whacked him a few good times on the back, no longer intimidated by him.

"Hey, let me have one of them with the cinnamon candies," Wayne said, reaching for the other platter.

"Eat your own damn cookies," Reel said, moving the plate out of his reach.

I took the platter away after they'd each had four cookies. I didn't want to put them in a coma. I watched the clock—smiling. Any minute now.

"Man, I'm still tired," Uncle Mike yawned.

"Me too." Reel nodded his head extra slow. Reel focused on his arm as he struggled to lift it an inch from the counter. "Shit," he slurred, looking up at me.

"Bastards," I said, as they both started to fall.

Bones grabbed Reel, and Rod caught Uncle Mike. Loading them in wheelchairs, using the one I came home in and Grandma's old chair, we moved them into the dining room.

"What's the plan?" Tansey asked.

"It's dress-up time."

Aunt Carol looked at me nervously. "Then what?"

"Then the park bench in town," I answered. "No keys, wallets, or phones."

"Holy crap," Colby mumbled. "What did you put in those cookies?"

"Just something to make them sleepy."

"What did they do to you? They hit you or something?"

"No, Colby. They would never hit me or you," I promised, looking him square in the face. "They paid the doctor to put a cast on my leg and told me it was broken."

"Damn," Colby said.

"Watch your mouth, young man," Loretta scolded, before turning to me. "You are one wicked woman," she winked.

"We get to take pictures, right?" Rod asked, getting out his phone.

"Oh, hell yes," Bones said, with his phone already out.

"Holy shit," Bridget said from the doorway. "I don't know what's going on, but can I play?"

"I'm not sure about this, Tweedle," Aunt Carol said. "Can we vote on it?"

"Nope, sorry. This isn't a democracy." I pulled Reel's boots off. "Don't worry, they'll blame me."

Aunt Carol seemed unsure but removed Uncle Mike's jeans as Rod held his body weight up out of the chair. I felt a bit awkward as I undid Reel's button on his jeans, and my face heated.

"It won't be the first time you've seen him naked," Tansey said as she stripped Reel's shirt off.

"He was ten. I'm guessing some parts have grown since then." I tried to look away as I pulled his jeans down.

"Yeah, I'd say you're right about the growing," Tansey said, snickering.

Rod covered Tansey's eyes and turned her away. I looked down and realized Reel's boxer-briefs were tented upward.

"Shit." I threw his shirt over his lap as heat raced up my cheeks.

Aunt Carol giggled. "Seems even sedatives can't keep all of Reel down."

~*~*~

UNCLE MIKE AND REEL SAT SIDE by side on the park bench with an arm thrown over each other's shoulder. Reel was dressed in an oversized ballerina outfit with a pink tutu and his hair bobby-pinned up in a makeshift bun. Uncle Mike was dressed in adult-size baby pajamas with a pacifier in his mouth.

"They're going to be pissed," Bones said.

"Bastards," I said, smiling.

Rod had strapped a rope around their waists and secured them to the park bench so they wouldn't fall over. Tansey and Bridget were still busy taking pictures with their phones. Townsfolk were emerging from stores and stopping their vehicles in the center of the street to watch.

"What did they do this time, Tweedle-Dee?" Old Man Mackerel asked.

"They paid a doctor to put a fake cast on Tweedle's leg," Colby answered for me.

"Fools," Mrs. Mackerel chuckled.

"Looks to me like Tweedle went easy on them. Remember the time that high school quarterback was put in his place?" Old Man Mackerel asked.

"I was the high school quarterback," Rod said, turning to look at Tansey and me.

"It was the year *after* you graduated," Loretta said. "You were away at that trade school."

"Nate Hoager?" Rod asked. "Didn't he move to Alaska or something?"

"Oregon," Tansey said.

"That boy was a marked man after Tweedle had his convertible filled with dead fish," Mrs. Mackerel said, nodding. "Don't know what he did, but it was only a matter of time before one of you Thurman brothers were going to catch up to him, so he skedaddled the night of graduation."

"Why do I feel the need to go to Oregon and punch him?" Rod asked Tansey. "And how come Uncle Mike didn't do it for me?"

"No one was stupid enough to tell Mike," Loretta said. "Besides, the girls handled it just right. Not only did Nate know not to mess with Tansey again, but so did every boy in town."

"Mess with Tansey?" Rod growled.

"We better get moving," Tansey said, giggling.

We gathered the wheelchairs, heading back to Grandpa's house. Uncle Mike and Reel would have to hitch a ride or walk back.

"How long before they wake up?" Wayne asked.

"I have no idea," I admitted. "The folks in town will keep an eye on them, though."

~*~*~

AUNT CAROL, TANSEY, AND ROD HELPED unload the boxes of files that Bridget and Tucker had "borrowed" from the former lawyer's office. They sorted the piles by importance, and Tucker dug into the financial accounts to figure out the what, where, and why of Grandpa's finances.

I worked on Grandpa's computer entering the expense receipts into the accounting software he used. I had three months balanced by the time I called for a break and went to the kitchen.

Filling the sink with hot soapy water, I was washing dishes when Reel and Uncle Mike walked through the back door.

"Tweedle," Uncle Mike nodded, as he waddled in his baby-suit into the dining room.

Reel stalked toward me, his eyes glaring. The effect was completely lost due to the sparkling silver eyeshadow. I snorted.

"You think this is funny?"

"Yes, actually, I do." I grinned. "Go clean up. Aunt Carol left some dinner for both of you."

"This isn't over, Tweedle," Reel said as he stomped up the back stairs.

His tutu bounced every time he slammed a foot down. I snorted again.

~*~*~

I was putting the last of the dishes away when Reel returned.

I decided it would be best if I said my piece first. "Do you remember when we were kids, and you told me I couldn't play baseball because I'd get hurt?"

"Yeah," he chuckled. "You threw the ball at my head. I had a headache for days."

"You shouldn't have had the doctor put a cast on my leg, Reel."

"I can explain," he sighed. "It was your uncle's idea. It was only to keep you safe. We didn't want—"

"You didn't want me to get hurt?" I glared, turning around to face him.

He held his hands out in surrender and took a step back. "We didn't deserve to be drugged and dressed up like idiots."

"You decided to act like an idiot, so that's how I treated you. You need to stop this controlling, overbearing big brother crap."

"I don't think of you as a little sister," Reel said, stepping forward and putting his hands on my shoulders.

"But you sure as hell didn't respect me enough to let me make my own decisions," I sighed, walking away.

Reel followed me into the living room where Uncle Mike was sitting on the couch next to Aunt Carol. She was sipping her tea, ignoring him as she read through some papers.

"Tweedle, you took things too far this time," Uncle Mike said.

"Before you think that you have a LEG to stand on in this argument, let me give you a warning. If either of you ever tries to manipulate me like that again, I have about fifty other ideas of how to settle the score. I might not be the smartest, or skinniest, or most coordinated, but you both taught me how to play a good game of revenge."

Both men sighed but didn't say a word.

Chapter Twenty-Three

Out of habit, I woke at the crack of dawn, showered, dressed and went downstairs to start baking. My grandmother was the original baker in the family and taught me everything she knew, though I think she only baked because she knew I enjoyed it so much. Her kitchen was state-of-the art with not one, not two, but three double ovens. I loved cooking in this kitchen.

I emptied the baking pantry onto the center counter and started whipping up a little of this, a little of that, and a whole lot of everything else. By the time Uncle Mike strolled into the kitchen, I had three dozen biscuits, a layer cake, a French silk pie, and about a hundred cookies of various flavors and designs.

"I see you're still mad."

"More like frustrated and disappointed," I said, beating cake batter into oblivion.

He filled a cup of coffee and topped off my cup before sitting on the other side of the breakfast bar.

"I'm sorry, Tweedle. I shouldn't have done it."

"It's not just the cast, Uncle Mike. You keep assuming that I can't take care of myself. That I can't handle being an adult."

"I don't want to see you get hurt."

"I know, but it's part of life. How old do I have to be before you let me live it?"

He sighed but nodded. "You're right."

"You think?" Aunt Carol giggled, walking past Uncle Mike to the coffee pot.

Loretta and Reel came down the back stairway, and Aunt Carol played hostess, filling coffee cups.

"Before everyone else starts gathering, we need to talk," I said, looking around.

"What is it?" Aunt Carol asked, setting her cup down beside me.

"Colby. He was the one behind the store robbery and the one who broke into the Burgess house. I need the charges to go away. He's just a kid. I don't know what he's been through, but I know sending him to juvie won't help anyone."

"Damn," Uncle Mike groaned. "I can't just make charges go away."

"I'll call the store and settle with the owner," Reel said. "I'm sure it's just a matter of agreeing to the right restitution."

"I can give Joan Burgess a call," Aunt Carol nodded. "I'll convince her to drop the charges. No one will need to know it was Colby."

"Thanks," I nodded.

"He can't stay with you while everything is going on," Uncle Mike said. "He could get hurt."

"He's safe here while everyone is around," Loretta said. "He can help with chores around the estate to earn his keep. It will be good for him. I'll stay out here until I know he's properly settled, and we'll figure the rest out later. Lord knows that Vince could use a young man around here helping out."

Reel leaned against a countertop, quiet, watching the floor. Without saying anything, Aunt Carol walked out of the kitchen, pulling Uncle Mike out of the room with her. Loretta motioned to Reel with a chin up and followed them out.

"I'm sorry," Reel said.

"No, you're not."

"Okay, maybe I'm not all that sorry. You need to be protected. I knew that if you were limited on being able to move around, you would be more agreeable."

"More agreeable? More like a dog on a leash!" I slammed my hand on the countertop. "What exactly were you hoping for Reel? That I'd be so dependent on you, I'd what? Move in with you?"

He didn't say anything.

"You're the one not understanding. For years, everyone whispered that you had feelings for me. For years, I've known that my birthday flowers came from you. For years, I waited by that dog-gone Ferris wheel, wondering if you'd show up. But when you finally reappear, you buy that creepy blue house? I'll tell you, I was stunned. You thought I liked that house?" I shook my head, angry tears burning my cheeks. "You don't know me at all. You just think you do."

I turned away, grabbing the eggs to crack them open into a bowl.

"The furniture you wanted me to pick out?" I continued, keeping my back to him. "The curtains? The dishes? You have it set in your head that you can waltz back into town and build a relationship between us. But did you ever stop to think that maybe I don't want you? That you waited too long? That I've changed into someone you no longer know?"

I was so angry that I fisted my hands, ignoring my own tears as I turned back to face him, pointing a finger at him. "I'm the one who gets to make the decisions about *my life!*" I yelled, storming out of the room.

I stormed through the dining room where everyone was gathered. "Aunt Carol, can you pull the bread from the ovens?" I asked, not waiting for an answer.

In the foyer, I was stopped by an angry-looking Grandpa. "Who the hell are all these people in my house?" he yelled. "Why the hell is there an IV in my arm and a hospital bed in my living room?"

"Bridget?" I called out.

"Yeah?" she answered, bouncing out of the dining room and into the foyer.

"Can you take a picture of me with my grandpa?" I asked, turning to stand beside Grandpa and face Bridget.

Grandpa quickly straightened his hair and slid the IV stand behind him before standing at parade rest for the photo. Bridget snapped a pic with her phone, only the edges of her mouth turning up in a grin.

"Now Grandpa, be aware that if you anger me more than I already am, I will have that picture sent to the local paper. You might want to take a look at your outfit before you open your mouth again."

I marched up the stairs with my head held high, turning the corner to go to my room. Down the hall, out of sight from the others, Tansey waited. She opened her arms and folded me in them as I cried.

"Bastards," I bawled.

"I know," she whispered.

~*~*~

"Okay, enough tears," Tansey ordered a good ten minutes later, shaking me by the shoulders hard enough to make the bed jiggle.

"Time to put on my big-girl panties?" I said, finishing the long-standing joke.

"That's right." Tansey shoulder-nudged me before standing up. "What did Reel say about the blue house and the annual birthday flowers?"

"I didn't give him a chance to say anything. I was too angry." I blew my nose and tossed the tissue into the trash.

"I have to get ready for work," Tansey said as she pulled clothes out of her duffle bag. "Did you want to come with me tonight?"

"Yes. But I need to do the adult thing and go downstairs to talk to Tucker and my grandpa," I sighed. I got up, checking to make sure that I had thrown away all the tissues before turning toward the door.

"That's the spirit. And, hey," she said as I neared the door, "I want a copy of that picture of Grandpa wearing the pink boxers."

"Deal," I said, waggling my eyebrows.

I went to the den, knowing I'd find Tucker and Grandpa there. Grandpa's shoulders dropped when he saw me.

"I still love you, Gramps," I said, kissing the top of his freshly showered head.

"I'm not sure why," Grandpa said, sighing. "Sounds like I put you and myself in a terrible position. Damn Marlians."

"You mean Martians?" I asked.

"No," Grandpa said, looking at me with a confused expression. "Why would I say Martians?"

I shrugged. "Because you've been running around saying that the Martians were dangerous."

"No, the *Marlians* are dangerous," Grandpa said sternly. "You must've misunderstood."

"Were you wearing all your teeth when you said it?" Tucker asked, chuckling.

Grandpa frowned. "I found my partials in the bathroom soaking, so probably not."

"Who are the Marlians?"

"They're a wealthy family over in Sarrosa County," Grandpa explained. "I did business with them about twenty-five years ago. I found out they were crooked, and Tucker helped me dissolve the business arrangement. I hadn't seen any of them since, until about three months ago. Randall, one of the kids, about your age, showed up. He was asking questions I wasn't willing to answer. I sent him packing, but I knew he'd be back."

"Why didn't you call Tucker or Uncle Mike? Hell, you could have at least told me. You put me in charge of your medical situation and then didn't warn me."

"It was stupid. I know," Grandpa said, shaking his head. "I thought I could deal with it on my own. But the next thing I knew, I couldn't think straight. I couldn't find my housekeeper, Adelle. The groundkeeper stopped coming. The drunk nurse wouldn't listen. I couldn't keep my thoughts straight."

"What did this guy want? When he visited you?"

"He wanted to know about his father and where his father stayed when he lived in town. Who he spent time with. Meaningless stuff, but he was asking too many questions."

"Uh-huh. So, really, he was asking about what happened twenty-eight years ago? Was that the timeframe he was trying to corner you about?"

Grandpa's sharp eyes pinned me to my seat, but I didn't look away. I nodded slowly.

"Tucker already knows, but how did you find out?" Grandpa asked.

"That my sister is my half-sister?" I asked, leaning back and crossing my arms over my chest. "When your lawyer died, Mother stopped getting her spending money. It wasn't hard to trick her into coming over here and answering some questions. I was trying to find out whether she was behind your poisoning. Never expected to hear that she had an affair almost three decades ago."

"You weren't supposed to know," Grandpa said. "It's not safe."

"Talk. Now," I ordered.

"She's right," Tucker nodded. "It's time."

Grandpa glared at Tucker but then sighed, realizing it was time to come clean. "Randall's father, Morgan, is a very dangerous man. Think gangster thug. By the time your mother realized she was pregnant, he'd already left town. She convinced your father it was his child, so he'd marry her. By the time I figured out the truth, she was already pregnant with you. I didn't want Darlene or you associated with that man. It wasn't safe. I've been paying your mother to keep her mouth shut ever since. I never even told your grandmother."

"But this Randall guy is snooping around, looking for answers. Why? What is he looking for?"

"Darlene was about six or seven when Morgan came back into town. He rented a house and stayed for a few months. I was having someone keep an eye on him but to my knowledge, he never talked to either of you girls. When I found out that your mother was visiting him again, I put my foot down. He left a week later. Your father must have found out about the affair too. He left around the same time. I don't know whether he found out that Darlene wasn't his daughter. But I suspected that Morgan figured it out."

"Was that the last time this Morgan guy came to town?"

"That I know of," Grandpa nodded.

"So Randall could have found out about Darlene through his father?"

"That was my theory, but then the meds started messing with my head."

"If it was Randall that was drugging you and ripping you off, we can get him put behind bars. Let's start there. We'll have the nurse ID a photo of him."

"What if people find out?"

"Lies and secrets, Grandpa, eventually float to the top of the water. It's time Mother tells Darlene the truth. She's an adult now."

Grandpa nodded, and his shoulders slouched another inch. I walked off to find Uncle Mike, finding him in the kitchen with Aunt Carol.

"I need you to get a photo of Randall Marlian and have the nurse ID him as the guy we're looking for. He came to see Grandpa before everything started going to hell. He has a vendetta against the family. You might want to look into the lawyer's death too. Wouldn't surprise me if this guy killed him."

"You sure?" Uncle Mike asked.

"That he killed the lawyer? No. That he attacked this family? Yes," I nodded.

I walked over and grabbed the house phone, calling my mother.

"Yes, dear. Did you get my checks straightened out?"

"Still working on it. In the meantime, it's been decided that you need to talk to Darlene and tell her about her biological father. *Today*. I don't want her hearing it from someone else. Her half-brother might be going to prison for stealing from Grandpa."

"What on Earth will I say?"

"Tell her the truth. You had an affair and got knocked up. Honestly, I'm surprised Darlene hasn't gotten herself knocked up yet, and she's older than what you were back then."

I hung up without saying anything else.

"Your mother had an affair?" Aunt Carol asked.

"Yeah. Darlene's my half-sister and both her biological father and his son, her half-brother, are criminals."

"You think your mother will tell Darlene?" Uncle Mike asked.

"She's still hoping to get her monthly checks rolling again, so yes, she'll talk to Darlene."

I walked upstairs and packed my bags. Then I walked across the hall and packed Tansey's too, since she had left with Rod for her shift at the bar. I carried all our bags downstairs, setting them in the foyer. Grandpa and Tucker stopped at the entrance of the living room. Aunt Carol, Uncle Mike, and Reel walked out of the kitchen and stopped at the dining room. Bones, Bridget and Wayne stepped in through the front door. Loretta and Colby walked down the stairs.

"Good, you're all here." I smiled. "I'm moving back home."

"We should wait for the ID," Uncle Mike said.

"No need, I know it was him." I shook my head. "Grandpa, this is Colby," I said, pulling Colby closer with an arm wrapped around his shoulder. "He's going to live here for a while and keep an eye on your grumpy old ass. Loretta will stay until she knows he's settled, or until I can set up other housing arranged for him. He has my phone number if he needs it."

Grandpa nodded at Colby, and Colby looked at me, unsure.

"His bark is bigger than his bite," I whispered. "And this house is plenty big enough for the two of you."

I turned to Bridget and grinned. "Thank you for coming to help. I know you all came as a favor to Reel, but I appreciate it." I hugged Bridget.

"If I ever need a good revenge plot, I'll be calling."

"If I ever want to learn how to pickpocket, I know who to contact."

All the guys checked to see whether they had their wallets. Bones, Reel, and Tucker went over to the tall vase to pull theirs out.

"Grandpa, get the books and legal documents sorted with Tucker. I'll come back in a few days. If you want me to be in charge, then be ready to explain the details of the estate."

"It's going to take about a week to sort it all. It's a mess," Tucker said.

"I can help," Colby offered. "I'm a fast learner."

"We will get it ready," Grandpa nodded, placing a kind hand on Colby's shoulder. "I'll make sure you and Tucker have all the information. I also called Adelle, and she's coming back to work."

"Good," I said. "Aunt Carol, can you drive me home?"

"Of course, dear," she said, grabbing her purse from the table and leading the way.

I walked out the door without looking at Reel. I just didn't have it in me to face him again.

Chapter Twenty-Four

It had been a long week, but it ended up being a good one. With the bakery under construction, Samantha and I started baking and selling goods out of my rental house. We arranged tables in the dining room and did takeout orders only. I didn't have as many ovens, but I had a built-in double oven and the standard oven that was part of the stove. Plus, we moved the oil cooker over to make donuts. Of course, Samantha made me fry the donuts, but it felt good. Familiar.

The sign on the front door was made out of cardboard and read: *The Bakery*. That's it. I didn't think it needed further explanation.

At the end of the week, Samantha and I split the profits, but she handed me back another hundred dollars to cover the electricity. I'd put her hundred and a hundred from my share into a Mason jar, setting it aside for when the utility bill came. I figured it would be at least six weeks working from home until the store was ready to reopen.

Until then, we'd continue baking.

But today we'd closed early so I could meet Grandpa and Tucker about grandpa's affairs, and I was eager to check in with Colby and see for myself that he was doing well. I'd called him every day, twice a day. Each time he'd said all was well, but I knew firsthand that Grandpa could be a big pill to swallow.

Walking up to the porch, I heard a car pulling into the drive and was surprised to see it was Samantha.

"Something wrong?" I called out.

"Something's been wrong for years," she said, laughing as she jogged up the steps. "I need to speak to your grandpa and my great-uncle. And you need to hear it."

"Well, this doesn't sound good," I said as we walked through the front door. "Hello?" I called out.

"Hey, Tweedle," Colby called, running down the stairs to greet me. "What took you so long? Vince and Tucker are cranky today."

"In the den, Tweedle," Tucker yelled.

"Samantha's with me. She says she needs a word with the two of you," I said, entering the office with my arm around Colby and Samantha on my heels.

"I hear it's a day of full disclosure," she said, slapping a thick file on the desk. "I thought you two better start with this."

"Now, Samantha," Grandpa huffed. "We planned on discussing the estate today. There's no need to go over anything else."

Colby looked at Grandpa and shook his head. "Vince, what did you do this time?"

"You, old fool," Tucker said, glaring at Grandpa. "You can't keep playing puppet master."

I got the clear impression that whatever everyone was talking about had to do with me, so I grabbed the file and opened it.

"Don't concern yourself with all that, dear," Grandpa said, trying to take the file away.

Colby pushed his hand away and leaned over my shoulder to read it at the same time.

"You're rich," Colby said.

"It's a trust account, payable to me," I said as I flipped through the papers. "The bakery is mine? What is this? What's with all this money in this bank account?"

"You're Grandpa bought the bakery when you were still in high school," Samantha said. "He doubled my salary as long as I pretended to be the owner, and he threatened to fire me if I ever told you the truth. Until this week, I was worried what I'd do if I didn't have a paycheck."

"Why the secrecy?" I asked Grandpa.

"The wrong kind of men would've seduced you for your money," Grandpa said with a nonchalant shrug. "I thought it best to wait until you settled down with someone who was worth your attention."

Colby barked a laugh. "He was worried you'd be swindled by a gold digger."

"Really? That's how naïve you think I am?" I said, throwing the file at him. "I guess it makes sense. I've been manipulated by my rich grandpa all these years."

I paced back and forth, hands on hips. I tried to rationalize the information. On one hand—he was old. On the other—I was pissed. When would everyone learn that I could stand on my own two feet?

"Is this why you never gave me a decent raise?" I asked Samantha.

We both knew that I could dance circles around her in the kitchen. But we worked well together, and she was better with the customers.

"I wasn't allowed. He wanted you working paycheck to paycheck."

"I'm done," I said to Grandpa, holding my hands up and shaking my head. "I refuse to be a pawn in your game."

"Now, just hear me out," Grandpa sputtered.

"No. You hear *me*. You are my grandpa, and I love you. I will be here for you if you need me. But you stay out of my personal life. No more interference. If I even hear a whisper that you are up to your old tricks, then I'll stop visiting you completely. And you can take the money from the bakery and shove it. I don't want it. And I don't want the bakery. You should sell the building."

I walked out of the office, through the living room, through the foyer and out the door. Getting into my car, I hit the gas and stones flew everywhere as I peeled out.

"Alpha idiots!" I yelled, hitting the steering wheel with my palm.

WHEN I GOT TO MAIN STREET, I pulled over to calm down. I was too angry to drive. Looking around to distract my thoughts, I realized I was parked in front of the old Michaelson building. A century before, it was the founding family's home. It had been remodeled several times for various business purposes, but each had failed. For the past few years, it had remained vacant.

I smiled up at the large building. I had an idea, but I'd need some help to make it happen. I texted Aunt Carol and Samantha to meet me at The Bar. I knew Tansey was already working.

"Ladies and gentlemen," I called out when I entered, "I'm selling my car. Spread the word."

"How much?" Eric Mickers asked, from one of the booths along the wall.

"Rod? How much is it worth?"

"About seven," he whispered.

"Seven thousand," I called out. "First one to hand me a valid check gets the car."

"Let me run home and get my checkbook," Eric said, jumping up and jogging out the door.

"What the hell, Tweedle? What are you going to drive?" Rod asked.

"I'm not," I said, frowning. "I'll have to walk wherever I need to go."

"From The Bar, back to town?" Aunt Carol asked.

I smirked. "I honestly didn't expect to sell my car that quick. I'll need you to give me a lift back into town."

Samantha arrived and tentatively walked up to me.

"I'm not mad at you," I told her, grinning.

"Thank goodness," she said, patting her chest. "I was so worried. I hated lying to you. You have to know that."

"I know."

I yelled over for Tansey to join us when she could spare a break but asked Aunt Carol and Samantha to meet me at the back table. I handed my car keys to Rod. "Can you get the keys to Eric when he comes back? And oh, can you gather anything personal from the car for me?"

"Sure," Rodd nodded, taking the keys. "Tweedle, is everything okay?"

"Yes," I said. "I think finally it will be."

I marched to the back table and leaned in to tell Samantha and Aunt Carol my plan. They both started squealing and clapping and soon, Tansey couldn't take it any longer and stopped to get the CliffsNotes of what was going on.

"Hell yes," she said. "What brought all this on?"

"I realized that Uncle Mike, Reel, and Grandpa are never going to let me be free until I prove to them that I can stand on my own two feet." I shrugged. "It's time to prove it to them."

Tansey smiled brightly and jogged off to the bar. She returned a few minutes later with four shots. "To standing on our own two feet," she toasted.

I looked nervously at my shot, unsure whether I should drink it.

"Your shot is only root beer," she whispered.

"You know me so well," I said before downing it.

Chapter Twenty-Five

I sold everything I could think of other than my bed and kitchen supplies. Samantha and I baked ten hours a day for six weeks in my rental, including taking catering orders in four counties. I didn't spend a dime more than I had to on anything. At the end of the six weeks, Aunt Carol met me at the bank, and we walked in together for our appointment.

I was nervous. My hands were sweating as I tried wiping them discreetly on the side of my skirt.

"What's the worst that could happen?" Aunt Carol asked, trying to calm me.

"They could say no," I whispered. "I'm not sure how much longer I'm going to get away with selling baked goods out of my house once the landlord realizes we aren't relocating back to the store."

"Then we'll come up with another plan," Aunt Carol said, seeming unconcerned.

We sat in the guest chairs and waited for Mr. Palmer. I had known Mr. Palmer my entire life but had never sat down across a desk from him.

"Ladies, please come in. I'm sorry to keep you waiting," Mr. Palmer said, gesturing for us to enter his office.

"You go ahead, dear," Aunt Carol said, picking up a magazine.

"But," I stammered.

"Go," she ordered.

"Shit," I mumbled under my breath.

"What was that?" Mr. Palmer asked as he closed the door.

"Sorry, just an itty-bitty sneeze. Allergy season." I smiled, taking a tissue from the box on the corner of his desk.

It couldn't be a good sign that he had tissue on the corner of his desk. How many people left this office crying? Was I going to be one of them?

"Well, bless you then," Mr. Palmer said. "Please have a seat. You were vague when you called to set the appointment. What can I help you with today?"

"I'm interested in buying a building for business purposes, but I need to find out what type of loan I could be approved for before I speak with the building owner."

"Of course," Mr. Palmer said. "Are you considering buying the bakery? I'm afraid it just sold. Someone's turning it into another antique store."

"I'm planning on opening a bakery, but not at that location. The building I'm interested in will require some minor renovations to bring it up to code, but the structure is sound. And I'm being vague because I don't want my grandpa to know what I'm planning. I'm afraid I'll have to require confidentiality before I speak any further on the matter."

I slid a nondisclosure agreement across the desk to Mr. Palmer.

"Well, this is a first for me," Mr. Palmer said, reading and signing the document.

He slid the document back to me and I handed him my business plan. He leaned back in his chair and read the documents. Forty minutes passed, and he hadn't made as much as a facial twitch. Finally, he set the folder down and looked up. I had my hands so tightly twisted together that my fingers ached as I waited for him to say something, anything.

And then he smiled.

I felt my breath whoosh out of me.

"Two immediate thoughts," he said, wearing a grin. "The new owner of the former bakery was in yesterday. He asked whether I knew anyone who'd be interested in buying the old kitchen appliances and tables. They want them out by this weekend."

"Good to know."

"The second is that your estimate for the purchase of the building seems high. Not high enough that we wouldn't lend the money, but maybe higher than what the seller would take."

"I've done a lot of research on the building and the owner. I'm hoping to get the price down about 30 percent. Most of the figures in the proposal were on the high side, just so I could prove to myself that it was doable."

"I think 30 percent would be pushing your luck," he said, laughing. "But get out there and see what you come up with. I'll get started on the loan paperwork."

"You'll give me the loan?" I asked.

"Easiest decision I've had to make in years," he said, standing to shake my hand.

I walked out of the office and tried to keep a straight face, but I couldn't fool Aunt Carol.

"Come along, dear. Let's go talk to the realtor," Aunt Carol said.

~*~*~

TWO HOURS LATER, I RETURNED to the bank with a copy of a signed purchase agreement. I signed the official application for the loan and paid the application fee.

"I can't believe you got it for that price," Mr. Palmer said.

"According to my research, they were eager to sell."

"Next time I go house shopping, I'm taking you with me."

"Is there anything else? I need to go talk to some people about buying some used commercial ovens."

"We're set. I'll call the realtor and set up the closing. We should have the title work and inspections done in about two weeks."

"Sounds good. The owner gave me permission to start working on the property right away."

"You'll be able to move the ovens and tables before this weekend then?"

"That's the plan."

~*~*~

MR. PALMER WAS RIGHT. The new owners of the old bakery practically gave away the kitchen equipment. I paid eighteen hundred dollars for about twelve thousand dollars' worth of appliances. And they threw in all the bowls and other cookware for free.

The only catch was that they wanted it all moved immediately.

I texted everyone in my phone's contact list and started hauling boxes down the street. By the time I returned for a second load, friends and family started arriving to pitch in and help. Folks in town noticed what was happening, and they pitched in too. Rod showed up with dollies, and the owner of the hardware store lent us two more. Colby showed up in town covered in sweat from riding his bike. He eagerly ditched the bike to take the box out of my hands. He was a good kid, through and through.

All the way down Main Street, to the other end, was a line of people either carrying a box or pushing a dolly to the old Michaelson building. And after everything was moved, they stayed to help me clean the place.

"Big strong, Rod," I said, squeezing his bicep and his ego.

"What do you need, Tweedle?" he asked.

"I was hoping you could pull the carpet in the foyer, dining room, and living room. Then I was hoping you could haul it to the dump for me."

"You sure? It looks to be in good shape," he said, walking around.

"Oh, I'm sure," I said, walking over to pull back a large section in the corner I knew was already loose. Of course, I knew this because last week I was the one who had pulled it loose.

"Holy crap," Rod said, grinning down at the flooring underneath. "That real wood or that fake stuff?"

"That's real wood planks, baby."

"I need manual labor out here!" Rod yelled.

A good half-dozen men joined Rod, and the carpet disappeared out the door.

"Have you been upstairs yet?" Tansey squealed, flying around the corner.

"You mean, do I know that your future living room has solid windows on two walls?" I asked, jumping up and down, clapping, in my best valley-girl cheerleading impression. "Yes, I do! Aren't you over the moon?"

"Oh, thank you, thank you, thank you. I know you should get first pick, but—"

Dropping the act, I held up my hand, palm out, to stop her. "You're an artist. I knew when I saw this place that this would be your apartment. Besides, I like the other side better."

"The other side is just a mess of offices," Tansey said, wrinkling her nose.

"For a few months," I said, nodding. "But after we get the new bakery ready, I can start remodeling my side."

"I'll help."

"Damn skippy you will. But first, I need you to figure out what paint colors to use downstairs."

I briefly described where the display counters, tables and chairs would be. The kitchen I'd handle myself, but I trusted Tansey to make the rest flow and look elegant.

"Do you want a mural or any particular patterns?"

"No, basic walls with accent lighting every six or seven feet."

"Really? Why?" Tansy said, looking around the large room.

"For your paintings, silly."

"But I thought the big room in the back was going to be the gallery."

"It is, but we want people to see some of your paintings out here, so they take the time to walk into the gallery."

Ten minutes later, I could still hear Tansey occasionally squeal while I wielded a wrench under the kitchen sink. I couldn't get the stupid P-trap to budge.

"My turn," Uncle Mike hollered from above me. "Go on, get out of there."

I slid out from under the sink and looked at him.

"If you can let the whole town carry supplies, you can let me fix the sink. I promise I won't take over or interfere with your business. But we're still family, kiddo."

I jumped up and hugged him.

"I'm proud of you, Tweedle."

"Thank you. Now fix the damn drain for me."

"You got it," he said, relieving me of my borrowed wrench. "You hear we finally got Randall Marlian in handcuffs?"

"I heard. Did he confess?"

Uncle Mike snorted and reached out for the bucket I held in my hand. He slipped it under the pipe and leaned out of the way before loosening the pipe that spilled stinky gray water into the bucket. "He lawyered up. Hasn't said a word. But we have enough evidence on him for drugging your grandpa and stealing from the estate. He'll be locked up for a few years."

"They holding him in Cooper City?"

"Until the trial," Uncle Mike said, nodding. "Seems his father, Morgan, is paying for the attorney but refused to help bond him out. Guess daddy wasn't too happy to hear what his son was up to."

"With daddy's reputation, figured it would be a proud father-son moment."

"I remember Morgan from years back. Evil, yes, but smart. He's probably pissed that his son was so sloppy about covering his tracks."

"What about him trying to kill me? How's that fit in?"

"No idea," Uncle Mike said as he stood and cleaned off the wrench with an old shop rag. "The way I figure it, Randall must have worried that you'd figure out what was happening before he stole enough to disappear."

I tossed a rag under the sink after pulling the stinky bucket out. I dumped the bucket off the back porch. When I returned, Uncle Mike was still standing there.

"Say what you feel you need to say," I sighed.

"Your grandpa has always been an ass, and you've loved him, anyway. He doesn't have many more years left. Best if you forgive him sooner rather than later." He grabbed the new plumbing parts and slid back under the sink. "And Reel is still in town. Might want to cut him some slack too. Saw him sitting on the park bench across the street not ten minutes ago."

"You hold grudges for years, but I only get six weeks?"

"You weren't built to hold a grudge more than a day," Uncle Mike chuckled. "We all know it's eating at you, so go clear the air."

He was right. Every day that had passed, the sickly feeling of guilt ate at me. I recrossed to the porch, spotting Reel across the street sitting on the park bench. He held my stare as I walked over and sat down beside him.

He nodded across the street as people scurried in and out. "Your Master Plan in action," Reel said.

"Per Grandpa's orders, I've put away 20 percent of my wages since my first baby-sitting job. Hated it back then, but he was right. It got me this far."

"You have enough money, then?" Reel asked with a raised brow.

"Yes," I nodded. "Tansey and Aunt Carol own half the building. We had enough to put down a healthy down payment and our start-up funds. The rest the bank owns until I can pay it off."

Reel nodded but didn't say anything.

"I'm choosing to forgive you, but I'm doing it for me, not for you. I miss our friendship."

"I don't want to be your friend, Deanna. I've been in love with you since you turned fifteen. I want you to be my wife, the mother of my children."

"I know you do," I nodded. "But the problem with that is you don't know me. You don't know what I like, dislike, or downright hate. You have this image in your head that I'd be the perfect wife for you. But I'm not that person."

"You're in love with me too. I know it. It's why you haven't dated anyone all these years."

"You're wrong. I haven't dated anyone in *this town* because you made it public that I was off limits. That doesn't mean I haven't dated. Had sex. Fallen in and out of love. I just had to leave town to do it. And you can't tell me that you haven't had your share of women over the years either."

"I only ever loved you," he whispered.

"I stopped loving you years ago. It was crushing the life out of me," I whispered before standing and walking across the street. I didn't look back. I didn't want him to see the tears streaming down my face. I had never lied to him before.

Colby waited on the front porch for me to return. "He hurt you?"

"No, Colby. He just wants me to be someone I'm not. And I'm too old to change my ways."

"I think you're pretty cool just like you are," Colby said.

"Pretty cool, huh? Yeah, well, mister, we haven't had the conversation about school yet. Am I going to still be 'pretty cool' after I force that one out of you?"

Colby didn't look for an exit, so I figured that was a good sign. "I like school. But what happens if the state makes me go back to live with my dad?"

"I get the feeling your dad used to hit you." I crossed to the porch glider and sat down, patting the seat next to me. "I can stop you from getting sent back to him, but are there other adult family members who'll want you to go back home?"

"Nah. My mom died of an overdose when I was still in diapers. I don't think I have any other relatives. I doubt my dad noticed I'm missing, or if he has, I doubt he knows how long I've been gone."

"Okay," I said with a nod. "Let's get the paperwork started. Loretta's a part-time social worker, so she can help us."

"If she's a social worker, why didn't she report me?"

"In the eyes of the state, she's not a very good social worker," I said, laughing. "And if your dad throws a stink about you staying here in Pine Valley, well, let's just say we have a few friends who'd be happy to pay him a visit to convince him it was for the best."

"For real?" Colby asked.

"We'll keep you safe, Colby. That's what this town does."

Colby looked down at the porch, and I knew he was tearing up. I rubbed his back and looked away to give him a minute to gather his emotions. Honestly, I needed a minute to gather my own.

"Colby, why don't you help me with the second-floor plumbing," Uncle Mike said from the doorway. "I could use a second set of hands."

Colby shrugged and led the way into the house. Uncle Mike gave me a nod before following in after him.

Chapter Twenty-Six

"This is the stupidest idea that you've ever had," Tansey said, as she gripped my arm tighter.

"Dumber than the time we went to that strip club and had our purses stolen?" I asked.

"Definitely dumber," she whispered as a man in handcuffs was led over to us and cuffed to the mounted hook in the center of the table.

"Who the hell are you?" Randall Marlian glared at Tansey.

"She's a friend of mine," I answered for her, sitting up straighter. "I assume you know who I am?"

"Sure," Randall nodded. "You're the granddaughter. What do you want?"

There was something unsettling about seeing him. It wasn't the fact that he was wearing an orange jumpsuit, or that we were sitting in the county jailhouse. It also wasn't the cold stare he directed my way, though something about it seemed familiar. I felt like I knew him, but at the same time, I was confident we'd never met.

"Have we ever spoken before?"

"No," he shrugged. "I saw pictures of you, though. You and *our* sister."

"Leave Darlene out of this," I said, leaning toward him. "Don't you even breathe her name. Ever."

"You afraid someone might hear that your sister's a bastard? I'm afraid the cat's already out of the bag on that one." He chuckled. "I only figured things out because of Pa's obsession with you. He has stacks of photos of you hidden in his desk. Since you were a little kid, only about knee high. I was surprised to find out Darlene was my sister, not you. He only had a handful of pictures of her."

"I don't give a damn who Darlene's father was. Fact is, she's *my* sister. And I'll make your life a living hell if you do or say anything to harm her."

"You think you can scare me?" He glared, leaning over the table at me. "Bitch, you don't know what fear is until you've grown up with my old man as a father."

His father. That was what was so unsettling to me. Those eyes. Randall's eyes. I had a feeling I'd seen them before, looking just as cold, staring at me with just as much hatred.

"Ah..." Randall's lips parted as he studied me. "You know my old man."

When I stood, Tansey rose with me. She was still gripping my arm tight enough to cut off circulation. My knees shook as I led us out of the visiting area. Randall's eerie chuckle echoed in my ears until the door closed behind us.

"That's it? What the hell, Tweedle? You dragged me all the way here, for that?" Tansey whispered as we walked out of the building and down the long sidewalk, enclosed on three sides by chain-link fencing.

"I'm going to tell you something, but you have to promise not to tell anyone," I whispered back as we waited for the gate to be opened so we could leave.

She nodded, but I waited until we were closer to the car before I said anything. "I don't think he's the one who was trying to kill me."

"*What??!*" she squealed.

"Hurry up and get in the car," I said, taking her keys from her to drive her newly purchased Subaru.

Her new Subaru was the same model as its predecessor and just as old and worn out. Maybe a bit less rusty. Rod was still arguing that she needed something newer, more reliable, but he couldn't argue with the fact that the vehicle could take a hell of an impact and keep us alive.

"What's going on?" Tansey asked as I drove us out of the parking lot and turned toward the highway.

I needed to collect my thoughts, and Tansey knew me well enough to give me the time to do so. I waited until we were halfway home before talking again.

"Get my phone out and Google Morgan Marlian. I need to see a picture of him."

Tansey did as I asked. "I can only find a group shot. He's the third guy from the left." She held the phone up, and I glanced at the picture as I drove.

Hitting the brakes, I veered to the side of the road as cars blared their horns, zipping past us.

"You trying to kill us?" Tansey yelled, with a death-grip hold on the dash.

I threw the Subaru in park and took the phone from her, taking a closer look at the picture. What I was looking at wasn't a man, though. He was a nightmare. A familiar nightmare that I had had on countless nights since I was a child. And in my nightmare he chased me while I ran through the woods to get away.

"It wasn't a dream," I whispered.

"Tweedle, you're scaring me. What's going on?"

I tossed the phone into my purse before looking over my shoulder for oncoming cars and pulling the Subaru back out into traffic. My hands shook, no matter how tightly I gripped the steering wheel.

"Did anything strange happen when we were kids? Do you remember me being scared or upset?"

"You're not talking about being scared of a movie or when a garter snake surprised you, are you?"

"You know I'm not."

"You don't remember?"

"Remember what?"

"You went missing one night. Reel found you in your tree fort the next morning and took you to Uncle Mike and Aunt Carol's. That was when you stopped talking for a week. Then you just woke up one day and were back to normal."

"Why?"

"I don't know. I was just a kid too. I heard Uncle Mike saying it might have had something to do with your father, but I never asked about it."

I exited the highway and turned toward Aunt Carol's house. I pulled up a few minutes later and got out of the Subaru.

"Tweedle, what's going on?" Tansey asked, hurrying beside me.

Aunt Carol opened the front door smiling. When she saw my face, she hurried across the lawn.

"Is it Mike? Is it your grandpa?" Aunt Carol asked, grabbing my hand.

"No," I shook my head. "Get Tansey inside and lock the doors. I need to go see Reel."

I set my keys and my purse on top of the Subaru and started walking down the long sidewalk to the end of the road. When I reached the end, I turned left and walked another block. I stood across the road, facing the blue house. I had stood in this same spot many times over the years, unable to force myself to step closer.

"Deanna?" Reel called, stepping out onto the front porch. "You okay?"

I placed one foot in front of the other and stepped off the curb. When nothing happened, I took another step. Then another. Before I knew it, I was standing beside Reel's truck, looking up at him.

"Deanna, you're shaking. What happened? What's wrong?" Reel asked, resting a hand on my cheek.

I heard a police siren and wasn't surprised to look up and see Uncle Mike's cruiser screech to a halt. The noise of the tires almost drowned out the noise of the gunshot. The bullet blasted the truck's side window into pieces, not two feet behind me.

"Gun!" Reel yelled, pulling me down and dragging me to the other side of the truck.

"Where'd the shot come from?" Uncle Mike yelled.

"The woods to the north," Reel yelled back. "We need to get Tweedle out of here. Pull your car up on the lawn."

I was still trying to process the fact that someone was shooting at me when Uncle Mike pulled the police cruiser beside us and Reel shoved me into the back seat and closed the door. Uncle Mike drove off the curb, and by the time I sat up, he was pulling into his driveway. I was dragged from the seat and into the house in a blink.

"What happened?" Aunt Carol asked, wrapping her arms around me.

"I have to go back and help Reel. Lock the doors," Uncle Mike ordered before leaving.

I walked into the living room and sat down on the couch. I stared at the beige and cream blended carpet, seeing all the different shades weaving in and around each other, forcing my brain to stop thinking of everything else if only for a little while.

By the time I looked up again, Reel, Uncle Mike, Aunt Carol, Tansey, Rod, Wayne, Bridget and Bones were all waiting and watching.

"There she is," Bridget said. "I told them to just give you some time, and you'd come back to us. You didn't look as out of it as last time."

Looking over at the big window, even with the blinds drawn, I could tell it was pitch black outside.

"I thought you guys went home." I asked Bridget.

"We did," she said. "Our bosses threw us on a private jet when Reel called."

"I need to go back to the house. The blue house," I said, standing up, only to feel dizzy and have Wayne reach out and steady me.

"Deanna," Reel whispered, wrapping one arm around my waist as he placed his other hand gently against my cheek. "Talk to me."

I nodded, looking into his eyes, but it took me a few minutes to breathe before I could speak. "Something happened when I was a child. Morgan Marlian. He was there. I remember him, but I can't remember what happened."

"He's the one trying to hurt you?"

"I can't prove it, but yes. And I have to know why. I have to go back to that house." I stepped away, clearing my throat. "I have been afraid of that house for years. I have to know why."

"I don't understand," Reel said, shaking his head. "You used to stare at that house for hours."

"Because it was evil. Until today, I couldn't step near it. I still don't understand, but I'm ready to face it."

"It's not safe," Uncle Mike said.

I looked at my uncle, the man who had been like a father to me most of my life. The man who was never far away whenever I needed him. I reached over and hugged him and heard him sigh. He knew I had already made up my mind.

"We should wait until it's light out," Reel said, stepping closer to me again. "It will be safer."

"I can't wait. I need to know."

"Wayne and I will go first to check the perimeter," Bones said. "Rod, stay with Tansey and Aunt Carol. Bridget, stay close to Tweedle." Bones and Wayne exited out the front door.

Reel searched my face. We stood in silence for a long time before he nodded and intertwined our fingers. "We do this together."

I nodded, and we walked out of the house and down the block, gripping Reel's hand so tight, my fingers throbbed.

"Deanna, we can wait until morning," he said.

"It was nighttime in my dreams," I whispered. "Why was I out so late?"

"What were you wearing in your nightmare?" Bridget asked from behind me.

"Pajamas," I answered, turning to glance at her.

Bridget took my other hand, stepping beside me. "And which direction was your house?"

I looked to the east, down the long block. I walked over to the east side of the house and started walking toward the backyard. I paused when the back porch was in view. The porch light was on, but in my nightmare, the light was off. I knew this because the only light was from the back door, left ajar and casting light onto the porch.

I let go of Bridget's and Reel's hands and crept up onto the porch. I tried to push the door open, but it wouldn't budge. Reel reached past me and unlocked the door. I slid inside without turning on the lights. Seeing from memory, I went to the basement stairs and stepped silently, one step at a time, down the stairs. Crouching down to look across the room before I reached the bottom. A memory played out in my mind. I watched in horror as the man I now knew to be Morgan Marlian buried the body in the basement.

Turning abruptly, I pushed my way past Reel and Uncle Mike and barreled out the back door. Landing on all fours, I retched in the grass, choking and gagging on bile.

"Dee," Reel whispered, wrapping his arms around me. "I've got you. I've got you."

"He's in the basement. All these years. He's been there the entire time. Just waiting for me to find him."

"Who, Dee? Who's been waiting for you?"

"My father," I said, looking up at Reel. "He's buried in your basement."

"Holy shit," Bones said.

"Tweedle, your father ran away. He packed his bags and took off," Uncle Mike said.

"Or was that just a story that her mother told us?" Aunt Carol asked, leading Tansey and Rod to our circle in the yard. "The timing is right. Her father disappeared the same night Tweedle ran away. We always figured she saw him leave and was upset. We should have pressed the issue."

"No, you did the right thing," Bridget said. "Her brain wasn't ready for her to process what she had seen. You could have royally messed her up by forcing her to face it."

Bones pulled Bridget into his side and kissed the top of her head. Uncle Mike, still wearing his uniform, called for backup to Reel's house and asked a squad car to pick up his sister and take her to the police station. He had tears in his eyes when he looked back at me.

I sat in the grass and pulled one of Reel's arms tighter around me. I wasn't leaving until my father's body was finally at peace.

CHAPTER TWENTY-SEVEN

"It's been two weeks," I complained, tossing the day-old biscuits into the tub to go to the church.

Colby walked into the kitchen, ignoring the argument between Reel and me and snatched a biscuit. I rolled my eyes and continued, "Morgan is most likely in another country by now."

"You don't know that," Reel said. "We need to keep you safe until we find him."

"And when will that be? Huh? A decade from now?"

"I don't know. I have people looking for him, but so far, nothing."

"I won't live this way," I said, shaking my head. "There's no point in him coming after me anyway. He was trying to kill me to keep me quiet, but now everyone knows. My father's funeral was like a damn media circus. Hell, my own mother confessed to covering up the murder and is sitting in a jail cell."

"You know she didn't know any details, right?" Reel said, walking up behind me and wrapping his arms around me.

"But she suspected," I sighed. "And instead of telling someone, she protected her lover by packing my father's clothes and getting rid of them, along with his car."

"I didn't say she was smart, or even a nice person, but she's not a murderer," Reel chuckled.

"Just a bitch," I mumbled, leaning into his embrace.

I had to admit, even if it was just to myself, that it felt good having Reel around all the time. He was warm, strong, and safe. But old feelings, feelings that never quite died, were resurfacing and I couldn't keep depending on him.

"No," I said, pushing away. "It's time for me to exert my independence. It's almost closing time, and I'll set the security alarm and stay indoors to work on the books tonight. But I need to start being alone again."

"I don't like it," Reel said, shaking his head.

"I can stay," Colby offered. "Vince would be fine home alone tonight. He's firing on all pistons these days."

"No, Colby. Thank you, but there's a difference between me being willing to step out on a ledge and me dragging you with me. If you need a break from Grandpa, you can go to Aunt Carol's or Aunt Loretta's."

"Fine. I'll just head home." He pouted, snatching a couple more biscuits before he lumbered out the door.

"That kid's going to be as big as a house," I said, giggling.

"We weren't done discussing you staying alone," Reel said, pulling my chin over to face him.

"You have to let me live my life, Reel," I said, placing my palm on his cheek.

He grasped my hand and kissed my palm. "Promise to set the alarm and not go anywhere?"

"That's the plan," I said. "Now, get your bag out of my spare room and go home."

"Your spare room?"

During my two-week protection detail, we had been renovating my share of the upstairs, converting the offices into a living space. So far, I had a makeshift kitchenette, an unfinished but framed bathroom and a framed room for a large bedroom. Reel had been sleeping down the hall on a couch in one of the untouched offices. It wasn't ideal, but we had made it work, and the renovations had helped take my mind off of a madman trying to kill me and the memories of my dead father.

"It's time, Reel."

"Are you sure? Maybe I should stay a few more days," he whispered, leaning his forehead against mine.

"You can't," I said, shaking my head. "I plan on soaking in the tub tonight, and the walls aren't finished."

"I won't peek."

Aunt Carol snorted as she walked past us and put a container of macaroni salad in the oversized refrigerator. "You need anything else before I take off?"

"No, I'm good. Take Reel out the door with you."

"Come on, Reel. You can give me a ride home. Mike took my car in for service this morning."

"Yes, ma'am." Reel kissed me on the cheek before jogging up the stairs to get his bags.

"You sure about staying by yourself? Tansey has to work tonight and won't be home until late."

"I'm sure. I need the quiet."

"Alright then. Call if you need anything," Aunt Carol nodded as I walked her to the door.

"Love you," I said, kissing her on the cheek as she left.

Reel returned and followed her out.

"Love you too, Tweedle," Aunt Carol said, leading Reel down the porch stairs. "Enjoy that hot steamy bath."

"I plan on it." I shut and locked the door.

I set the alarm, not because I didn't feel safe, but because I'd promised. Walking through the bakery and deli shop, I checked all the windows and doors to make sure everything was buttoned up for the night. I still had cleaning to do, but tomorrow was Sunday, and we didn't open until 10:00, so I would do it in the morning.

Tansey was only working Friday and Saturday nights at the bar now. She worked the rest of the week in the deli with Aunt Carol. Samantha covered the bakery side, and most of the time I was happily tucked away in the kitchen baking. Special orders from five counties kept me busy, on top of the town's donut and pie consumption. Profits were actually better than expected, and Tansey was selling her paintings regularly too.

Turning off the downstairs lights, I looked around the shadowy rooms one last time before climbing the stairs. Entering my apartment, I smiled. The drywall had been hung on my new bedroom walls. Reel and Rod had been upstairs earlier in the day and must've installed it while I worked.

I crossed to the bedroom which still lacked a door. Even with the walls unfinished, they'd put together my bed, complete with sheets, blankets, and a single rose lying on top of one of the pillows. I finally had some privacy to sleep—on the same night I'd kicked everyone out.

Stripping off my clothes, I dropped them in the washer on my way to the bathroom. I started the water, dumping some bath salts into the tub and setting a towel on the floor. I didn't wait for the water to fill, getting in and letting the warm water rise around me.

When the water reached my shoulders, I shut the faucet off and relaxed.

My phone rang from my purse, sitting on the kitchen counter.

"Damn it."

Wrapping the towel around me, I ran to answer the phone, dripping water across the floor. As I pulled the phone out, my foot slipped, and I landed on my butt. My towel had sprung loose, and I was sitting naked in a puddle of water.

I sighed and looked at my phone, still resting in my hand, but no longer ringing.

I hit call-back and wasn't surprised to hear Tansey's voice answer immediately. "I can't reach Rod or Reel, and their father is three sheets to the wind and needs a ride. Can Reel come get him?"

"Reel's not here, but I can come pick him up. Just let me throw on some clothes."

"Are you in your PJs already?" Tansey asked.

"Actually, I'm sitting naked on the kitchen floor, but the story that goes along with that isn't so great. I'll be there in ten minutes."

"How are you going to get here?"

"I'll find a ride and then drive Everett's truck home. Don't sweat it."

After disconnecting, I turned over on all fours to crawl up off the floor. I stomped carefully into the bedroom and found a hot pink sweat suit that was ugly as hell but clean. I left my hair up in a pompom-style ponytail. I didn't care what I looked like. My nice relaxing night at home had been interrupted, and I was grumpy.

Not able to find clean socks, I stuffed my feet into a pair of flip-flops and marched out the door. I walked into the middle of the street and waited for the next car to come. A blue SUV slowed and stopped, and I walked to the passenger side and got in.

"Miss Tweedle," Mr. Palmer, the bank manager, said wearing a grin.

"Mr. Palmer," I greeted him back, pointing down the street. "Tansey called me and asked if I could drive Everett home. Can you drop me off at The Bar?"

"My pleasure," Mr. Palmer nodded, resuming his drive down Main Street. "Still don't have a car yet?"

"No. I haven't really needed one. Maybe I'll keep Everett's truck for a days though."

"He'll think he misplaced it," Mr. Palmer said, chuckling.

"I doubt anyone would rat me out," I said, nodding. "So, anything new lately?"

"All the gossip the past few weeks has been centered on you. Oh, except your grandpa tried to pay off your mortgage. I told him to go to hell."

"Thanks. I appreciate it."

"I enjoyed it. Your grandpa is a good man except when it's about money. Then he's a pompous ass."

"Alpha idiot," I mumbled.

~*~*~

Everett wasn't the only drunk who needed a ride home. Tansey laughed out loud and rolled her eyes at me when she saw me in my neon pink outfit, then pointed to the back of the bar. I winked at her as I pushed through the crowd, moving to the back wall where Darlene was eagerly being groped. I grabbed what I hoped was an exposed elbow and pulled her out, away from the man who was feeling her up.

"Hey, what the hell?" the drunk yelled.

"Come on, Darlene, the night is over," I said, dragging her along.

The drunk grabbed her other arm and jerked us both to a stop.

"Take your hand off my sister," I demanded, stepping between Darlene and the drunk.

"And if I don't?" he slurred.

"Davey," the bartender yelled.

The drunk looked briefly at the bartender with blurry eyes before dismissing the warning. He jerked Darlene's arm again, and I saw red. Swinging my arm back, I let my heavy purse swing like a wrecking ball into his family jewels. He caved to the floor, instantly puking as he cupped his nuts.

Several men and women laughed as I guided my sister's drunk ass through the bar, grabbing Everett on my way past and pulling them both out to the parking lot and toward Everett's truck.

"Everett?" I said, holding my hand out.

Everett handed me the keys, knowing better than to argue with me. I opened the passenger door and helped both of them into the pickup before I shut the door and walked to the other side. As I went to open the door, I heard something from the edge of the tree line. I looked, but it was too dark to make out what caused the noise. Probably a coon scrounging up dinner. I shrugged and climbed into the truck, turning it over to hear its low rumble. After carefully backing out of the lot, I drove toward Everett's house. Darlene, unfortunately, would probably be sleeping at my place tonight. She was too wasted to be left alone and with Mother in jail, I had inherited the problem.

Turning down River Road, I slowed for a sharp curve. High-beam headlights turned on behind us, glaring into the mirrors and windshield. I hadn't noticed anyone driving behind us, but now I could see the bright lights approaching fast. The curve up ahead was too sharp to speed up, and I watched helplessly as the vehicle behind us slammed into the back of our truck.

The tail of the truck veered into the center of the road, but I tucked the wheel tight and accelerated as we pulled out of the curve. She straightened out on the other side.

"What the hell?" Everett yelled.

"Seatbelts," I yelled back. "Help Darlene get buckled in."

I dug into my purse, finding my phone. I hit redial and put the phone on speaker as I sped up and prepared for the next turn.

"The Bar," Casey, the owner, answered.

"Casey! Tell Tansey to call for help. I ran into trouble on my way to Everett's house. Someone's trying to run us off the road."

The vehicle behind us slammed into us again, sending us skidding toward the side of the road. I dropped the phone as we all screamed. I struggled with the steering wheel, trying to keep us partially on the pavement. Jerking the wheel hard, the truck skipped over the graveled edge so all four tires were once again on asphalt, but we had lost speed. Before I could put any distance between us and the other vehicle, it rammed us again, sending us spinning in circles in the other direction, launching us over the edge and down a steep hill.

Darlene grabbed my hand as we both screamed. Trees and brush flew past us at an alarming rate as the truck continued straight down. Everett leaned forward, grabbing the wheel, jerking it toward his side. A large tree scraped down my side of the truck, flinging the side mirror off as we passed. The friction slowed our speed, but not enough to stop us from slamming into the large evergreen that stood in front of us. Everything turned fuzzy as my eyes closed.

~*~*~

My ears rang, and I felt nauseated. I looked up to see Darlene was standing over me and appeared to be yelling. I couldn't understand what she was saying, but Everett helped her drag me up out of the brush, and they pulled me deeper into the woods. I felt heat on my back and turned to see the truck ignite. I forced my legs under me and turned away from the truck. I started running on shaky legs, pulling them with me.

"Shit, shit, shit," I mumbled, when we stopped near a stream.

I pulled Everett and Darlene down beside me. We would be hidden from sight, but any fool would be able to track us. I looked down at my feet, realizing my flip-flops were long gone and my feet were covered in mud and bloody scrapes.

"Who the hell was that?" Everett asked, peeking out to see whether anyone approached.

"My guess is that it's Morgan Marlian."

"My father is trying to kill me?" Darlene squealed.

I covered her mouth with both my hands and pulled her down into the mud beside me.

"No," I whispered. "He's trying to kill *me*."

"Why?" Everett whispered.

"Because I witnessed him kill our dad."

Darlene pushed my hands away and glared. "You mean your dad."

"That man loved you like his own. Don't you dare disrespect his memory."

She bit her lip when it started to tremble. I had been so busy with everyone and everything else, I had never made the time to see how Darlene was handling everything. She might have been a bitch, but she was still my sister. I should have been there for her. Maybe during the funeral I had been too big of a mess to help her, but afterward, I should have been there.

"It's going to be alright," I said, throwing an arm around her. "But we are sitting ducks here. We have to get moving."

"If we try to circle back up to the road, he'll spot us for sure," Everett said.

"Isn't this the creek that heads up to Reel's fishing cabin?"

"Might be," Everett said, looking around. "Can't say as I've been sober long enough the past few years to come out this way."

"I'll recognize it when we get closer. If I'm right, it should be about two miles up the creek."

"Two miles?" Darlene whimpered.

"If we stick together, we'll make it. Come on," I said, as I pulled her up behind me.

We stayed low for the first mile and close to the creek. If anyone was following our trail, though, they'd have an easy time of catching up with us. After another half mile, the ground started to flatten out. We were losing our cover.

"We need to move faster. Let's run for it," I called out to Everett, who was leading the way.

"You sure?" he asked, looking back at me and the dark woods surrounding us.

"It's our only chance. We'll be exposed as the ground flattens out, anyway. We need to hurry."

"Come on, Darlene," Everett said, pulling her by her other arm. "Let's hightail it across, but stay together."

We took off running along the bank of the creek. The ground flattened out in a valley, and a gunshot split the silence. The bark on the tree next to me ricocheted around us as we kept running as fast as we could. Another shot rang out, and Everett went spinning to the ground. Darlene and I both grabbed him under an arm and hauled him along with us.

Passing three pines in a clump by the creek's edge, I ordered Darlene to turn right. We had to run, dragging Everett uphill, but when we reached the top, we could see the cabin.

"Hurry," Darlene cried out.

Everett was conscious but didn't seem to have the use of one of his legs. "Leave me. You can make it if you leave me."

"Not happening, old man."

"Who's out there?" a male voice called from the front porch, holding a rifle.

"Friends of Ryan's!" I yelled. "There's a man trying to kill us!"

Another shot rang out, kicking the grass up against my back as we ran.

"Drop to the ground!" the man on the porch yelled.

The three of us dropped, throwing our hands over our heads as shots rang out over us.

"Move! Now!" the man yelled.

Pulling Everett up with us, we followed orders and resumed our dash across the yard to the fishing cabin. Once we were close enough to the porch, the man jumped off the side and took over getting Everett inside as we all barreled in and locked the door.

"Storm shutters," the man ordered.

Darlene and I ran through the small cabin and locked the windows and interior storm shutters. The only light inside the cabin was a small fire in the fireplace. Everett laid on the floor in front of it, sweaty and pale. Filling a bowl of water and gathering some rags, I rushed back as the stranger was ripping a hole in Everett's jeans.

"Leo, come in. Leo, it's an emergency," I heard Reel's voice over the nearby CB radio.

"Get that," the stranger said, taking the rags and water from my hands.

"Reel, we need help," I answered over the radio.

"Is Leo with you?"

"If that's the man mending up your dad, yes."

"We're on our way. What's happening?"

"We were run off the road. We made it to the cabin, but your dad was shot in the leg. We are locked inside."

"Tell Leo that I have guns hidden in my room under the bed. We are fifteen minutes away."

"Reel, I'm scared," I admitted, my hands shaking.

Darlene walked over and took the CB.

"Reel," she said over the CB. "He was right behind us when we got to the cabin. You have to hurry. I will never forgive you if you don't save my sister. She's the best person I know."

"I'll get there, Darlene," Reel answered before the CB squawked and cut out.

"Did you hear that?" Leo whispered, looking around the cabin like he was trying to see through the walls. "You," he said pointing to Darlene, "Help me drag him into the hallway. He'll be better protected there."

"The name is Darlene," she said, hurrying over to help drag Everett. "This is Everett, Reel's dad. And that's my sister, Deanna. But everyone calls her Tweedle."

"I'm Leo," he nodded. "Let's hope we all live long enough to have made it worth the time wasted on introductions. Deanna, get the guns."

I ran down the short hall into the bedroom and shoved the bed out of the way. The gun storage unit was already open, with a gun missing. Probably the rifle that Leo had shot to give us cover to get to the cabin. I grabbed two handguns and checked the clips.

"You know how to shoot that?" Leo asked, taking the other handgun.

"Yup. And I'm not planning on aiming for his toes either."

Leo looked at me curiously but then moved back down the hall. Darlene held the rifle, watching the living room. Leo stationed himself against the wall so he could watch both the living room and the bedroom.

I crouched down next to Everett and wiped the sweat off his forehead with my sleeve. He was unconscious. "How is he?"

"Wound isn't that deep, but the bleeding isn't slowing down."

"He's a tough old bird. He'll make it," Darlene said, not turning her attention from the living room as she answered.

A gunshot blew a hole in the door, but the latch held it closed. Darlene and Leo returned fire. After several rounds, they stopped and waited. A side window was shot out in the living room.

"He's baiting us," Darlene said. "Looking for a read on our location."

"Or trying to make an opening large enough," Leo whispered.

"Large enough for what?" I asked, dreading the answer.

"To drop something inside and torch the place," Darlene whispered.

"It would be the smart move," Leo nodded.

"The smart move? Who the hell are you?" I whispered.

"An acquaintance of Reel's who isn't stable enough to be let loose on the world."

"Should I be pointing my gun at you?" Darlene asked, raising an eyebrow.

"Naw. You're too cute to kill," Leo said.

I set the gun down and crawled back into Reel's room. I opened the top dresser drawer, finding some socks. Crawling to the closet, I dug around for some shoes and was both happy and annoyed to find a pair of women's tennis shoes.

"What are you doing?" Leo whispered, poking his head in the bedroom.

"If I die out here, promise me two things," I grumbled, as I slid the shoes and socks on.

"What?"

"First, get these damn shoes off me. Second, punch Reel. And I mean *hard*."

"Wait—Ryan and Reel are the same person, right?"

"Yeah," I nodded, lacing up the second shoe.

"And why would I punch him?"

"Hand him the shoes and he'll know why."

I crawled back into the hall and waited.

"Whatever you are thinking, it's a stupid idea," Darlene said.

"He wants me. Not any of you. When he tries to shoot out the next window or door, I'll make a run for it in the other direction. He'll follow me away from the cabin. He won't waste the time to light it on fire first."

"I'll go," Leo said, holding my arm to stop me.

"Won't work," Darlene said. "She's right. He wants her." She passed the rifle off to Leo and took his handgun. "But you're not going alone. I will go with you. Then Leo can get Everett out of here and to a hospital."

"No deal. I can move faster on my own. Reel will find me in time. Stay with Leo and help get Everett out. If you see Reel, tell him I'll take the trails to the east for as long as it's safe to stay on them. He knows these woods."

"And if Reel doesn't find you in time?" Darlene glared, her eyes shining with unshed tears.

"Then get your shit together and make me proud, sister," I said, pulling her in for a brief hug.

A shot rang out through the bedroom window, and I ran for the front door before anyone could argue. Throwing the door open, I jumped off the side of the porch, stumbling before I got my feet back under me again. I started for the east trail as I yelled out behind me, "Come and get me asshole!!"

A shot rang out, shredding a chunk of bark on a tree as I ran past. I ran faster.

Chapter Twenty-Eight

I was slowing. I couldn't help it. My jelly legs were unaccustomed to so much exercise. Okay, they weren't accustomed to any exercise. And neither were my lungs, as each breath seemed to burn in my chest like I was inhaling flames. Sweat dripped off me and ran down my forehead into my eyes, making it even harder to see in the near blackness.

I knew I had to turn off the trail and attempt to hide before he caught up with me. I might have been almost thirty years younger, but he had been gaining on me, and the shots were getting closer and closer. Ducking to the left, I raced down an open hill and crossed into a patch of trees as another shot rang out. I couldn't hear where the shot had landed and glanced over my shoulder to see whether I could see anything. As I ran blindly forward, the ground disappeared under my foot, and the next thing I knew, I was rolling down a steep bank, landing in a muddy gulley.

I scampered to the side of the gulley, trying to pull myself up the other side. I made it about ten feet before I dropped to my knees, unable to keep going. I turned, leaning my back into the muddy slope, nestled between two scraggly bushes, and waited. I could only hope that I was covered in enough mud to hide me in the dark. I wasn't so lucky.

"Trying to hide in a hot pink jogging suit is a bit silly," a man's voice called from above me. "Even if most of it's covered in mud."

"Yeah, well, I'm tired," I answered, breathing heavy. "I just can't run anymore. Maybe if you leave and we try this again in another month or so, it will be more sporting for you."

"You're funny," he said humorlessly as he jogged down the bank beside me. "Your dad was funny, too."

"Is that why you killed him? You have something against people with a sense of humor?"

"I had something against a man trying to raise another man's daughter as his own," he snapped. "Darlene was my daughter, not his. He had no right."

"So, he did know? That Darlene wasn't his?"

"He knew alright. Said he knew it the moment he saw her, but he didn't care."

"Ever hear of filing for shared custody? You didn't have to kill him."

"I would have just taken her, if it weren't for your grandpa," Morgan snorted. "He had evidence against my brother and me. We would have gone to prison. Killing your father was the best option."

"For what purpose? You still didn't have a relationship with Darlene."

"That was your mother's fault." He slid the last few feet down the bank to stand in front of me in the muck. "Evil bitch. She said she had proof that I murdered your father and that if anything ever happened to her or Darlene, her lawyer would turn the evidence over to the police."

"If anything happened to them," I mumbled, repeating the thought aloud.

"Oh, you picked up on that did you?" He laughed. "She never once offered to protect you. I would've killed you years ago, but it appeared you'd forgotten all about that night. But when that fella of yours bought the house, I realized it was only a matter of time before you remembered, so I decided your time was up."

I snorted. "You make a terrible hitman," I said, thinking of all the times he'd tried to kill me. "I mean, the Ferris wheel? The snake? Tampering with my accelerator, chasing me with your truck, the gas leak, and let's not forget the number of times you shot at me—*and missed. Really?* Mrs. Crookburn came closer to killing me with her Buick at the bakery."

"I'm much better at killing people up close," he said, pointing the shotgun at my head from only four feet away.

"Just answer one more question before you pull the trigger."

"Make it quick."

"Why does my mother hate me?" I asked, looking up at him, hoping to understand after all these years.

He laughed, lowering the gun. "That's easy. Because after she had you, she was stuck in this town for the rest of her life. Forever doomed to live in boredom. She knew your father, your uncle, your aunt, and your grandpa would never let her leave and take you with her. You were the anchor that choked the life out of her."

I sat in the muck in silence, thinking about what Morgan said. Maybe it was true. Maybe I was the final weight that held my mother imprisoned in a life she never wanted. Or maybe he was full of shit. I'd probably never know.

But I knew the rest of what he said was true. My father, my uncle, my aunt, and my grandpa would never have let her take me away from them. They would have protected Darlene the same way. It made sense that my father gave his life trying to protect her. I was willing to do the same.

I looked back up at Morgan and nodded that I was ready. He slowly raised the gun again, and even in the shadowy darkness, I could see his eyes shine in excitement. What he didn't know, was that I planned on taking him with me.

Raising my own gun, I expected him to shoot me immediately, but he was startled by a deep growling-hiss from his left. Covered in dark fur against the muddy bank, the creature stood only a few feet away from Morgan. I couldn't make out the type of animal in the blackness, but its long, sharp canine teeth glowed against the dark background. Morgan and I both froze, watching it.

The animal continued hissing and moved side to side, seeming to pace within only a few feet as it watched Morgan. Morgan broke his stance, taking a step back, and the creature leapt, sinking sharp fangs into his thigh as its front claws struck out. Startled, I jumped back, leaning into the muddy bank behind me, and unintentionally pulled the trigger of my gun that was still aimed at Morgan. He fell backward screaming, and I watched in horror as the creature jumped from Morgan's leg to his face as it attacked. He screamed, trying to tear it off.

"Shit, shit, shit," I whimpered as icy chills ran down my back and I turned to furiously climb up the side of the bank, trying to block out the hissing, growling, and screaming behind me.

Needing both hands, I tossed the gun and sank my fingers into the muddy tufts of grass to pull myself up. At the top, a solid set of arms lifted me and turned me away from the ledge.

The blackness of the night prevented me from seeing who held me, but I knew by the scent and feel that it was Reel. "Got-t-t, tt-ttt-ooo, l-l-leavvve," I stammered, gripping tight to him.

"I've got you," he whispered. "Is that Morgan down there?"

"Mmm-monnn-st-tt-ter, got-t-t-t, 'im," I stuttered, trying to calm my shaking.

"Holy shit," Leo said from beside us, leaning over the ledge with a flashlight. "She's not fool'n'. Something is attacking the shit out of him. I think he's dead."

"What?" Reel said, leaning toward the edge.

"Noooo!" I yelled, beating on his chest and pulling us away from the ledge. "You, take me home," I cried. "Right now. Damn it, Reel. *Take me home.*"

"You heard her, Leo," Reel said, picking me up and carrying me in his arms. "Time to get my girl home. She's as strong as they come, but when she's done, she's done."

"Yeah, no problem. I promised Darlene we'd find her and bring her back. The quicker the better before she causes any more trouble."

"Still can't believe Darlene punched Rod."

"She thought he was you."

"That's why it's funny."

"And you think I'm the crazy one."

I listened to their banter as I held Reel close, and my body trembled from the horrific scenes playing in my mind.

"Shhh," Reel whispered. "I'm right here."

I was with Reel. I was safe.

I drifted off to sleep.

Chapter Twenty-Nine

I woke in my own bed, curled up tight against Reel. I knew I should move away, but he felt warm and safe, and I needed more of that.

"You okay?" he whispered, sensing I was awake.

"No," I answered, feeling another round of tears coming. "I killed him, didn't I?"

"No, babe," he said, kissing my forehead, before dragging my body up on top of his so he could see my face. "You didn't kill anyone."

"But he's dead?"

"Don't know yet," Reel said, shrugging. "I hope so, but the search party waited for daylight to go look for a body."

"You stayed here? With me?"

"No place I'd rather be," he said, cupping my face in his hand. "I love you, Deanna."

"You don't know me," I said sighing and resting my head on his chest.

I felt his chest rumble as he laughed. "You love to bake because it keeps your mind settled and your hands busy. You easily forgive and seldom anger. You find humor in almost any situation. And when you love," he said, pulling me up again to face him, "it's forever. Because you only know how to go all-in."

He kissed me. Not the quick peck on the lips or a calming kiss on the forehead, but a passionate kiss. His tongue and hands searching desperately, finding the truth in my response as I clung to him, my hands running through his hair and stroking his chest. I deeply inhaled as the kiss broke and he looked at me.

"Tell me you love me," he panted.

"I love you," I whispered back, my heart pounding in my chest.

He rolled us so he rested above me.

"Tell me again."

"I love you," I repeated, grinning.

He leaned in to kiss me again when a loud pounding on the wall interrupted us.

"Excuse me, but not only is there not a door on her bedroom, but do you really think it would be okay to deflower my niece while we are all waiting for her in the living room?"

I heard Aunt Carol snort from the other room.

"I'm not a virgin, Uncle Mike," I said, rolling out from under Reel and getting out of bed.

"Careful," Reel said, warning me as I stood.

Sharp pain lanced up my feet, forcing me back down on the bed. "Shit," I said, looking at the shredded pads of my feet.

"Good thing you found those tennis shoes, or your feet would really be toast," Reel said as he sat up.

I tried to stop myself, I really did. My arm flung forward, and my fist slammed into his mouth. Intentional or reactionary, it didn't matter. I was mad. I forced myself onto my sore feet and limped into the other room.

I heard Reel cussing and Uncle Mike laughing.

"Deanna," Reel called, following me out.

"Don't talk to me," I snapped, flopping onto the couch. "The least you could have done was thrown out your old girlfriend's crap before declaring your love for me."

"They are *your* tennis shoes!" Reel laughed, holding the back of his hand to his lower lip. He tossed a muddy shoe onto the floor in front of me. I looked down and tried to understand. "You were eighteen and drove out to my fishing cabin to seduce me, remember?" Reel said, sitting next to me on the couch.

"Damn, I forgot about that."

"*What?*" Uncle Mike yelled.

"I don't know this story," Tansey said, leaning forward in her chair. "What happened?"

"She had been drinking. I paddled her ass for driving and then took her home. She had taken off her shoes when she got there, though, and I was so mad I hadn't noticed."

"You noticed other apparel being removed though."

"It's been burned in my mind for years. I'm not likely to forget."

"You left two days later," I sighed.

"I had to return to the Army. You knew that. And I wasn't going to start something I wasn't sure I could finish," he said, pulling me over and tucking me into his shoulder. "I can't believe you sucker-punched me."

"You somehow deserved it, even if my reason wasn't accurate."

"Probably so," he chuckled.

"Look at how cute of a couple you two make," Rod said, turning his devilish eyes on Tansey.

"Not happening," she told him, shaking her head.

"A bet's a bet, Tansey," Rod said.

"What bet?" I asked.

"I was sixteen! It doesn't count!" Tansey yelled, getting up from the couch and tossing a throw pillow at Rod.

"What bet?" I asked again.

"She agreed to date me if you and Reel ever hooked up," Rod said.

"How did I not know about this?" I asked, turning to watch Tansey.

"Like it was ever in the realm of possibilities," Tansey said, throwing her arms up in the air. "Besides, I can't be held accountable. I wasn't even old enough to vote yet."

"No, I think Rod's right." Reel chuckled. "A bet's a bet."

"He's laughing again," Wayne said as he entered the apartment with Bones and Leo. "That's so damn freaky."

"Did you find him?" Reel asked, the laughter draining from his face as he pulled his arm tighter around me.

"No. Sorry, man," Bones said, shaking his head. "We found a lot of blood, the guns, and what looked like badger tracks, but he must have crawled away after you left."

"But I shot him," I said, looking up at Bones.

Everyone turned and looked at me.

"In the foot or the knee?" Bridget asked.

"In the chest," I answered. "When the creature attacked, I jumped and shot him on accident. But I was already aiming the gun at his chest."

"Umm, Tweedle," Uncle Mike said, scrubbing his hand across his forehead. "Did you have your eyes open when you pulled the trigger?"

"Of course not, but I opened them right after, and he had fallen backwards, so I must have hit him."

"What?" Wayne asked, seeming confused.

Aunt Carol, Tansey, and Bridget broke out laughing.

Reel sighed and leaned his head back on the couch. "You never told me that you close your eyes when you shoot."

"She closes her eyes when she catches a ball too," Uncle Mike chuckled.

"I shot him!" I yelled. "I know I did. Why else would he have fallen backward?"

"Tripped on a root?" Leo said.

"Slipped in the mud?" Wayne said.

"Surprised that you pulled the trigger and tripped over his own two feet?" Bones said.

"Fell over laughing," Reel said, which earned him an elbow to the ribs. "Ow! Sorry, babe."

"I shot him," I pouted.

"I believe you," Bridget said. "Close your eyes and think back for a moment. What noise did you hear right after you pulled the trigger?"

I sat up straighter and closed my eyes, concentrating on the moment. I pulled the trigger and right before I opened my eyes again, I heard Morgan.

"*Air*!" I answered loudly. "I heard air whoosh out of Morgan as he fell backward."

"See! She shot him. Might not have been a fatal shot, but she hit her mark. He's at least wounded," Bridget said.

"Way to go, sister," Darlene said, offering me a high-five.

I slapped her hand as the room went silent. I looked around at all the surprised faces. "Darlene and I are good again."

"For the moment," Darlene added.

"So you're not a bitch anymore?" Tansey asked.

"Oh, I'm still a bitch. I just don't hate my sister anymore."

Tansey shrugged and went to fill her coffee cup.

"What's next? How do we hunt this asshole down?"

"No clue," Reel said.

"I called Kelsey," Wayne said. "She figures he'll either go somewhere safe to hide and lick his wounds or he's already trying to find a way to get to Tweedle."

A cold shiver raced up my back. Reel rubbed his hand up and down my arms to comfort me.

"So where would he hide?" Darlene asked.

"His son might know," I said quietly. "Randall hates his father. He might tell me how to find him."

"How would you know that Randall hates his father?" Uncle Mike demanded.

Tansey was about to sit when she veered the other direction to leave the room. Rod hooked an arm around her waist and stopped her.

"Talk," he ordered her.

"It wasn't *my* idea," she insisted.

"It never is, dear," Aunt Carol said, shaking her head. "But at some point, you need to learn to put your foot down when Tweedle starts to steer you down a dark road."

"You talked to my brother?" Darlene asked, scuffing her foot over the floor.

"He's an asshole," I nodded. "And he tried to kill our grandpa, but he's nothing like Morgan."

"You mean, *your* grandpa," Darlene sighed.

"No, I don't," I said, rolling my eyes. "Both Dad and Grandpa knew you weren't biologically related, but they still tried to protect you. They considered you family. Dad died trying to protect you because he loved you as his own daughter."

Darlene looked away.

"I'm family," Tansey said, giving Darlene a pointed look. "And there's not a drop of blood linking us."

"But maybe the reason I've never felt like family is because I have my biological father's bad genes."

"Bullshit," Bridget said. "My father makes yours look like a saint. But he has no hold over how I live my life. If you feel like an outsider, it's because you've treated everyone like you're an outsider. Trust them and they'll trust you. It won't happen overnight, but it can happen. And it can change your life for the better." Bridget walked out of the apartment and down the stairs.

Bones shifted to the door, following her out.

"I need to go see Randall," I said more to myself than anyone else.

"No," Reel said, shaking his head. "Don't argue, please. I just need you to be safe for a little while before you leap into doing something dangerous again."

"I'll go. He's my brother," Darlene said.

"That's not a good idea," Tansey warned.

"He's a little obsessive with you," I said, shaking my head.

"Why wouldn't he be? He's just as shocked as I am to find out we're related. I'm curious about him too, even though, yeah, he must be a little crazy to try to kill my grandpa."

"A little crazy?" Tansey shuddered. "The man is downright creepy."

"I'll go with her," Leo said, watching Darlene.

She nodded but didn't say anything.

"I'll go too," Tansey offered, retrieving her purse. "I already know the drill from when I went with Tweedle."

"You'd do that?" Darlene asked.

"For now, I'd do that as a favor to Tweedle," Tansey answered. "It'll take you not being a bitch to me for at least a day before I do you any favors."

"No promises," Darlene said, following her out the door.

We watched them walk out and close the door behind them. I hoped that Darlene meeting her brother didn't cause more damage. She had enough feelings she was trying to sort through.

"Rod, how's Everett?" Aunt Carol asked.

"Detoxing," Rod said.

I grinned and turned to Reel.

"Don't get too excited. We've heard Everett promise before he was done with the drinking."

"But not in a long time," I said. "This might be the big one. The one that ends it for good."

"You are so optimistic," Reel said, snorting.

"It's all rainbows and sunshine," Uncle Mike said, rolling his eyes.

"Don't forget the unicorns," Aunt Carol added while filling everyone's coffee cups.

"What?" Wayne asked.

"Her bedroom at her aunt and uncle's house," Reel explained. "She had Tansey paint a big sun on one wall, and the rest of the walls were plastered with rainbows and unicorns."

"How in the hell do you know what my girl's room looked like?" Uncle Mike yelled.

"I guessed?" Reel said as a question, shrugging. He couldn't stop the grin that crossed his face.

Uncle Mike threw the apartment door open and stomped down the stairs.

"What time is it?" I asked in a panic.

"Almost 8:00, dear. We put a sign up that the bakery would be closed today."

"Like hell," I said. "The gossipmongers will buy everything we can stock just to get a peek at me to see whether I'm alive. For a small town, this is great marketing. And I have a mortgage to pay."

I stood and carefully stepped over Reel's outstretched legs as I wobbled on the outsides of my feet toward the bedroom. "Everyone out. I need to get dressed. Shoo. I don't have any doors yet."

Chapter Thirty

By noon, the seating area and the front porch were standing room only. We were selling everything before we could put it in a display case. The deli was sold out of chicken salad, macaroni salad, and egg salad. Aunt Carol was scrambling to make more, and I had every oven baking something, bread sitting off to the side rising, and had been feeding the deep fryer for hours.

Samantha and Bridget were serving customers and running the checkout counter until Tansey returned and jumped in to help. We were too busy for me to ask how the prison visit went, but Reel stepped off the back porch with a comforting arm around Darlene.

We were only open for four hours on Sundays, just 10:00 to 2:00, but it took us another hour to get everyone to clear out.

"That was insane," Aunt Carol sighed.

"But makes for one hell of an extra payment against the mortgage," Tansey said, smiling as she counted out the cash from the register drawer.

"We did okay, then?" I asked.

Tansey nodded, continuing to count.

I sat at one of the tables and propped my feet up. "Where did all the pictures go?"

Reel pulled out the chair next to me, sitting. "A friend of mine swung in and bought all of them. He's an art fanatic and fell in love with them. He's going to show them to some art dealers he knows."

I leaned over and kissed Reel on the cheek. "Thank you."

"I didn't do it for you," Reel said. "I did it for the commission."

"What commission?" I asked, concerned for Tansey.

"Snickers bars," Tansey said, laughing as she tossed a dozen of them on the table in front of Reel. "Seems you're not the only one addicted to the damn things."

Reel tore a bar open and bit into it. "What? I won't allow myself to buy junk food, but it doesn't count if someone gives it to me."

"If you get fat, I'm firing your ass," a man said as he walked down the back hallway and into the seating area. He was clean cut, wearing a pressed button-up shirt and gray dress pants. But his eyes held a seriousness that absorbed everything around him.

Reel choked on the candy bar he was eating. I thumped him on the back before standing.

"Are you Donovan? " I asked. "Reel's boss at the security firm?"

"Yes. You must be Deanna," he said without extending a hand or a smile.

"I have a question, and I want an honest answer," I said, placing my hands on my hips.

"If I choose to answer the question, I'll answer honestly," Donovan said, squaring his already tense shoulders.

"Is he safe when he's out on assignments?"

"No. None of them are safe. But we do everything we can to take precautions and back each other up. I'd take a bullet to protect him."

"And is he good at his job?"

"That's a second question, but I'll answer it because I think you need to hear the answer. He's not good at it, he excels at it. He's saved a lot of lives. Both clients and co-workers."

"And if he ever showed signs of being reckless?"

"I'd send his ass home in a heartbeat," Donovan said.

I reached out and hugged him. "Welcome."

Donovan laughed, hugging me back. "I like her."

"I'm glad; now take your hands off my woman," Reel growled. "Deanna, get off those feet. You should have spent the day soaking them instead of working."

Reel pulled out a chair, and I obeyed, sitting and propping my feet up.

"Donovan, what the hell are you doing here?" Reel asked.

"Kelsey sent me. She didn't like what she was hearing. She wanted to come herself, but Nicholas threw a fit."

"Can't say I blame the kid," Reel said. "He just got her back. It's going to be awhile before he feels safe again."

"Her son?" I asked.

"Long story," Reel nodded, grabbing my hand and intertwining our fingers.

"I also heard that Bridget is stealing wallets still." Donovan glared across the room at Bridget.

Bridget cringed, and Bones looked at the floor, chuckling.

"She's teaching us to stay alert to our surroundings," I defended Bridget. "She doesn't keep the wallets but reminds us of how easy it is to have someone deceive us. It's been helpful."

"I'm a cop, and she's snagged mine three times now," Uncle Mike grumbled. "Tweedle's right. Bridget's good for us. If you don't want her working for your firm, I'll get her a job at the police department."

"We'll see how it goes," Donovan said, shaking his head. "Now fill me in on the case."

"We have a possible location of where Morgan is hiding, but we have to wait until nightfall," Reel said coldly, as he leaned forward in his chair.

"What are you talking about? What don't I know?"

"It's fine, babe. Darlene got a possible location out of her brother, so we are going to check it out. This is what we do, remember?" He looked at me, trying to reassure me, but I could see the rage simmering behind his crystal blue eyes. He was distancing himself, pulling back so he could focus on Morgan Marlian.

"You can't kill him," I whispered.

Multiple sets of eyes turned toward me, but no one spoke.

"Reel, he's Darlene's biological father."

"If we can take him alive, we will," Wayne nodded. "But we won't take a chance of him coming after you or Darlene. If there's a choice that has to be made, I'll drop a bullet in him myself."

I scrunched up my nose, not liking that answer, but knowing it was the best I was going to get. I nodded at Wayne and heard everyone around me release the breaths they held.

"Come on," Reel said, picking me up out of my chair and carrying me. "I hear you have a freezer full of Klondike bars and every season of *The Big Bang Theory* waiting for you upstairs."

"You're kicking me out?"

"No," Reel said. "I'm letting everyone else talk about work while I curl up with you in bed and watch TV."

"Don't get any ideas," Tansey said, passing us to run up the stairs. "I'm also going to be in that bed, so no hanky-panky allowed."

"Wouldn't expect anything else," Reel grumbled, rolling his eyes.

"I have doors for my apartment on order," I whispered to Reel. "They should be here next week."

"Do they have locks on them?"

"They will after you install them."

Chapter Thirty-One

"I'm bored," I pouted to Tansey.

"No. We are not sneaking back downstairs again. The house is filled with trained military men. Every time we've tried, they've caught us, and we've looked like idiots."

Reel had watched TV with us for a little over an hour before he got a text asking for his presence downstairs. Every time we went below, we were sent back upstairs like teenagers.

"Why won't they tell us what's going on? And why did Darlene tell you that she didn't get any information out of her brother, when obviously she did?"

"I was right there with her, so it makes no sense to me. He told her he didn't have a clue where his father would be hiding, and I believed him. When we got back here, Reel pulled her aside, and they argued. But I don't know about what."

"So I'm just supposed to sit here like a good little girl?" I pouted again, throwing my lower lip out for added effect.

"Let's go over to my apartment. You can read in the window seat while I paint," she said, grabbing my hand and pulling me out of my bed.

Grabbing a book from one of my unpacked boxes, I followed Tansey down the hall and into her apartment. Every time I entered, I was shocked by all the sunlight streaming in. She had decorated the apartment in earth tones, with tons of comfortable cushions that Aunt Carol helped her sew together, and tall plants scattered around the apartment that Uncle Mike and Rod helped carry upstairs. It was the perfect Tansey-paradise. Even her paintings seemed more uplifting lately.

I strolled over to the open window with the deep window seat and curled up. But before I opened my book, I heard voices in the backyard.

"We have to tell her," Reel said. "If we don't and anything happens to him, she'll never forgive us."

I turned and looked at Tansey as she carried a glass of water over to me. I raised a finger to my lips to silence her, and she crept over beside me to look down.

"We can't tell her," Uncle Mike snapped. "If she knew that her grandpa had been taken, she'd do anything the madman wanted to try to get him back. Her grandpa wouldn't want that."

"Then how the hell will we know for sure that the place he's referring to is the blue house? The message says to meet him at the place where she came the closest to death. We're only guessing that he meant the blue house. He could have meant the cabin. Or he could have meant the muddy gulley."

"Look, I get it," Uncle Mike said. "She'll be pissed. But she'd be guessing just like us. We have men at all three locations just waiting for him to show his face. We'll catch him, rescue her grandpa, and then tell her."

"And if it all goes to hell? If Vince dies?"

"Then it won't be us she'll blame. She'll blame herself—and we may never get her back. So let's not screw this up."

"Shit," Reel sighed.

"We need to figure out who stays behind tonight to protect the girls," Uncle Mike said.

"Leo said he would stay. I trust him, but he's not ready for mission work yet. He's been through some shit. He'll step up if the girls are in danger, though."

"You sure?"

"She's my life, man," Reel said, running his hands through his hair. "No way in hell would I leave her if I didn't know he'd keep her safe."

"Then let's get back inside and go through the plans one more time. The note said to meet at 9:00, so we only have a few more hours."

Reel nodded but waited a few minutes, staring across the quiet yard before sighing and walking back inside. I turned to Tansey and saw the tears streaming down her face.

"You can't go, Deanna," she said, shaking her head. "For once, let them protect you. Stay home. Play it safe."

"And if Morgan kills our grandpa?"

She dropped her head into her hands and cried quietly. I threw an arm around her in comfort and looked up to see Darlene standing in the doorway.

She stepped into the apartment and closed the door, walking over to us. "I wanted to tell you. Reel made me swear to go along with his plan. What can I do?"

"Find Aunt Carol," I whispered. "Tell her I need a gun; the boys have mine. Then get back here. Leo's our babysitter tonight. I'll need you to distract him."

Darlene looked shaky and pale, but nodded before slipping back out of the apartment.

I pulled Tansey's face up so she would see me. "The way I figure it, they'll leave Rod here too. He's not trained for the military stuff. I think it's best if you play like you have the flu. Go change into pajamas, grab a pillow and blanket to curl up with on the couch. It will help explain why your face is so blotchy," I said, grinning at my friend.

She nodded, sniffing as she got up, and walked silently to her room, closing the door behind her. Minutes later, Leo and Rod walked in, looking around.

"Where is everyone?" Rod asked.

"Darlene had some errands but will be back soon. Tansey doesn't feel well, so she was going to change and lie down for a while. I was just about to go back to my apartment to read in my room."

"Tansey's sick?" Rod asked with concern.

Tansey walked out of her room, dragging a blanket and carrying a pillow. She tossed the pillow on the couch and curled up on top of it with her face turned away from everyone. Rod walked over and rubbed her back and kissed the top of her head before he declared that he was going to make her some soup. Leo opened the door as I moved back to my own apartment.

"How sick is she?"

"Maybe a touch of the flu. Or it could just be exhaustion. It's been a wicked couple of months."

"Yeah, I get that," Leo nodded. "So Darlene's coming back over? Were you two planning anything special?"

"No," I said, shaking my head. "She'll probably watch TV in the living room. I don't want her out alone while Morgan is still on the loose. She agreed to sleep on the couch tonight so I wouldn't worry about her."

"You're a good sister."

I snorted but didn't explain our history. "Can I ask you something?"

"Sure," he answered, seeming nervous and looking away.

"Why was Reel keeping you hidden out at his fishing cabin?"

He opened my apartment door, holding it for me and closing it behind us. "Figured that would be your question," he sighed. "When I got out of the Army, reality and make-believe got a bit confusing for me. I was captured the day I tried to kill their friend Kelsey. I was told she was a terrorist when, in fact, I was being played. If Reel wouldn't have volunteered to bring me here and watch me, I'd probably be six feet under right now."

"Shit. I don't know what I was expecting to hear, but the fact that you're an assassin wasn't anywhere in the top ten of the list."

I stepped back, not scared, but unsure of my instincts. I had felt comfortable around Leo the moment he stepped up to protect us. But what if all the crazy stuff going on in my life was causing signals to get crossed in my brain?

"I know what you're thinking, but I'm better now."

"Can I bet Darlene and Tansey's lives on that?"

"You don't have to decide. You know Reel. He'd never leave me with you if he didn't trust me."

"You're right," I nodded. "And if Reel thinks you're well enough to integrate back into the real world," I said stepping in front of him, "then I say, welcome to Pine Valley. I hope you decide to stick around for a while." I reached my arms out and hugged him. He stood stiff, uncomfortable with the embrace, but made an attempt at patting my shoulder.

Chapter Thirty-Two

When Darlene returned, she wasn't alone. Aunt Carol followed her in with her overnight bag and knitting bag.

"I heard there was a sleepover tonight," Aunt Carol said, passing Darlene and heading straight for the bedroom. "I'm taking the bedroom. I'm the eldest. You girls can fight over the couch in here and in the guest room."

"I'll sleep in the guest room. I'm going to read and then go to bed early. Tansey's sick and already in bed. I'm feeling a bit worn out, too."

"I'm sorry to hear that," Aunt Carol said. "I'll gather some of your things so you are more comfortable. Should I check on Tansey too?"

"No," I said, shaking my head. "Maybe later. Rod's making her some soup."

"Well, Leo," Darlene said, bumping her hip into his. "Looks like it's just you and me fighting over the remote tonight."

"I don't watch much TV."

"Maybe you haven't been watching the right shows. Ever heard of *The Real Housewives of Orange County*?"

Leo looked nervous but sat on the couch as Darlene turned on the TV. I followed Aunt Carol into the bedroom and gathered some clothes, a pillow, and a blanket. Aunt Carol stuffed a small bag into the pillowcase before carrying the pillow as she followed me down the hall. The office down the hall held an old green metal desk and a scratchy couch along one wall. What Leo didn't know, but Aunt Carol did, was that it was the room that had the emergency drop-down chain ladder that Rod bought for us in case of a fire.

"Alright, tell me what the hell is going on," Aunt Carol whispered.

"Morgan has Grandpa. I overheard Uncle Mike and Reel arguing about whether to tell me or not. Morgan sent a note saying for me to meet him. The boys are guessing the location and are hoping he shows, but they didn't understand the message. Morgan was counting on me overhearing or being told and sneaking out to meet him."

"Why is he still so obsessed?"

"The only thing that makes sense, is that I'm still the only witness. Maybe he figures that if I'm dead, a decent lawyer can get him cleared."

Aunt Carol fisted her hands and placed them on the top of her hips as she thought about my reasoning. "You're probably right," she nodded. "What's the plan? You're not seriously thinking of meeting him, are you? With no backup?"

"What choice do I have? It's Grandpa. I have to try to save him."

"Vince wouldn't want this. He wouldn't want you to risk your life for him."

"But he'd risk his life for me."

"As would everyone else in this town. How will I explain it if something happens to you? How will I live with myself?"

"You will remember that I'm an adult and have the right to make my own decisions," I said, kissing her on the cheek before pulling out the bag hidden in the pillowcase.

"Where are you meeting him?"

"I can't tell you that," I said, shaking my head.

"I won't tell your uncle, or Reel, or any of the rest of the men. Promise."

I didn't want to tell her. But she'd never broken a promise to me before. "The old bakery. He said to meet him where I came closest to death. When he was holding me at gunpoint, I had told him that Mrs. Crookburn had come closer to killing me with her Buick than he had with his multiple attempts."

"You told him that?" she asked, trying to hold back the grin. "Only you would be crazy enough to insult a madman."

I laughed and nodded as I pulled the guns out of the small bag. Aunt Carol had brought me a small gun with an ankle holster and a revolver with a belt clip. I changed my clothes and strapped the guns on. My shirt was long enough to hide the gun at my lower back, but Morgan would guess that I'd be carrying. Hopefully he wouldn't suspect I'd carry an ankle gun as well.

"Are those Reel's bags?" Aunt Carol nodded toward the wall where several duffle bags were stacked.

"Yeah," I nodded. "And maybe Leo's. He stayed last night too."

Aunt Carol walked over and picked the bags up, searching them. She smiled when she found what she was looking for, pulling it out of a duffle bag. "Flak jacket."

"You want me to wear a bulletproof vest?"

"Humor me. I'm already agreeing to let you walk into the lion's den. The least you can do is wear this."

"Fine. Help me get it on; I'm running out of time. And Leo's going to get suspicious if you don't return soon."

"No, he won't," Aunt Carol said, rolling her eyes. "Do you know how addictive *The Real Housewives of Orange County* is? He'll be glued to the TV for at least six hours."

She helped me strap the vest on and then kissed me quickly on the cheek. "I refuse to watch you leave. Just get in and get out. And, damn it, don't you die on us." She hurried from the room, and I took a deep breath.

Checking my watch, I saw it was almost 9:00. I pulled the emergency ladder out from under the desk and dropped it down the open window. The chain rattled, but it seemed louder outside in the quiet night air than inside the house. I threw one leg out the window, finding the first rung, before I turned my back and climbed the rest of the way out—remembering on the way down that I had told Rod I'd likely break my neck using the ladder.

Miraculously reaching the ground, I wiped the sweat off my hands. I crossed the backyard, followed by the next two yards, until I reached the side street. I walked the edge of the street where it was the darkest until I came to the back parking lot. It was one long, but narrow, parking lot for employees and owners for all the Main Street storefronts. I crossed in the shadows to the other end until I stood facing the back door of the old bakery.

I stood frozen, staring at the door, trying to force myself to walk through it. I had to be brave. I had to face Morgan and try to save my grandpa. But I was in over my head, and I knew it. I'd likely get both of us killed. And in the meantime, trained professionals were only a phone call away.

I reached for my purse to pull out my phone, realizing for the first time, I hadn't planned this out at all. I didn't have a phone. I was alone without a way to contact anyone. Even if I screamed for help, it would be unlikely anyone would figure out where the scream came from as the downtown businesses had closed hours before. I was totally screwed.

"Chickening out?" a familiar deep voice whispered from behind me as a gun was placed tight to the back of my head. "Too late."

"I thought you were inside," I said without turning.

I felt him pull the gun I had holstered to my back. "I figured I'd hide out here and make sure you came alone."

"Smart," I admitted before turning to face Morgan. "Wow, you look awful. Those bite marks must hurt like a bitch."

Morgan had a large bloody and yellow gauze patch on his left cheek, another on this neck, and several on his hands and arms. He was pale with a tint of yellow and had dark circles under his swollen eyes.

In the shadowy parking lot, I could still see Morgan's eyes flare in rage, as he nudged me with his gun toward the bakery door. "Inside. Now."

"My grandpa?"

"Trussed up like a turkey. Though it's not like that crazy coot would know he was even in danger. Sad really. He was a formidable enemy once upon a time. Now I'd be surprised if he knew how to tie his shoes."

Turning my back to Morgan, I hid my smirk as I opened the back door of the bakery and walked in. So, Grandpa was playing mental possum. That could be helpful. I grinned wider when I saw the old bakery prep table was still in the kitchen, covered with construction tools. With any luck, the shotgun was still in its cubby. I looked over at Grandpa, then glanced quickly over at the table. He blinked quickly before looking back at the floor and pretending to be distracted by the tiles.

"Nice jacket," Morgan chuckled from behind me.

"I thought a bulletproof jacket looked good with my jeans."

"Doesn't matter. I've been trying to decide between shooting you in the face or slitting your throat. Either way, the jacket doesn't save you."

"Has anyone ever told you that you're insane? I mean really, really insane?"

He smiled, pulling a large knife that had been resting on a shelf.

"Not out here," I said, shaking my head. "The front room. I won't let you kill me in front of my grandpa."

"What? No begging me to release him?"

I moved toward the door then pushed it open to cross to the other side. He followed me.

"I was an idiot to come here. When you found me frozen outside, that's when it finally hit me. You'd never let him go." I turned to face him. "You were going to kill us both all along."

"It was only a matter of time," he said, shrugging. "Even if he is screwy in the head now, he still deserves to be punished for what he put me through years ago."

"My grandpa is loving, loyal, protective, and dedicated to his family. You've shown your own son none of those traits. You've left him in a cell to rot, even when you knew what he was doing the entire time. You actually hoped you could pin both our deaths on him, didn't you?"

"I'll admit, it was convenient that he was targeting your grandpa." Morgan shook his head. "Useless boy. Randall lacks the intelligence to survive in this world. It was no sacrifice to use him as my pawn."

"Now what? You think that my family, my friends—they'll forget and forgive? That they will let you walk away after you kill me? Even if you don't go to jail, they'll hunt you down and torture you."

"You must be referring to your boyfriend. What's his name? Ryan? But everyone calls him Reel?" He chuckled a sinister sound. "Him and his friends have bigger concerns right now."

His eyes were cold black, but the grin that spread across his face was the one I remembered from my nightmares. It was the same look that had me, as a little girl, running blindly through the blackened forest. Even now, as an adult, every instinct in me screamed to run. Telling me that he was pure evil.

Reaching into his coat pocket, he pulled out a cell phone, holding it up.

"I'm guessing they went to the cabin or the old house where I killed your father. Well, I left them a little surprise. Unfortunately, by the time they realize it—BOOM—they'll be blown to bits."

He pressed several keys on his phone, and my brain slowly processed that he was talking about a bomb.

"No, no, no, no," I cried, grabbing a Tiffany lamp from a display table and barreling toward him, aiming for his head.

He dropped the phone to knock the lamp out of my hands before he pushed me backward, forceful enough to throw me to the ground.

"Too late. They're gone."

"*NO!!!*" I screamed.

I thought of Reel, Uncle Mike, and all the others. They didn't deserve to die. They didn't deserve for this monster to win. No longer caring what happened to me, I rolled onto all fours, turning my back to him as I climbed up from the floor, pulling the gun from the ankle holster. I stood, turned, and held the gun aimed at him.

He laughed, still holding his own gun on me. "Déjà vu? I think the last time we were in this position, you shot me in the shoulder and left me being attacked by a badger."

"Looks like the badger is still working his magic on you. Those sores look infected."

"I'll live," Morgan said. "The question is, will you?"

"I think she's got a pretty good chance," Grandpa said, walking through the door with the shotgun aimed at Morgan.

"I'll second that," Tucker said, walking in through the front door.

"Better odds by the second," Darlene added, entering with a Glock pointed at him.

"Your odds seem to be decreasing rapidly though, Morgan," Tansey said, holding a rifle.

"What the hell?" Morgan whispered.

"It's called family," Aunt Carol said, holding her favorite revolver on him and moving to stand next to me. "You messed with our girl. That wasn't too bright."

The room rapidly filled with familiar faces. Faces I'd known my entire life: Mrs. Crookburn, Old Man Mackerel and his wife, Sarah Temple, Mr. Palmer, Buck Peaton, Loretta Hines, Betty Fergin, Eric Mickers, Casey Pritchard and so many more. And each one of them aimed a gun at Morgan.

The store filled shoulder to shoulder with neighbors, friends and family. I looked out toward the window and saw that more townsfolk waited outside, fully armed.

I walked up to Morgan, taking his gun from his hand. He knew it would be suicide to act now and gave it up willingly. I handed both our guns over to Tucker.

"The bombs?" I asked Morgan, tears streaming down my face.

"They're all dead, honey," Morgan said.

"The bombs at the house and at the cabin? Shit," Leo rolled his eyes. "Any kid who's been through basic training would've found and disconnected those wimpy-ass bombs. Besides, I already called the boys, and they were on their way back to town as soon as you snuck out the window."

"They're alive? Are you sure?" I asked Leo, running over to grip his shirt sleeves.

Leo pulled out his phone and called Reel, putting the call on speaker.

"Tell me she's safe, Leo," Reel yelled into the phone.

"I'm safe," I yelled toward the phone. "How about you guys? Everyone okay?"

"We're fine. We're a block from Main Street. Where are you?"

"I'll let Leo fill you in. I'm in the middle of something." I turned back to Morgan. I stepped forward, driving my leg up, and slamming my boot-covered foot into his testicles.

"SCORE!" Loretta shouted, and everyone cheered.

I laughed as he fell to his knees. I stepped back, looking down at him. "That was for threatening the people I care about." I forced myself to take another step back. I wanted to inflict more damage. Wanted him to pay for what he had done to my father, my grandpa, my sister, my friends.

"Don't do it," Darlene said, walking up beside me and grabbing my arm. "You'll feel all guilty and shit about it tomorrow."

I glared over at her, then looked over at Tansey.

Tansey shrugged. "She's right," she said, rolling her eyes. "You'd be all mopey and question whether you were a bad person or not."

"But luckily you have a sister who has a more relaxed view of the world," Darlene said right before she hauled her leg back and kicked Morgan in the face, flinging him backward.

Everyone cheered, and Darlene threw an arm over my shoulder and led me out the front door.

"That's so not fair. Why'd you get to kick him in the face but I didn't?"

"You mean he's still alive?" Reel panted, jogging his way through the crowd.

"He's missing a few teeth now," I said, pointing at Darlene.

"And he'll need an ice pack for his nuts," Darlene said.

"Sheriff is slapping cuffs on him. The party is over," Aunt Carol said, walking up behind us with Tansey.

I turned to grin at her, and Reel stepped up behind me, throwing an arm around my chest to pull my back into him.

"Tweedle!" Colby yelled, running up and throwing his arms around me.

If it hadn't been for Reel bracing my back, I would have been flattened to the ground. "I'm okay, kid. No worries," I said as I held him.

Reel moved his arm to wrapped it around both of us. "Anyone hurt?"

"Nope. The plan went off without a hitch," I said, smirking.

Several sets of eyes glared at me.

"Okay, so *their* plan—to save me from *my horrible plan*—went off without a hitch."

"You are in so much trouble," Reel said, sighing.

"You better spank her," Mrs. Crookburn yelled.

Chapter Thirty-Three

"This is by far the stupidest thing I've ever agreed to do for you," Tansey whispered loudly, crouched over, sneaking down the side of the road beside me.

"This is not half as stupid as the time we snuck into Michael Shanner's backyard to peep in the windows to see whether he was making out with Suzy Zemple."

"That was an important mission. I knew he was lying to me. The bastard."

"If you knew he was lying to you, you should have just dumped his ass," I whispered, grabbing her arm and pulling her along at a quicker pace. "Come on. You're moving too slow."

We followed the dark shadowy edge of the road, having parked about a mile back on a side street.

"Tell me again why we couldn't just drive up and ring the damn doorbell."

"How are we supposed to eavesdrop if we ring the bell announcing we're there?"

"You could just demand they tell you whatever is going on."

I snorted and turned back to face her. "You really think Reel, Uncle Mike, and Grandpa are going to admit whatever they are scheming? *Please.* In fact, this whole town has been acting shady. I'm not sure what the hell's going on but I—"

The ground under my right foot gave out, and I started sliding down the hill.

"Shit—" Tansey yelped, trying to grab my upper arm as I clawed at the ground trying to stop my fall.

She lost her grip, and I slid several feet down the steep hillside before my feet hit a hard root, stopping me. Unfortunately, my backside had been pointed out away from the hill, so when my feet stopped, my ass kept going, rolling me head over feet several times before I stopped with a splash.

"Damn it!" I yelled.

"Tweedle? You hurt?"

"Hurt? No. Just squishy," I moaned, trying to sit up and falling back over. "Eww, it smells."

"What did you land in?" she yelled from somewhere above.

"Some type of water runoff." I didn't have a choice but to turn on all fours to try to get up. Rolling over and getting my knees underneath me, I slid again, face first into the stagnant water. I blew the water out of my face and forced myself up again. Half walking, half crawling, I made my way back to the edge of the bank and climbed up to the dirt road.

"Oh my God. You reek!" Tansey exclaimed, backing away.

"A little help here?" I said, holding out my hand for help up off the ground.

"No way," she laughed. "I'll make it up to you. Six boxes of Klondike bars or a case of Snickers, but I'm not touching you."

"Some best friend you are," I mumbled, forcing myself to my feet.

I looked down at my left foot, wondering why the stones were cutting into my skin, and realized that I had not only lost my shoe but the sock as well. Damn it.

Thoroughly ticked, I stormed in the direction of my grandpa's house.

"Maybe we should go back home so you can shower," Tansey said, as she jogged along on the other side of the road. "I mean, do you really want to confront them when you smell like that?"

"I'm too angry now to turn back," I snapped, rounding the corner and seeing my grandpa's house up ahead. "Good, they're still there."

"No, no, no, please," Tansey cried trying to keep up as I jogged across the yard and up the front porch.

I ignored her pleas to turn back, and without ringing the bell or knocking, I threw open the door and stormed inside.

"Ryan Reel Thurman, where are you?!"

I turned to the right and my heart stopped. Resting on one knee with a ring in hand, Reel was waiting for me. Behind him appeared to be the whole town, waiting for my reaction.

"ROD!!" Reel yelled, getting up and approaching me.

"Not my fault, bro," Rod said, jogging through the door and stopping next to Tansey, who stood several feet away from me. They were both plugging their noses. "You told me to stay back, so she didn't see me. I was too far away by the time she started sliding down the hill."

Reel glared at him and then looked at me. "Are you hurt?" he asked, carefully plucking some type of green goo out of my hair with his thumb and index finger and dropping it on the foyer tile.

I looked around again at all the people in the room. Despite trying to hold my composure, I was exposed when my lower lip started to tremble.

"Tansey?" Reel said.

"Clothes, I'm on it," she said scurrying down the hallway.

Reel reached out and lifted me in his arms, carrying me up the staircase.

"Rod?" Reel called down below.

"I'll find you something to wear," he chuckled.

"Aunt Carol?"

"We'll clean this up," she called out.

I felt the tears start to flow and tucked my head into his shoulder.

"You've done worse," he chuckled. "Remember the time—"

"Don't you dare finish that line, Reel Thurman!"

He chuckled again but didn't say anything as he carried me into the bathroom, placing me on my feet inside the bathtub. He reached down, turning the water on full blast, directed at my head.

"I'm still dressed," I complained, turning my face away from the hard water pressure.

"Leave your clothes in the tub. I'll have Rod burn them later."

Reel picked up a bottle of shampoo and took the cap off, dumping the entire bottle over my head and body.

"Stop it. I'll finish myself."

I started to strip off my clothes, and he closed the curtain, turned on the fan, and walked out. I heard him laughing all the way down the hall.

I spent twenty minutes scrubbing with every soap, body wash, shampoo and conditioner I could find. By the time I got out of the shower, I smelled like a mixture of strawberries, jasmine and skunk.

I looked at the countertop and sighed at the clothes that were topped with a note that read: *Sorry. These were all I could find.*

I didn't keep many clothes at Grandpa's house, so in the stack were clean underwear, my Metallica T-shirt, baby blue yoga pants, and a pair of flip-flops.

"Oh, what the heck," I said to myself. "It's not like you're going to answer yes anyway, Sullivan."

This would be the fourth time Reel had asked me to marry him. Every time he asked, I answered with a no and got just a little bit angrier.

As far as I was concerned, he'd spent years disappointing me and needed to step up his game. Simply proposing wasn't going to cut it.

"You about done?" Reel asked from the other side of the door.

Already dressed, I opened the door as I slid my feet into the flip-flops. When I looked up, I tried to keep an annoyed look planted on my face, but I was struggling.

Reel always looked hot, but never more so than when he was still wet from a shower. He smirked and without saying a word, grabbed my hand and led me downstairs.

Downstairs, every window and the front door was propped open, yet several people still held hands over their faces, trying to cut off the lingering smell.

At the entryway to the living room, Reel got down on one knee. "One more time," Reel said. "Deanna 'Tweedle-Dee' Sullivan, will you do me the honor?" he asked, holding the ring out.

"Of course not," I answered, grinning down at him. "What kind of girl do you think I am?"

Grandpa and Uncle Mike clinked glasses from their spot next to the bar.

Uncle Mike laughed. "Told you."

"Rod?" Reel said.

"Got it." Rod chuckled, jogging over.

Rod handed Reel a long black scarf. Stepping behind me, Reel tied it over my eyes.

"What are you doing?"

"Trust me," Reel chuckled, leading me blindly off in another direction.

Having run wild in my grandpa's house since I was knee high, I knew when we passed the foyer, walked through the kitchen, stepped out onto the back porch, and crossed into the backyard.

I could also hear everyone following behind us.

"Hit the lights, Leo!" Reel called out.

With the blindfold still on, I could see shimmering neon lights, light up the backyard. I tore the blindfold off when I heard the carnival music. Before me stood the Ferris wheel.

"You didn't," I muttered, looking up at Reel.

"I wasn't about to wait a year for the carnival to come back into town, so I brought it back myself," he said, grinning.

He led me to the Ferris wheel and helped me into the first bucket seat, sitting beside me and closing the door. Rod jogged up, checked the latch on the door, and then grabbed a nearby chain and padlock, securing the door extra tight.

I laughed, appreciating the gesture.

Leo flipped a switch, and slowly the Ferris wheel went up and around while everyone watched below. On the third loop around, the bucket stopped at the top.

"Now, Deanna 'Tweedle-Dee' Sullivan, will you make me the happiest man on Earth?"

"That's a lot to ask of just one person."

"I think if anyone can pull it off, it's you."

"Is that diamond real?" I asked, raising an eyebrow.

"You know damn well it is," he growled.

"What about all the conversations we haven't had? Where will we live? How often will you be away for work? How many kids will we have?"

"We'll finish the upstairs and live there until we start a family. Then we'll live in the house I'm having built on the street behind the bakery. And we can have as many kids as you want or none at all. It's up to you. As long as I have you, I'm happy."

"It's up to me?"

"Yes, but I do have one request." Reel kept his eyes locked on mine. "I want Colby to move in with us. He can still work part time for Vince, but he needs you. And I've gotten pretty attached to the kid."

"You mean it?"

"It's what I want," Reel said, smiling. "What do you say? Will you marry me?"

I shrugged. I wasn't ready to cave yet. "What about your work?"

"I've already talked to Donovan. I'll take the shorter assignments so I can be home more, but I'd like to keep working. If it gets to be too much, I'll quit, though."

"You'd quit a job you love for me?"

"I'd do anything for you, Dee."

"What about the blue house?"

"It's being demolished next week. A small playground will be installed on the lot."

"Ryan 'Reel' Thurman?"

"Yeah?" he asked, cocking one eyebrow.

"You got yourself a wife. Don't screw this up."

"Don't plan on it." He laughed, leaning in to kiss me.

The kiss was brief, and he pulled back quickly.

"I know." I giggled. "I still reek."

"It's horrible," Reel coughed as he laughed. "What the hell did you land in? A sewer?"

He slid the ring on my finger, and everyone below us cheered.

"Till death do us part," I whispered, holding my hand out to admire the ring.

"The smell might send us both to an early grave." Reel threw his arm around me and kissed me again.

Chapter Thirty-Four

TANSEY.

I watched my best friend, high in the sky, surrounded by the neon lights, get engaged to the man she fell in love with when they were too young to even understand the meaning of the word. Tears flowed freely down my face and the faces of many of my family members.

And that's what they all were. My family. My father ducked out of my life before I was born. My mother, too consumed with depression, chose to die rather than to see me grow up. But the people who stood around me had taken me in, accepted me as one of their own, and helped raise me to be the woman I was today.

A hand slipped into mine, intertwining our fingers. I looked over at Rod, standing strong with a jolly grin as he wiped my tears away.

"We'll have to hurry," he whispered.

"Hurry? To do what?"

"Date. We have to be an official couple before they get to the actual wedding."

"I can't date you." I laughed. "You can't be serious."

He pulled me by the hand away from the crowd, away from the lights. I didn't know what he was doing, but something drew me along, something stronger than his grasp on my hand.

When he turned to face me, for the first time, I didn't see humor in his eyes. I saw passion. I saw desperation. I saw vulnerability. And then he kissed me.

And that's when I knew, as I leaned into his heated body, that I'd spend the rest of my life madly, crazily in love with Rod Thurman.

Hope you enjoyed spending time with Tweedle and friends. These characters were a hoot to write.

Though *Slightly Off Balance* is a standalone novel, several characters (including Reel/Ryan) are in the original Kelsey's Burden Series. And near the end of that fan-favorite series, Tweedle-Dee herself makes a guest appearance.

Start the series with book one, **Layered Lies**.

Were you already reading *Kelsey's Burden Series* and took the detour to *Slightly Off Balance* after book five?

If so, next up is book six, **Day and Night**.

Already binged the *Kelsey's Burden Series*? Flip to the next page where you'll find a summary of more of my books.

Until next time, best wishes!
Kaylie Hunter

Books By Kaylie

Kelsey's Burden Series
Ex-cop Kelsey Harrison is on the hunt for her enemies—the people responsible for taking her son.

Slightly Off Balance
When small-town baker Deanna Sullivan finds herself in danger, Reel Thurman returns home, vowing to protect her.

Diamond's Edge
Raised on the wrong side of the law, Diamond Campbell knows how to navigate within the criminal world. And when someone targets her in a deadly game of cat and mouse, they'll get what's coming to them.

Davina Ravine Psychic Crime Series
Amateur small-town psychic Davina Ravine is in over her head, stumbling her way from one mystery to the next, while unraveling dark family secrets.

Made in United States
North Haven, CT
25 April 2025